MORDECAI'S FIRST BRUSH WITH LOVE
NEW STORIES BY JEWISH WOMEN IN BRITAIN

Edited by Laura Phillips and Marion Baraitser

LOKI BOOKS

LOKI FICTION

Series editor: Marion Baraitser

MORDECAI'S FIRST BRUSH WITH LOVE
NEW STORIES BY JEWISH WOMEN IN BRITAIN

Edited by Laura Phillips and Marion Baraitser

LOKI BOOKS

In association with the European Jewish Publication Society

LOKI BOOKS

First published in Great Britain as a Loki Book paperback original in 2004 by **LOKI BOOKS LTD**, 38 Chalcot Crescent, London NW1 8YD.

The European Jewish Publication Society is a registered charity, which gives grants to assist in the publication and distribution of books relevant to Jewish Literature, history, religion, philosophy, politics and culture. EJPS, PO Box 19948, London N3 3ZL.

Elisabeth Russell Taylor's *Present Fears* was first published in the *Critical Quarterly,* Vol 37, no 2, Summer,1995, then by Arcadia Books, London, 1997.

A CIP catalogue record for this book is available from the British Library.

ISBN: LOKI 0 9529426 6 6

Printed and bound by Biddles,Woodbridge Park Estate, Woodbridge Road, Guildford, Surry GU1 1DA.

Cover drawing by Alexandra Baraitser

Contents

Introduction

There is little encouragement of the writing of short stories in Britain. No prestigious awards exist. Stories may or may not be published in little magazines, then disappear from view. Global publishers feel they do not sell as well as novels—and the present publishing market is dominated by big finance rather than by what is small and original like short stories, which are nearer to the poetic end of writing. Many writers themselves are wary of short stories as a genre—they see them as too slight to matter in a body of work, or assume that they are easier to write. The latter is a misconception: though new writers may find the genre more approachable than writing a novel, the writing of a successful short story is a highly demanding task requiring its own disciplined form and concentrated language, and its own intention. In fact, readers enjoy short stories—you can read them between tasks, or on a tube, and their intimate nature evokes an immediate cry of recognition.

As editors and writers for a small independent press,we decided to go against the grain. We wanted to discover and encourage new talent, as well as celebrate established Jewish writers in an area that has been neglected. Our aim was not to retreat into the ghetto, but to announce a new confidence and ability among disparate authors bound by a common culture, gender, history and, sometimes, faith. This seems to be part of a current Jewish cultural renaissance. Jewish women seem happy to express one or more identity in their writing. Though they know themselves as Jewish, their cultural identity is still fluid and linked with the 'outside', with migration.This is reflected in the settings of many of the stories, and in the birthplaces of their authors. The writing is infused with a Jewish sensibility that binds the collection together, though the stories are written for a wider public. There is little self-hate in the work, and this allows room for self-criticism, and for an openness to Jewish and female identity.

Jewish women's writing in English, surfaced in Britain as early as the late eighteenth century with poets like Jael Henrietta Mendes and Emma Henry-Lyon. There were a number of recognised Jewish women fiction writers in the early nineteenth and early to mid-twentieth centuries: Grace Aquilar (1816-1847), Naomi Jacob (1889-1964) who wrote *The Golanze Saga*, Ada Leverson (1865-1936), Gladys Bronwyn Sterne (b.1890), Betty Miller (1910-1965) and Gerda Charles (Edna Lipson, b. 1915). There were also British women immigrants who wrote in Yiddish in the 1930s and 40s: Esther Kreitman, Katie Brown and Dora Diamant.

Perhaps the best known Jewish woman writing in Britain in English in the nineteenth century is Amy Levy.(1) Levy is remembered particularly for her novel *Reuben Sachs*, which brought her fame, and notoriety among certain Jewish readers who accused her of fowling her own nest. The novel criticises Jewish bourgeois values of expediency and materialism, and laments the fact that for a Jewish woman of the time, marriage was her only certainty. Levy felt that the position of women was changing in British society, but not in Jewish society. In the novel, consciousness shifts significantly to that of the heroine Judith, as Levy paints the horror of a woman trapped in a loveless marriage. The novel is a political, socialist and feminist statement, hence a 'novel of revolt' rather than a novel by a self-hating Jew. Judith cannot reach self-understanding until it is too late: she cannot face the radicalism, that includes not marrying a Jew, dictated by her real needs.

Amy Levy grew up in Britain at a time when the making of fortunes was balanced by the rise of trade unions and the new British Labour Party. Male patriarchy was also being dismantled.(2) Born into a wealthy Bloomsbury Jewish family in 1861, Levy was the first British Jewish woman admitted to Newnham College, Cambridge. As a woman, she was barred from sitting the examinations. Students rioted when she tried to gain admission. Unlike our generation, Levy was part of the new upper middle-class Anglo-Jewry who had escaped the East End. One of the last short stories she wrote, *Cohen of Trinity*, concerns a scholar who writes a book that brings him fame, then takes his own life.(3) It was prophetic. Levy, an incipient melancholic, committed suicide in 1889 aged twenty-seven.

Opportunities and social attitudes have changed since Amy Levy's time and this is reflected in the stories in the collection.We are better educated and more culturally confident, which allows a new pluralism and diversity of self-expression and openness in Jewish women writers. We still do not seem to have escaped the old dilemma of the split-personality of the Jew who (in Amy Levy's words, as quoted by Cheyette) 'has his being both without and within the tribal limits.' Although we no longer feel oppressed, we are coming to terms with our sense of being outsiders within another culture.

In this collection, we included stories tackling problems that come with post-acculturation, pluralism and intermarriage. A pregnant Catholic wife sits at her new husband's *seder* celebration table in *The Woman who was not Elijah.* Jewish humour and wit surface in *Mordecai's First Brush with Love.* In *Birthing,* a daughter imagines her own birth through her mother's eyes. Motherhood, marriage, food and eating (*Patchwork*), are all prominent as subjects. Though the stories are mostly non-political, *Yom Tov* is about the plight of an Arab Israeli taxi driver misunderstood for saving a Jewish child.

We chose tales that are literary and stay in the mind. As Susan Hill found in editing her collection of contemporary women's short stories for Penguin, the work is 'quiet, small scale and intimate... (The stories are) about everyday but not trivial matters, about the business of being human and about the concerns of the human heart.'

The work in this collection often concerns identity in which the Jewish element survives as a kind of awareness of compassion, justice and guilt. Certain writers seem prepared to be more open about the violence in their everyday lives. *A Violent Tale* describes the destructiveness underlying pre-adolescent sexuality. *The Sin of the Father* is a tale of a narcissistic, wealthy London Jewish mother's abusive betrayal of her rebellious small daughter.

Some stories are concerned with Jewish subjects. *Something Chronic* deals with a Jewish wife's traditional, but sadly misplaced loyalty to her husband. *Naomi's Lament* updates the biblical story of Ruth and Naomi to modern times. Other writers choose a subject unrelated to their Jewishness. *Jerusalem Pictures* presents an Orthodox stance of a younger generation who have chosen to leave the diaspora for Israel.The ritual of a Jewish life long since abandoned becomes a powerful bond between characters in a non-Jewish world in *The Night Watch.* The Holocaust casts its long shadow in *Cherries, The Mezuzah*

Gatherer and *A Small Number*. The remnants of a generation in Eastern Europe whose lives were broken off by persecution, are embodied in a compelling portrait in *The Newspaper Man*. *Toot, Toot, Tootsie* is a personal response to mothering that is suffused with a Jewish sense without naming it. *The Glamorous Aunt* tells the story of infatuation, marriage, and the politics of Jewish family life. *The Book of Life* deals with the power of the writer's imagination and the need for compassion in our dealings with others, while *Recipe for Moussaka* is about Jewish identity and a young woman's steps towards recovery after a bereavement.

In each story we found something that we instinctively acknowledged was 'true' but had never been expressed before in quite that way, giving a moment of extraordinary, memorable insight into a private world that has bearing on one's own and the world of the *other*.

1. Cheyette, Brian, *From Apology to Revolt: Benjamin Farjeon, Amy Levy and the Post-Emancipation Anglo-Jewish Novel 1880-1900*, Jewish Historical Studies, 29, 1988, 265.
2. Showalter, *Sexual Anarchy: Gender and Culture at the 'Fin de Siecle'*, Virago, 1992).
3. New, Melvyn (ed), *Amy Levy: The Complete Novels and Selected Writings: 1861-1889*, University Press of Florida, 1993, Bloomsbury.

Marion Baraitser
Laura Phillips
2004

Erica Wagner

Erica Wagner was born in New York City and lives in London. She is the author of a book of stories, *Gravity* (Granta, 1997), *Ariel's Gift: Ted Hughes, Sylvia Plath and the Story of Birthday Letters* (Faber, 2000). She is Literary Editor of *The Times.*

'Every morning when I walk to work, I pass Fashion Street in the East End—and the house where my great-grandmother, Rebecca Siegel, was born in 1888. When she was six, she and her family left for the United States—where I was raised, an American, in a family that no longer considers itself Jewish. But I have returned to London, to live not far from Rebecca's birthplace, and perhaps that means something after all.'

Toot Toot Tootsie

'There you go.'

Dr De'Freitas smiled with her dark eyes. She held the microphone against my belly and the echoey gallop of my baby's heartbeat rushed out into the room. I smiled too.

'Still there,' I said. 'Always life.'

'Of course,' Dr De'Freitas said. The first time I met her, more than fifteen years ago, I had liked her right away. With her neat chestnut hair, small hands and solid ankles, she looked like she would be a good cook.

'He's just fine. Or she. You're sure you don't want to know?'

'I think a nice surprise would be a good thing,' I said.

'How are you doing?' she asked.

'I'm okay,' I said. 'My head feels very full. I'm organizing things all the time. A funeral. Moving. Buying strollers. A cot. I guess this is what being a grown-up is all about.'

'It's hard for everything to come at once,' she said. 'Do you have help?'

'Oh yes,' I said. 'People help. I just have to remember to ask them.'

She looked at me with a sternness that was only half-joking. 'You have to ask. You should be taking it easy. I know that may be difficult, but really, you have to try. Promise me you will.'

'I promise,' I said. Dr De'Freitas did not look convinced. 'Come back next week,' she said. 'If I don't see you in the hospital first. It could be any time now.'

I kept my face still when she said the hospital, but my mind filled with my mother, the high-sided bed, the lights, the machines. I looked at her and didn't speak. Maybe she knew what I was thinking.

'You'll be just fine,' she said. 'You both will. That's my promise. Go on; get dressed. I'll see you next week.'

****

'You know, I'll be there if you want,' Nick said. It was a couple of hours after my appointment with Dr De'Freitas, and I was sitting on the floor of my old room in my mother's apartment with a pillow behind my back and another one under my legs. Nick was lying on his back underneath the cot he had just assembled for me, checking all the screws were tight. 'You could page me.' He yanked at something and grunted. 'But I guess you maybe want a girl there.'

'Don't worry,' I said. I didn't know if I wanted anyone there. I still wasn't certain I wanted to be there myself. 'But that's awfully sweet of you. I'm really grateful. I am. Not to mention this, and everything else. All this handyman stuff is a little less handy now you don't live upstairs from me.'

'It's only a subway ride,' he said, 'and it's a pleasure. Better than algorithms any day.' Nick was a freelance programmer. He'd lived upstairs from my old apartment on Sullivan Street, the one I knew I'd have to leave when I discovered I was pregnant; the one I did leave when my mother died and there was suddenly somewhere to go, even if I didn't want to go there. On Sullivan Street, Nick had collected my packages from the post office, repaired my sink when it flooded the kitchen/living room/dining room/bedroom—I shut the door of the bathroom—and once brought me won ton soup from Hunan Paradise around the corner when I had the flu. Once he had even proposed to me, but we had drunk two bottles of red wine and in the morning, we both agreed that marriage would probably be a mistake. I got pregnant about a month later. Nick was not involved.

'There you go,' he said, pulling his long body up from the floor. 'All done. It's nice.' It was a plain beech-finish cot, with rolling beads along its curved end rails for a baby to play with. My baby.

'It is,' I said. 'I just can't quite believe someone's going to be sleeping in it.'

'I'd feel the same,' he said. 'May I?'

I nodded, and he put his large, warm hands on my belly. We both stared down at it, as if waiting for the curtain to rise. Sure enough, my tenant obliged with a wriggle that reminded me of an old man settling into an armchair. Nick laughed delightedly.

'Now I have to pee,' I said. 'Help me up.'

I braced my feet against his, took his hands, and he hauled me upright. Everything took longer, was more effort; I could not get used to it. Getting up, sitting down, lying flat—even sleeping was a task to be approached and accomplished.

'Look,' Nick said, when I came back into the bedroom. 'You're all hooked up.'

He had taken the baby listener out of its packaging, put in the batteries I'd left lying by it, and plugged in the baby unit. It had a night-light that gave a feeble glow against the bright March sun streaming through the blinds. 'This one in the bedroom?' He held up the parent unit with its detachable listening pod. The listening pod was rechargeable; it had a clip you could attach to your belt. You could carry it anywhere. Nick was heading for what I still thought of as my mother's bedroom.

'Not there,' I said quickly. 'Back there.' I pointed towards the kitchen, where there was a small third bedroom; it would have been a maid's room. I had put in a single bed, pushed against the wall, and a night table with a lamp. There would be room for a Moses basket on the floor. Nick plugged the parent unit into the wall and set it on the little table.

'Kind of… Spartan in here,' Nick said.

'Close to the kitchen,' I said, 'for making up bottles in the night.'

Nick raised an eyebrow. 'This apartment may be bigger than your old one,' he said, 'but it's still a Manhattan apartment. Everything is basically not too far from the kitchen.'

I sighed but didn't say anything. I was tired of explaining, even to myself.

'Wait there,' Nick said. Then he walked back through the kitchen and down the hall to the baby's room. That's what it was now; that's what I should call it. There was a click and then the little speaker on the table woke up, flashing an array of tiny rainbow lights like a fruit machine on Coney Island. And then Nick's disembodied voice, crackly and tuneless, singing:'Rock-a-bye baby, on the tree top, when the wind blows the cradle will rock…' Rustling. I imagined him, his mouth and beard close to the microphone, sunlight from the window on his one gold earring. 'Hello baby, hello baby… come in. This is Nick calling Ella's baby… come in, baby… come in… the water's fine…'

Half-singing, half-speaking, then laughing. I looked at the small round speaker. It was as if I could see Nick curled up inside it, just like my baby was curled up inside me.

****

Louis. 'Lovely Louis,' Nick said into his sea-misted eyes. Seven pounds, fifteen ounces. A really good-sized chicken; a somewhat inadequate turkey. No longer tenant, now co-owner, of me, of everything—with a squashed-flat face and a drawn-out head. And for a while I moved out of the past and into a continuous present. When he came down with a cold at three weeks and I called the doctor at four o'clock in the morning and she told me to come to the hospital, I thought we would always be this way: always in a taxi to the East Side, always in a brightly lit room, always with an oxygen monitor clipped to his toe—and then, when he was well (because of course, he was fine, really) it was all as if it had never happened. The first time he smiled, I couldn't remember a time when he hadn't been smiling. He was his own self, always staring at the world with those wide eyes, and when I thought back to the first time I had seen them, I knew there had never been a time when I hadn't known their gaze.

Mrs Rosenfeld, the neighbour I had regarded with terror from the time I was seven and had bounced my super-ball repeatedly against her door, never thinking what it would sound like inside until she emerged and shouted at me, brandishing a ruler—Mrs Rosenfeld brought me meat loaf from Zabar's and gave Louis a ten-inch-high glow-in-the-dark statuette of the Virgin Mary to guard his slumbers. (Mrs Rosenfeld had reverted, apparently, to a native faith after the long-ago death of Mr Rosenfeld). Antonia came down from her Massachusetts retreat bearing packets of medicinal herbs that I put away carefully and promptly forgot about, and an electric breast pump with hoses and suckers and tubes that made me imagine I was standing in a milking parlour.

In the clean pale air of spring I took Louis to the Hudson River, sat on a bench and gazed at the George Washington Bridge upstream, drinking coffee from a paper cup while my son slept seriously, with a little frown, as if sleeping kept him very busy indeed. We went to the park and watched softball games, or sat by the Bethesda fountain. The days passed quickly, and so did the nights. Louis liked to sleep at night; when he woke I'd feed him, taking him from his Moses basket and into my bed where we'd fall asleep together, fitting into each other like jigsaw pieces. It seemed possible to be always moving forward. The George Washington Bridge could belong to Louis's childhood, not mine; the park was his, too, and Broadway, and the rest. Every path was a new one. Nothing was easy, but I welcomed the difficulty. It was distraction, it was difference, it was a whole new life.

When he was not quite two months old, and the heat of the summer had just begun to push down on the city, he got too big for his basket. He liked to sleep flat out on his back, his arms spread out by his head; suddenly his elbows were crowded. But for the first week, the cot in his room—my old room—seemed too big for him. He flailed. It was a sea of sheets and blankets. There were not enough edges. I lay on the floor by his side, my hand poking up through the bars until my fingers went numb, continuing to sing to him even as I fell into sleep. But on the eighth day, he slept.

I was wakeful, in my little maid's room. (Suddenly not to hear him at the foot of my bed.) The red eye of the baby listener winked at me. No rainbow lights. Silence. It was possible to turn it all the way up so that I could indeed have heard his every breath, but I'd told myself this was not the point. The point was to hear if he cried. Still, I leaned close. Nothing. Then – a flicker of light, just for an instant. I looked up. I looked at my watch. Only 11 o'clock. Traffic noises drifting up from the street below. The microphone was very sensitive.

Then, another flicker. And this time—my neck stretched, my ear right up to the speaker, very faintly, not crying: singing.

At first I was hardly startled. It seemed so natural. I knew the words so well.

Toot toot tootsie
Goodbye—
Toot toot tootsie
Don't cry—
The choo-choo train that takes me—

Not a song I had ever sung. I had whispered him to sleep, told him stories, invented names. I was not a singer, not me. But the words of this song were threaded through me.

Away from you—
How sad it makes me—
Kiss me, Tootsie, and then—

It was so faint, I held my breath to hear, all the while wondering if perhaps I wasn't really asleep and dreaming. I turned up the listener. The voice grew no louder. Only now I could hear the breathing of my son. Soft, soft, soft. Sound asleep.

I got up. I walked to his room in the glowing city dark, the wooden floors cool and smooth on the bare soles of my feet. I pushed open the door to his room and stood looking down at him, a mother looking down on her sleeping child. As if another set of eyes was looking through mine. I shook my head to clear my vision. His chest rose and fell beneath an orange blanket. There was no one singing. His nightlight, above the listener's microphone, burned pale yellow.

I walked back to the room where I slept, but when I lay down on the bed I imagined another room, my mother's room, a room which I had hardly entered since she died. I had just left it alone, as if she might walk back in to repossess her dressing table, its top left-hand drawer—I was sure—still stacked with her expensive, engraved stationery. SALLY WHEELER it said along the top; that was all: the letters deep indigo, the type something called Cloister Open Face, I had learned once long ago, I do not remember why. Beside the paper, a banded pile of envelopes, blank but for a blue border along the triangular opening edge. I knew that stationery like I knew her voice. For me it was her voice, in a way. Pulling open the envelopes at school, always careful never to tear the blue line. I couldn't tear the blue line. Not ever. Opening the folded paper and looking first at the top right, just below the line of her name, where the name of the place the letter had been sent from was written in her looping hand. When I was younger I kept a map with pins. Duluth. Key West. Santa Rosa. *Darling baby girl—*

Finally I fell asleep. Louis woke me with his crying, the rainbow lights full on, and I brought him into bed with me so I could sleep curled around the future.

****

I kept meaning to put the apartment on the market. I meant to do it before I went back to work, but every day I'd found a reason to put it off. But the morning after I'd heard—or dreamt—the singing voice, I put Louis in his stroller and walked across town to the real estate agent Antonia had recommended. Three days later I got the first call. A couple, no children, a dog. I said I would be home, I'd show them around.

They were in their fifties.They had a house in Westchester; but he was retiring, and she liked to go to the theatre. They wanted to travel. The dog was with them, tucked under the woman's arm neatly, like a furry purse.

'It needs some work,' I said. Louis was asleep in his cot. When he slept in the daytime I always felt that I was not quite real, that I was in suspension, waiting for him to wake. 'The master bathroom hasn't been retiled in about a thousand years, and you'd probably want to put in a new kitchen. But the space is very good.'

The woman, Mrs Foote, nodded, peering at the wooden floors, the mouldings, the window sills. Mr Foote smiled at me and kept his hands in the pockets of the neatly pressed chinos that were slung below his belly.

'It was my mother's apartment,' I said, because it was something to say.

Mrs Foote turned her gaze to me. 'Wasn't your mother Sally Wheeler?'

'Yes, she was,' I said, startled. 'How did you know?'

'Oh, Cynthia told me,' she answered. Cynthia was the realtor. It hadn't occurred to me that selling Sally Wheeler's apartment might be easier than selling any old apartment, but Cynthia, presumably, knew better. 'I was so sad to read that she'd died.' There had been a small obituary in *The Times*.

'We used to go hear her downtown,' Mr Foote said. 'We were fans. Once, for our anniversary—was it our tenth?'

'Eleventh, Howard, I think,' Mrs Foote smiled.

'Our eleventh anniversary, we went to San Francisco. And wouldn't you know, in a little place right by our hotel, Sally Wheeler was singing that night. It was magical. One of those moments.'

'She was special that night,' Mrs Foote said.

'The night was special.'

'And this is her apartment.' Now Mrs Foote looked around, not at details, but all around her, inhaling deeply, as if she might pick up some scent or essence of my mother. Or at least, of the woman she thought was my mother. Would she want to know about the dozens of cans of ravioli and baked beans stacked in the kitchen cupboards? The crate of bloody Mary mix? The ancient stick of cocoa butter by her bedside table? The red felt slippers, dusty, disintegrating, she'd had since I was a little girl? For Mrs Foote my mother was a presence, a caramel voice in a black silk sheath, a scarlet mouth, peep-toe shoes, a loop of real pearls always around her left wrist. Once, when I was about seven, I tried to rub them against my teeth. That was what you did with pearls, though I didn't know why. My mother had just got out of the shower; I was sitting on the edge of her bed. 'Don't,' she said, her red-tipped fingers snatching the string from me, clutching them to her, to the pink towel wound around her body. 'Be careful.'

'I was,' I'd said. 'I was careful.'

I must have looked forlorn because she came and sat beside me and put a damp arm around my shoulder, squeezed. She still held the pearls in one hand. 'They're my lucky beads, honey,' she said. 'I'd be lost without them.'

What would I be lost without? I had wondered then. I couldn't come up with an answer. Once I had been given a rabbit's foot on a chain, dyed green, but it only seemed strange and sad and I lost it fairly soon. I had wished I had something to believe in, like lucky beads. Where were those pearls now? They must be in a drawer somewhere. I should look for them.

'It must make you sad to sell it,' Mr Foote's voice had a sheen of conscious sensitivity.

'Oh, I don't know,' I said. 'Really, she was hardly ever here.' And if she had been, would I have felt differently? It was impossible to imagine. Then she wouldn't be my mother.

I had clipped the baby listener to my belt; now it hissed and moaned. 'My son,' I said. 'He's waking up. I won't be a minute.' I left them in the hall while I went to get him; he lay blinking in his cot and I scooped him up and brought him out, perched against my shoulder, his head twisting like an owl's to see.

'What a lovely little baby!' Mrs Foote said. Her manicured fingers tickled his chin and he squinted at her. The rest of the tour was conducted with Louis in my arms. To cover the awkwardness I felt. Why? As if I were revealing too much of myself, or of some history these two people, fans of my mother, were not entitled to—I more than occasionally addressed my remarks to Louis, in a way which seemed to me idiotic but over which I had apparently no control.

'You see,' I said in a serious, grown-up voice when we stood in my mother's bathroom. 'It needs retiling. And plastering.' Then, to Louis's apparently interested gaze: 'Doesn't it?' My voice high, nearly a shriek, baby-talk. 'Doesn't it need retiling? And plastering? Yes it does, it does!'

When the Footes left, an echo of their admiration remained, and the apartment seemed oppressive. It was drizzling, but I tucked Louis into his pram and put on a jacket and we went out, strolling up and down Broadway. I bought a coffee. I thought about going back to work. How quickly I had got used to this new life, this non-life. There was so much to do, and so many things to think about, and most of them I didn't want to think about at all, and I certainly didn't want to have to explain them to any one else, which is why I had kept reaching for the telephone and then not picking it up. It was easy enough not to think about Louis; there was so much to do for him that thinking was barely feasible. But suddenly, on 99th and Broadway, I wondered what being his mother meant. What would he accept of me and what sort of person would that make him? I had accepted my mother's absences, her essence transmitted through the mails, her visits to my boarding school, the solitude I had cultured and nourished as so much more reliable than any contact with another human being. What would Louis culture and nourish? He lay in his stroller, gazing up at me with his dark blue eyes, keeping his own counsel, waiting.

****

This time it was nearly dawn when it started. I had been up three times in the night; Louis was restless and hungry, or restless, anyhow, and always happy to attach himself to me for a little while before we both fell into a doze. I hadn't brought him into my bed; resolutely I had gone into his room, sat up in the chair, listening to the muted noises of the city at night, the hiss of cars rushing, whatever the hour, up and downtown; a fire engine somewhere to the east. I looked out over the string of coloured lights, like Christmas bulbs, that marked the western edge of Manhattan before the tarry strip of the river, the low twinkle of New Jersey across the water. Sometimes my eyes dropped shut, and I would jump awake again when my chin fell towards my chest. But at dawn, the fourth time of waking, it wasn't Louis's cries that pulled me out of dream.

Kiss me, tootsie, and then—
Do it over again—

A breathy voice, a voice like a wooden flute, a voice I recognized and yet did not recognize. It was a young voice.

Watch for the mail—
I'll never fail—
If you don't get a letter then you know I'm in jail—

It was my mother's voice. But her voice, I knew suddenly, as I lay listening in the dark, hearing my son stir but not wake, before I had known her. Her voice as it had been when the picture of herself she kept on her night table had been taken: a picture by Bruno of Hollywood showing a girl with marcelled waves in her close-cut hair, extra-long eyelashes retouched on to almost oriental eyes, a mouth so dark in the black-and-white picture it was easy to imagine its deep blood red. A gold gypsy bangle on her wrist.

In the ignorance of my youth, I had often wondered why she kept this picture out. To me it seemed like it would be a reproach, this former, airbrushed self, vanishing into age. Suddenly I knew I had been wrong. That self had never vanished at all.

Toot, toot, tootsie
Goodbye—
Toot, toot, tootsie
Don't cry—

My mother's voice sang to my son from a time that existed as vividly in my imagination as if my own memories were being conjured. The Bon Soir, The Embers, The Maisonette and The Persian Room. Panelled walls, a piano, the string of pearls, smoke curling up towards a low ceiling and waiters at the edge of the room, waiting for each song to end. A burst of laughter and applause, the rustle of silk and wool and the sound of ice cubes swirling in a tall glass. It was how she met my father, a man with a Martini who sat in the front row of The Half Note for four nights running in 1961. Someone else's husband who died of a heart attack when I was eight, who left the trust that sent me to school. She hadn't talked about him, not really, only sung me the songs she must have sung to him, too. I had one picture of the two of them, on a picnic in upstate New York, which always looked more staged to me than the Bruno of Hollywood portrait. Where was that photograph? Maybe with the string of pearls.

I lay still, listening to her sing. Louis was quiet now. Over on the east side, the dawn was coming. I wondered if the Footes would make an offer for the apartment. I wondered if I would take it, if they did. I could retile the bathroom myself. I might get to like baked beans. I might even get to like canned ravioli. There was a hiss and crackle. The voice faded and vanished with a soft hiss like something dropped into the sea. I pressed my ear close to the speaker and heard my son's breath; only that, deep and regular and sure.

Rachel Castell Farhi

Born in London as a matrilineal Jew, Rachel Castell Farhi has written much about dual identity. After re-discovering traditional Judaism, she is now also happy to affirm her non-Jewish roots. Her short stories have appeared in two collections, and her journalism has been published in *The Jewish Quarterly* and *Daily Telegraph*. She is married with a family and lives in London.

'To me, good writing transcends gender: I also write in a male persona, and I write to find the common denominator, however small, between us all. I love being a Jew but I am proud of being British. Judaism tugs at my heart like a guilty child wanting attention; Englishness is my father in his military uniform, standing on a Remembrance parade in silent dignity. Both need nurturing. Judaism will still be here in a thousand years time, but the Englishness I cherish will not, and that saddens me greatly.'

The Mezuzah Gatherer

One

She asks me if I am Jewish and I hesitate. 'No, yes—I mean, not really, any more.' The stumbling answer surprises me as much as her question. She takes no notice, brushes aside any objections on my part and continues.

'We must all be ready for *Mashiah* and do our bit to hasten his arrival. Can I give you this leaflet on *misvoth* in the home? I see you haven't got a *mezuzah.*'

Her finger pointing at my doorpost annoys me but I feel unable to tell her to buzz off. I analyse my weakness—something about being caught out on an error, a school girl shyness at the bubba headmistress, the baby crying inside.

'Look I'm not a believer anymore. I'm really busy. I have to go.'

It's so simple to say; it's what I think, believe. I'll blurt it out, quickly, get it over with—this doorstep evangelism .

'If you need a *mezuzah*, I can get one for you from our office. Very reasonably priced. Hundred per cent *kasher*, certified by *Rav* Menashe—'

I grab her leaflet, say thank you and close the door. A moment later, I hear her ring our neighbour's doorbell and the spiel starts again. David glances up at me, holding Tanya across his shoulder. Her crying is petulant, insistent, demanding me, not him. I take her from him and she calms, but our Sunday afternoon peace is irretrievably shattered.

'What's that?'

'More paper for the recycling bin.'

'Not that bloody *Lubavitch* woman again. I thought she'd given up on us.'

'Us, yes. Me, no.'

'Next time I'll answer the door. You're too soft. You should just say piss off we've become Catholics.'

David doesn't understand. David has *chutzpah.* He can tell it like it is and not worry about the reaction he provokes. I worry and wither, my words waste away like unused wine down the plughole. Powerful feelings, lousy delivery, might as well give it up.

'Anna—the darkness. I'm afraid of the darkness.'

'Hush, quiet. No need to be afraid. I'm with you.'

'But tonight, Kol Nidrei. I'm scared the Angel of Death will come for me. I've done so many bad things this year.'

'You're just a baby. What could you have done wrong?'

'Lots, Anna. Lots of things. I have. Will I be punished?'

'God doesn't punish babies.'

'Promise?'

'Promise.'

'But I'm nearly seven. I'm not a baby any more. Am I Anna? Am I?'

The fumes will fill the room, silently, just a hiss like Eden's serpent let loose for its revenge. Invisible. Deadly. Poisonous air killing the oxygen, consuming it, consuming us. Death waits for sleep, sleep becomes death. The first choking breaths start then.
Who will die by fire and who by flood?
Children died first, the book said. Lung capacity small, they breathe in faster. Ingest the carbon monoxide quickest.
Who by famine? Who by the sword?
If I starve myself on 'Yom Kippur' and the day after and the day after that... If I die too, what will he become?

'Anna—is it me? Is this for me?'

The clock says three but my mind starts, alert and ready, as if it were morning. Breath is hard to catch, mouth sucking in air that isn't there for me. Clumsy panic takes me to the window; I push open its casement and swallow in the chill night. The cold fills me, shocks my warm body with its presence; I shiver, longing to return to the warmth of our bed, to sleep beside David again, but I am afraid to, afraid of something I cannot name. Out in the night, in this still London air, the comfort of suburbia envelops my anxiety. The scorn I feel in the daylight for my dull neighbours has been shamed by my need for them; the stability, the routine, the predictability of their existence, so many sleepers in so many beds, reassures me. The world is as I left it last night. No surprises, no demons. No angels either. Calmer, I look across at David who sleeps like a man with no conscience—a worker's sleep, deep, deserved, satisfying. Even Tanya, restless Tanya, sleeps like one who has worn out the day to its limits and is now enjoying its reward.

'Does the Angel of Death come for children?'

Stop. It's over. There's nothing here but peaceful silence. And in a few hours, everything will be alive again. You must believe that.

Two

The train from Liverpool Street takes me eastwards, through London and out to my job on its periphery. I have never noticed the journey, caught as I am between the last shadows of sleep and the glaring white pages of files whose contents I must consume in lieu of breakfast. In this transit, I have no identity, no name. No number. An hour ago I was Susie and Mummy, in another hour I will be Mrs Abraham from the Education Department. At this moment, only the ticket collector will be interested in my being here.

The sun is bright and high already. I can't concentrate on the files today. Something is dragging me away, pulling me from the pages I should be reading, taking my gaze from the names—all those sad histories of children's failed expectations—and focusing me elsewhere: Bethnal Green, Hackney Downs, Clapton. Names that mean little to me now but sound a resonance in my past. I hardly knew my grandparents but these names, these places were part of their legend. My parents had been busy expunging them from their children's hand-me-down tales, replacing them with upwardly mobile places from northern suburbs.

'Thank God, you'll never have to set foot in Dalston,' my mother once said.

She'd worked hard to take the East End out of her accent after she'd met my father.

'Heaven knows why you want to go and work in those sort of places. They're not romantic you know. Poverty and dirt aren't romantic. Diamonds are romantic. En-suite bathrooms with showers are romantic.'

My mother believed that a semi-detached in Edgware, and a husband who could pass for Cary Grant in a bad light, was romantic. I remember my father fondly, not for his shadowy resemblance to a film star but for the way he encouraged my mother's dreaming with his own successes.

'All the success in the world but you can't buy your destiny. A man may have it all and then lose what is most precious to him and he's as good as over.'

Who said that? Who told my father that? Or did they speak it then, behind his back, when the *shivah* was about to start? Words, phrases. They come uninvited into my head at the moments when I most need clarity, uncluttered thinking. Thoughts that come into my head when I don't want to think, when I want simply to feel. Feel David's warm breath against my breast. Feel myself again.

Susie, Susie, Susie!
When Susie was a baby, a baby Susie was,
She went wah, wah, wah-wah-wah!

That playground song in my head.

Where is Anna? When was Anna here?

There is no break to my day. It is a fluid chain of interconnecting events, punctuated by my desire to eat or take a piss somewhere. The children, the parents, the faces, the names: Mehmet Ali, Mahmood Ali, Alisa Begum. I have five children called Begum on my caseload, all from different branches of the same family and none of whom attend school regularly. Then there's Shaun Mitchell. His mother called me a lousy bitch but I still have to talk to her. I don't want to talk to her. I want to shout at her. I want to say: 'Look Mrs, no wonder your boy's a little shit, he gets it from you.' I'm supposed to be trained.

I'm supposed to be calm, controlled, professional; not to pass judgement.

'It's the parents to blame,' my mother says. 'Kids aren't born devils; they become them. No proper families anymore. No roots. If children don't know where they belong, how can you expect them to give respect to those who do?'

I argue with her. Bring out the old sociological chestnuts about economic deprivation; middle class value systems judging working-class ones as invalid; difficulties with English not being a first language. Mum cuts through the crap as only she can. 'My parents were all those things you've just said—and we made it through school all right. You're only a teacher now because of the sacrifices they made in some stinking tailor's sweatshop in Whitechapel. Think on that before you start bringing your Socialism home here.'

Dad will smile. He doesn't think the word 'socialist' is a term of abuse but he'd never call himself a sympathizer. 'Our Susie a socialist? Well, every Jewish family's got one.'

I'm not sure I believe the arguments anymore. I trot them out like *responsa* to a catechism, tell myself I did the thinking out part back then, back in Dr. Wasserman's lecture room, when the world seemed black and white, the enemy—class—to be squared up to wherever I encountered it. In those days—God, did I really write that, I sound more like my mother than is good for me—I loved my job, believed in it. Teaching is an honourable profession—even the religion I don't have says so. Not that that should have mattered, because by then I was an atheist, but it was nice to be confirmed in my mission. My mission's changed now, though. Today's mission: roll out at Liverpool Street station, take the tube to a middle-class Jewish suburb and survive my daughter's bedtime tantrums before this starts all over again tomorrow.

They've made an announcement. A fire on the track. All services suspended until further notice. London Underground apologises... The platform guard answers me impatiently, basically wanting me to sod off and let him get on with his job. I note his tone and decide I should adopt it with the *Lubavitch* woman when she comes to call. 'Yo lady!

Ain't you just heard? *Mashiah* ain't comin' cos there's a fire on the line. Take a bus instead.'

The fire part disturbs me more than it does the other commuters. I decide not to hang around, surface instead into the green-glassed metrodome of shops above the station and try to find a taxi.The queue for taxis is long: a line of male suits interrupted by an occasional female suit, each disappearing into a mobile black unit, selfishly enclosing themselves from the rest of the world. I look in my purse and decide I can't really afford to take a cab at all, but if I could share someone else's... This suggestion to a pinstriped neighbour is met with disdain. Ten years ago I might have sought to challenge him with arguments about gender and ecological soundness. Tonight, I just want to get home.

'Tell me Anna, is it far to go? Are we nearly there?'
'I don't know.'
'Will Mama and Papa be there? Eh, Anna?'
'No.'
'When will they come, then?'
'I don't know.'

Three

I am standing alone outside a green door. Its paint is blistered with age and the letterbox, a rusted iron slit, hangs to one side like the lopsided mouth of a cretinous face. The scaffolding over my head doesn't worry me, but it should—a sudden gust of wind and it would shake precariously, stop me thinking my crazy thoughts, perhaps knock them into focus again. I take the risk. I've become very good at taking risks, not out of bravery or principle but just to liven things up. It's warm this evening; my dress clings to my shoulders like a little devil hanging on my conscience.

- *Go on, knock.*

The face at the little window upstairs is old and dark, swathed in cool white robes that look cleaner than the house should allow.

- *Say it, go on. Ask.*

The old man looks frightened, his beard a tangle of virtues I don't understand, his eyes hollow and set like someone without reason to trust a stranger. I didn't think anyone lived in the house; it looks condemned.

'I didn't think anyone lived in the house.'

The old man calls out behind him in a language I don't know, but keeps his gaze fixed upon me as though I am a predator come to claim her quarry. A moment later, a younger man appears at the window and the elder retreats behind him.

'Yeah?' he asks suspiciously.

- *I can't.*
- *Go on. You must.*

'I thought the house was empty. Is it yours?'

'Who are you?'

'Just a tourist. Is it your house?'

'No,' then, slightly eased, 'My grandfather's. What do you want here?'

This is excruciating but the devil eggs me on.

'I want a souvenir. This was once my grandfather's house also.'

The head disappears from the window and a moment later emerges from behind the weather-beaten door, eyeing me with suspicion. I am overwhelmed by myself, that a thought I have held inwards has become a reality, has brought this stranger to talk with me, to help me with my odyssey. Lies slip off my tongue as easily as the truth does from a young child's lips. Why do I lie about my grandfather?

'Your family lived here?' the younger man asks.

I see now that he is not young at all, but in contrast to the old man, he seems so. There is a chasm of difference between us, and it isn't about the colour of our skin. He has eyes that know and watch, eyes that wait for the right moment, then pounce. He has that toughened look that I've seen before, in the schoolchildren, in their parents.

David has it, my mother has it. I feel momentarily threatened, then the lies seem to take over and win my confidence back.

'A long time ago. Before the war.'

He believes me but says nothing. The old man appears from behind the gloom and stands at his shoulder. They converse.

'My grandfather says if you want to look inside, you can.'

The invitation surprises me. It isn't what I came for. What have I come for?

- Go on, ask for it. Ask for the mezuzah.

'I want that.' My finger points towards the doorjamb before my eyes have a chance to follow it to know if it is really there. It is. A rusted cheap tin box nailed at an angle perhaps a hundred years before. A careless brush stroke of apple green paint has swept across its breadth. It stands worthless, unnoticed for half a century, un-kissed, un-worshipped, like a woman past her prime, and suddenly, three pairs of eyes are upon it as if for the first time.

'The doorbell doesn't work but it's part of the house,' the younger man begins. I interrupt.

'It isn't a doorbell. It's a religious symbol placed by Jewish people on their houses. It should have been taken down by the family, unless another Jewish family was moving in straight after.'

The old man says something else, more furtively than before.

'My grandfather says the Jews keep money inside them. You can have the box but he wants the money.'

I am unsure of my reaction, but there is anger within me tempered by amusement. Do they really think that of a *mezuzah*?

Flashback: a classroom; kids try to bait me.

'Why don't Jews eat Quality Street, miss? Cos they're made for sharing.'

Titter, titter.

'Why do Jews build their synagogues square? So they can hide in the corners when the collection plate comes round!'

'Laugh, miss, go on. There ain't no Yids in the class.'

The black kids laugh along with the white ones. Black and

white united—a teacher's dream?

'How many Jews can you fit in an ashtray?'

Six million.

'What?'

The younger man is asking me something. I explain.

'There won't be any money inside. Only a piece of paper with some prayers written on it.'

The old man reaches over and pulls at the doorpost with his horny fingers. The *mezuzah* comes away with little effort; the nails holding it to the rotting wood fall away noiselessly at my feet. Underneath the paintwork is yellow and clean—its first exposure to daylight for many years. The old man turns the *mezuzah* over in his hand slowly. It leaves a rusty deposit on his skin like henna, which he blows off; then he peers inside the top of the object at a rolled up piece of parchment. He attempts to prise it out but the paper is old and flaky.

'It's very bad luck to take it out,' I say instinctively.

He seems to understand and after a few moments he passes the *mezuzah* to me, assured that it is worthless to him.

'Take.'

His voice is weak but proud. I believe he has understood everything all along but chooses silence as the prudent course. It is one kind of survivor's trick on another—he is a survivor who recedes into the background to become part of the whole, one who doesn't draw attention to himself, but forms part of the picture anyway. I know I am neither sort.

Four

I know that Anna is cold, if indeed there is anything left of Anna. Because they won't talk about her, never visit her, say they don't know where she is. But I know. I know because I used to talk to her, still talk to her when I need to, when those nights come when the air seems thick and un-breathable and the night blinds me with its darkness. I talk to her when the kids seem at their most hateful and David won't listen because he's too tired and we haven't made love for weeks.

- Anna, Anna. You were never meant to know any of this.

My father cannot discuss her at all because she was young and clever and used to put him to shame with her brightness. My mother will never discuss the past unless it's a golden country to be revisited for pleasure. Anna's name is never linked with pleasure because Anna wasn't her child. Anna is the past's un-gathered recollection. I shouldn't know about her, but I do.

When David and I first met we discussed our families and which Old Countries were old countries for them, as Jews seem to do. He told me about his parents and their flight from Holland as the Nazis moved closer; of immigrant ships and British soldiers pushing old women and girls back to their persecutors because no-one wanted to take them in. He spoke of his father in a detention camp in Cyprus, in sight of the promised land; of his mother disguised as a convent girl in Switzerland until the war was over. And I told him about Anna who was gassed in the war and was buried in an unmarked grave.

'I thought your family were in England during the war,' he said.

'They were. Anna was my father's child from his first wife. She suffocated in her sleep because of a faulty gas fire in her room. And she was buried in a wartime mass grave because there was no money for her to have her own. My father never talks about it and my mother respects that. Do you believe in spirits?'

I told him that I used to think about Anna whenever there was a programme on about the Holocaust, that somehow she seemed to have died there. Gas, an unmarked grave—it all seemed too coincidental to a child.

'For me the Holocaust will always be personified by Anna. I used to talk to her as a child, whenever I was scared.'

'And what used to scare you?'

'Being Jewish. And going to sleep.'

'No child of mine will ever be scared of either,' David affirmed that night.

And as he said it, I felt safer, not just for myself but for David's future children, which I had a sense would be mine also.

'Are your family very *frum*?' he asked when our relationship got closer. I told him no. His weren't either.

'They used to be. But the war put them off. It must be the same for yours.'

'My father won't even put up a *mezuzah*,' I said. 'But that's got something to do with Anna. Apparently, the rabbi said that God looked the other way that night because the *mezuzah* on her room wasn't *kosher.* My father got angry and said he'd never put one up in the first place.'

'Well, I'm not interested in having one in my house,' David said. 'It's all nonsense anyway.'

I gather *mezuzoth* like so many un-recollected thoughts. I keep them in a drawer at home, the ancient harvest of twilight adventures whenever the trains aren't running properly or my job takes me to a former Jewish corner of an East End street. I have collected them from demolition sites, when doors have been replaced by yuppie house owners after I've assured them that they weren't a priceless original feature; and from superstitious Bengali men who worship the same God, only differently, and feel a respect for the object which has no meaning for those it ought to have.

They are all shapes and sizes, these relics. Some have their parchment missing; others are damaged through time and the elements. I showed them to the Lubavitch woman one day and she was impressed in a way that misunderstands.

'None of them are *kosher*, you know. The parchment has to be completely intact and undamaged. So don't put them up or it's bad *mazzal*. But it's a sort of *mitzvah* what you've done. They ought to go in a *genizah.*'

'What's a *genizah*?' I asked.

'It's where we bury sacred books and scrolls. We never burn them or throw them away when they can't be used any more. The *Torah* is life, we mustn't burn life.'

I keep them, still. My drawer has a box in it and they lie within, undisturbed, until a new arrival comes. I kiss each one as it is collected, fingers to my lips first, then lightly touch the case. Respectfully. Dutifully. Receiving these unknown into a cherished place, as I hope God received Anna.

Lana Citron

Originally from Dublin, Lana Citron is the author of the novels *Sucker*, *Spilt Milk* and *Transit.* **She has published short stories and poems, broadcast on Radio Four and scripted the award winning short film** *I was a Cigarette Girl.*

'A writer! My inner Jewish mother coming to the fore on the birth of my son wishes I'd been a professional—a lawyer, or say, a dentist. But what can you do? Never mind the fact I was brought up in Ireland, so I have been exposed to a generous measure of both Catholic shame and Jewish guilt. On the bright side, I thank God I have enough neurosis to be creative.'

Mordecai's First Brush With love

Mordy carried on him a fit of despair: never in the whole of his life, one of fourteen summers, had he felt so wretched. Mordecai Levison, son of Jason (and Marlene) Levison, an antiques dealer on the Kilburn High Road specialising in shiny *shmattes* and affordable *khazeray*. Jason had a good business, nay, a great business: so, imagine his disgust when, one day, Mordy, his own flesh and blood, announced he didn't want to work in his father's shop anymore. 'What! You crazy? *Oi,* that's real smart working for nothing in a second hand store,' he said.

'Dad you're making such a big deal out of it.' Surely his father should have been proud of his son's initiative in securing work experience, albeit unpaid, in a record store in Camden. For Mordy this was but a stepping-stone, a way into a world he 'obsessed' about, which, more importantly, provided access to the female sex.

'Am I?' his father roared. 'That my own child should treat me this way, after everything I've sacrificed!'

Mordy hated his father: besides, it wasn't like he ever paid Mordy, either.

Marlene, sucking on a Prozac, sick to the teeth of the arguing, shouted, 'Leave him be; he's a growing boy.'

Mordy also hated his mother, not because she was of a nervous disposition, in a constant state of worry, obsessed with food—she, skin and bone herself—but, just 'because.'

In truth, Mordy hated most people: as I've said, he was only fourteen, and all this putrid emotion was but a pot brimful of misplaced frustrations. For although Mordy had witnessed love before—gleaned from the pages of magazines, videos, his friends coping off at parties—love evaded him. He had yet to succumb to the pleasures of a good woman, or any woman for that matter. The 'bottle' spun out of his reach; his mother still sent him Valentine cards. God, how he ached, wished, yearned! His grandfather, on his mother's side, Mordecai Snr, had been a tailor, and of late, Marlene would look at her son and cluck, 'If only your Grandpa could see you now!' She was always saying stuff like that as if it somehow meant something.

Mordy had only met his grandfather once, in a dream. He'd said to him, 'I had a *shiksah.* Her name was Sheila. What a lady!' This had been the night before Mordy's *bar mitzvah* and halfway through reciting his portion of the *Torah,* he went blank. His tongue wagged, soundless; his spittle dried. The Rabbi tapped him on the arm: 'Take a deep breath, kid.' Mordy glanced up toward his mum; she smiled kindly at him; then, at his sister, who made a jeering face. He hated his sister; it was mutual. She made his life a complete misery and never let him into her room when her friends called by. So he'd answered her contempt by finding courage, and continued with his portion of the *Torah*. His voice rose, fell and then broke on the final 'Amen'. And so it was on that special day Mordy officially reached manhood. He peacock-paraded from the *bimah*, across to the s*hul* hall, enjoying the attentions as a young man should. Yet when the disco lights dimmed, it was only Marlene who deigned to slow-dance with him. The fact was—Mordy was a slow developer, puny and pimply, puberty waving to him from afar. His nana, Irma, would shrug her shoulders and say: 'All in good time,' but this is all she ever said—she, patiently waiting for death in an old age home, to which Marlene would drag Mordy once a month.

'All in good time', and then it happened—it happened—Mordy's first brush with love.

On a night with a full moon, Mordy, shackled by despair, had run panting from the arms of his love Rachel Reuben, back to the safety of his warm home. Beautiful Rachel Reuben, the object of his desire, of his confounding heartache, daughter of Louie and Rena (ten years divorced), now living with her mother and older sister in West Hampstead: and only thirteen. Mordy first noticed Rachel in the record store, flicking through LPs—doltish brown eyes, long lashes, black hair tied up in a pigtail, and already a chest one could knead—and as for her tush... *Oy* how the front of his trousers twitched! Mordy understood these stirrings and swore to himself that Rachel would be his. One day he would press himself close against her and she wouldn't... resist. Over the ensuing weeks he had slept well on sweet dreams of hope—of how he could coax her out on a date. Then two Saturdays later, her face half hidden by a raised LP, their eyes met, and Mordy muttered a feeble 'I've seen you around.'

Rachel batted her eyelids. 'My name's Rachel.'

'Mordy,' He pointed to himself. 'Looking for anything in particular?'

'No,' came her teasing reply.

A further three Saturdays passed before they met again. As a God sent angel, as a vision, she reappeared, and Mordy waved at her over-enthusiastically, dreadfully self-conscious. He grinned at her showing his trained, tracked teeth and spluttered: 'What you been up to?'

'Just things.'

She giggled mischievously, a coy look on her face, a hand masking her mouth. (The flirt. The little vixen. I'll have her for sure, it's certain.) And right there and then, Mordy surprised himself and asked her out, his voice rising in pitch.

'Do you want to come to the cinema tonight?'

'With you?'

'Yeah.'

'I'll have to ask mum.'

'Okay.'

They exchanged mobile numbers and it wasn't until closing time that she called and arranged to meet him at the Odeon, Swiss Cottage, later, that very night.

Later, that very night...

'Where the hell have you been?' His mother was near to tears when finally Mordy pushed his key into the key-hole.

'Cinema,' he muttered.

She was pacing the sitting room in her pink dressing gown.

'I've been out of my mind. Why didn't you call?'

Mordy shrugged off her questions and made for the kitchen. Marlene could tell something was up: usually he would shout back at her.

'Mordy what happened?'

Why does life have to be so complicated? There he was waiting outside the cinema for Rachel, two tickets in his grubby palm. She arrived fifteen minutes late; they bought ice cream and popcorn and Mordy, in a sweat, couldn't believe his luck. They watched the latest spy-thriller, and at a scary moment, Rachel had grabbed his hand and squeezed hard. Then, at the end of the film, as the credits rolled, he leant toward her, praying his breath didn't smell, praying her breath didn't smell, praying she'd open her lips. And they had: her lips opened and their tongues swam in unison, and never, ever, in his whole life, had Mordy felt this good.

'Mordy, *feygele,* answer me. I'm your mother.'

Mordy slunk down in the kitchen chair.

'You hungry? Want something to eat?'

As every Jewish mother knows, food is love and love is food. How attractive is a fridge? A *Yiddishe* boy's pornography.

'See how full it is,' says Marlene to her son, 'What would you like? What can I get you? You want cake? There's some left over chicken? I could heat the roast potatoes in the micro?' The Levisons' fridge was stacked to capacity, overflowing with the goodness of Sainsbury's supermarket.

'Aw Mum.' Mordy just wanted her to go away.

'You've gone off food… You have a temperature?'

She checked; he didn't.

Marlene couldn't understand this, and went for the full frontal. She opened the freezer compartment too. 'You want a Marks and Spencer ready-made?'

Ah how they had kissed in the darkness of the cinema—wet, wild, eager, clutching one another. So this is love, thought Mordy, and whispered though her tousled hair: 'Rachel, you're so beautiful...'

The micro wave tinkled and Marlene took out his favourite, chicken *korma* with rice, broke a sprig of parsley from the window-box of herbs and went to sit beside Mordy to watch him eat.

'So then—what, Mordy?' asked Marlene (all the while thinking: I'm losing my son, my only son— already a man!)

'I... we...' and it was at this moment that Mordy realised exactly why he hated his mother: she was the one he cleaved to and always would.

'We left the cinema...'

'Were you holding hands?'

'Yeah... Mum it was awful. We crossed over to KFC to get some food and ...'

'What Mordy, she doesn't eat out?'

'No... We're standing in the queue; I turn to her, to ask if she wants something else and I see...'

'What Mordy?'

'I see... Oh God it was horrible!'

'You can tell me. It doesn't matter.'

'Mum, she has a moustache. I've fallen for a woman with a moustache!'

Marlene looked at her son, thinking: A nice Jewish girl: what did he expect? She placed her hand upon his and said, 'Don't worry—you'll get yours soon.'

Though beautiful, intelligent and destined to be the controller of the BBC, three miles down the road, in floods of tears, choking on snot, with her mother's Jolen burning her upper lip, was the young Rachel. Throughout her life this humiliation would always plague her, and she would wax, pluck, Immac, and have electrolysis until, aged thirty, finally, she could afford laser treatment.

Joan Michelson

Joan Michelson was born in Boston, MA, USA and has lived in England since 1970. She is a tutor in Creative Writing at Birkbeck College, University of London, and has been the recipient of numerous writing fellowships. Her work has been published in two volumes of the British Council's *New Writing.* Her poetry chapbook *Letting in the Light* (2002) was an Editor's Choice prize publication.

'My sense of a cultural Jewish heritage was informed, strengthened and directed by a year as an undergraduate at the Hebrew University of Jerusalem, and my first encounters with survivors of the Holocaust. My experience in Israel drew me to Europe and Britain where I arrived as a young adult. For a decade from the mid-seventies I lived in a West Midlands town. If there were any other Jews around, they were hidden, at least from me. In these circumstances, as a writer and lecturer, I found myself drawn towards the history of the Jews in the twentieth century. This led to research and publication within Holocaust Studies as well as the development of taught courses in this subject area, and it heightened my sense of Jewish culture and history. Also, I have a daughter who, born and brought up in Britain, has chosen to be a part of a Jewish community. Issues around this have helped to shape the story *Birthing*, written for this anthology.'

Birthing

'On the day you were born, I had to find a synagogue. I don't know why,' my mother said.

'That was me.' I said. 'I wanted to go.'

'Could be,' she said. 'Like a voice from afar.'

'No,' I said, 'not like that. I was inside you, trying to get out.'

My mother continued.

So you were, my lovey, and so you did. But the fact is I hadn't put a foot in a synagogue since your Aunt Judi and Uncle Barry were married and they'd just celebrated their tenth anniversary with an overnight in a Boston harbour hotel. I told Judi when I telephoned, which wasn't something we did every day or week or month. You can't imagine how it was before the computer age. A call to overseas came with Big Operator Charges. At least for those of us who lived outside the cities. It always takes England a little longer than America to get its wires straightened, although I suppose even in those days, if we'd been in Manchester or Birmingham or London, we could have dialled direct for something like a reasonable cost, say a cup of coffee with a scone.

Of course on the day you were born, we phoned everyone. Or your father did. The night before I thought you'd died because you were so still, and then you came back to life and I was wide awake at some crazy hour. Then I had my bloody show and phoned Judi waking her up because it was after midnight in Boston. Then it was dawn of the day so misty with heat I could picture the sea all around us although we were in the middle of the country and the sea was over there, where Judi lives. I told her I had packed my overnight bag and was taking it with me because I had every intention of keeping my appointment. I was following clinic instructions to the letter. As the British say, I told Judi, I was being a good girl.

On the other hand, I wasn't a complete dodo. I understood that the hospital preferred their mothers to deliver on weekdays between nine and five, and if they were thinking of keeping me in on a Thursday, the chances of undergoing an induction to speed things up were about one hundred per cent. I don't think I have to tell you, my lovey, that I was opposed to this along with other offerings: prods, injections, inspections, drips.

Of course there was your father to think of. Naturally he was growing impatient. Given that I needed the car at my disposal, he couldn't plan his work schedule because he didn't know where he had to be when. Yet he remained sympathetic. He only swallowed when I told him I'd prefer to squat beneath the apple tree in our back garden and deliver you on the grass. It didn't matter that it was a scraggly old Spartan and that the apples were worm-eaten. Then he said that sometimes nature could use some help. I think he was referring to the tree and also pushing me towards the hospital, which sometimes gives nature a helping hand, so to speak.

'You didn't tell him about the synagogue alternative?'

'What synagogue alternative?'

'But you spoke to your sister that morning. You must have known it was the New Year. Aunt Judi would have said something. 'Happy Holidays. Happy *Rosh Hashanah. Hag Sameyah.*'

'All right. Enough.'

All right. Enough of my mother for the moment. I'm taking over here.

I understood that there was no Jewish community in the town where my parents were living. In fact, according to my father who grew up in that part of the Midlands, there weren't any Jews, or there weren't any that were recognised. In the heyday of his youth, my father confused Jews with Americans, or that's what he says. And that's why he married my mother.

I could also sort of understand that since my father had defected to non-believer and my mother was gaga about him, at least until I came along, my mother let go of who she was. Or had been. But then I was there, and she became a Jewish mother. On top of that, my mother told me this, she had a connection to the Midlands.

This was through her mother's father's brother. Around 1900, escaping from a summons from the Tsar's army, and on his way to New York, he stopped somewhere in the middle of England. He was in England for at least a year. That's all we know. But it's possible that he fathered a child. Stranger things have happened. For all I know, the young woman sitting beside my mother in the Birmingham Liberal synagogue could have been one of her own cousins four generations removed. Family, it's like that. At the WUJS conference this past winter, World Union of Jewish Students, I found a cousin I never knew about.

Perhaps on the day I was going to be born my mother felt a forgotten connection. So she caught the train she was supposed to catch, carrying her overnight bag but then, on the train, sharing a table with her, she met a woman and a little girl who was colouring in animals for Noah's ark. She asked the little girl some questions about Noah and the Flood, fell into conversation with the mother about missions to East Africa where her Bible College was going to send her in the winter and, missing her hospital clinic stop and leaving her overnight bag on the train, she got off the train with them at Birmingham New Street station.

What happened to the overnight bag? My father collected it from Lost Property later in the week.

Cities are alike, my mother told me. Or the cities I know. Or maybe it was because of the heat. It might have been the beginning of autumn, but it felt like the middle of August, smog-white and so moist, the air dripped sweat. There was that city smell, things all mixed up, sweet, sharp, sickening, bland, indefinable. Invisible fumes hung suspended in the air. The daylight made things blur.

I didn't know where I was going. The theatres went past, a maze of narrow streets with low brick terraces, homes and shops, pubs pressed in among them. Endless. Then a turning. I found myself on the side of a wide dusty road. Maybe it was the time of day. But it felt like a place people avoided. Some boarded up buildings. Warehouses. Discount stores. Some from the 60s or 70s with plate glass windows. That's what I recall. Hardly any traffic. A feeling of wilderness. Of abandon. On one side of a flattened lot, a remnant wall propped up with iron supports. Glass in some of the windows, the frames painted in pastel gloss with edgings of old floral print wallpaper.

Then, alive, a Victorian school surrounded by a high iron fence.

Children on break time were racing around on the tarmac as if let out of hell.Then I saw it, tucked behind the school with two men in front guarding doors. A synagogue.

The men let my mother in as if they recognised her as one of their own. She climbed the women's stairs to the balcony and found a seat in the back row. Of course by then, the contractions she wasn't taking very seriously, were not the practice ones she'd been feeling for a week, the 'prodromals', as they are called. So she didn't stay seated for very long, just long enough for the rabbi's wife to bring her a prayer book and whisper a blessing if that's what she did; and for a young woman to attach herself like a sister, a young woman who might have been me.

I know how my mother ends the story.

She walked into one of the warehouses, a furniture discount store with an invitation to the public to buy at wholesale prices. She rolled onto the nearest bed and that was it. So I was born there. Or in the back seat of a taxi rushing her to hospital. On my birth certificate the place named is New Cross Hospital but certificates are filled out that way regardless of the truth. And if I ask for my mother for the truth, she only smiles, which makes me see red.

So here's my version.

I was at university and a UJS rep, Union of Jewish Students. The rabbi had invited us to join in the Holiday services. I'd left the halls of residence a little late, arrived a little late and so, like my mother, I slid into a seat in the back row. I was late but she was even later, so when she arrived, I was there. I moved over. I gave her a lot of room because, although she is a small woman, she was big. She's told me I was a big baby, the biggest in the ward and I needed an ocean to swim in, because I was already a swimmer . That accounted for it—me and an ocean inside her.

She was wearing a white smock, a tent of a dress made of Indian cotton. It was wet and clinging to her. I couldn't help looking. Well maybe I was staring, that high-rise blimp settled on her thighs and those breasts settled on the blimp. I'd never seen anything like it, at least not up close. I don't know how the rabbi's wife got wind that a stranger had joined us. Shoshana, which is what the rabbi's wife asked us to call her, was sitting at the front with a good view of the goings on below—the rabbi, the cantor, the elders, the opened ark lit up, the silver shields of the holy scrolls gleaming, and sitting or standing in front of the mahogany benches, men and boys with fringed white silk shawls wrapped around their city clothes. Some of the boys were stealthily moving about, conferring with one another. The smallest were being rocked in their fathers' arms. It was something to look at.

But hardly had my mother lowered herself onto her seat, when Shoshana, the rabbi's wife, her black onion dome hat falling forward, was leaning over my mother planting a kiss on my mother's hair, which was uncovered against synagogue practice. Shashona seemed to be saying, 'It's all right. All things are forgiven.You are welcome. Your child will be one of us.'

I like to think Shoshana mouthed something like this into my mother's ear before laying an open prayer book on her lap. Lap? Right on top of me, you could say, where I was punching and kicking. Shoshana pointed to the place on the page that the rabbi was reciting and returned to her bench.

My mother was confused and lost. I could see that. Her daughter in the guise of a stranger, I put my finger in the place in her prayer book. It was then that she first spoke to me. She sounded ashamed. 'I don't know where I am.'

'Never mind,' I said, 'We can read it together.' I pointed to the words one by one and whispered them aloud. I thought she was following but when I looked, her face looked tight and red as if she was about to cry.

'It's no use,' she said. 'I've forgotten all my Hebrew.' Then was time for a standing prayer. I put my arm out to help her up. 'I'm sorry,' she said, keeping her seat. 'I have to sit.'I didn't know what was happening. I could hear her breathing as if she'd run up a hill. Then she pushed herself up and went to the cloakroom behind us.

She didn't come back. I pictured her sitting behind the curtain on the bench under the coat hooks. Just in time, I saw her come out and turn towards the stairs. I went after her but keeping my distance so that she wasn't aware.

She had chosen exile. I was chosen to bring her back. I was at peace with myself yet I was afraid. Against our mothers, it is hard to speak out. She moved slowly up the road and so did I.Soon I too was wet with sweat, short of breath and felt my heart beating at a furious pace as if I was the unborn that she was carrying.

My mother reached a furniture show room walled with picture glass, and went in, straight to the nearest bed. It was a doublebed with a shiny brass headstead. She put her hands out, heaved herself onto the naked double mattress and rolled to the side with one leg sticking out. A short grey-haired salesman hurried towards her and so did I.

I rushed in and shouted at him to order a taxi. We'd go to the rabbi's house. Someone would be there to let us into the garden where our women's group had raised a tent. We had made it ourselves for the new moon, and the new year. For *Rosh Hodesh* and for *Rosh Hashanah*. It was of red canvas hung on a wooden frame with blankets for a floor, pillows for chairs, a box of bowls and plates, instruments to play, and a bucket of water. When the moon rose, we would wash our hands and eat. Then we would wash our hands again, sing and dance and tell our stories.

This was the place for my mother to give birth.To celebrate my birth into the community and to wake my mother to her own renewal. Everyone would help, sisters, friends, mothers, daughters and the rabbi's wife, Shoshana. We would make a circle. We would be together, loving and learning and laughing and hugging. The force would be in us: belonging.

It was my twenty-first birthday and the Day of Remembrance again. My mother came to Birmingham to take me out.

'And what happened afterwards?' I asked her.

'What do you think?' she said. 'Your father drove us home. Then I spoke to Judi on the phone. And then I rang my mother.'

'But she never came.'

'She never stepped onto an airplane.'

'But I was being born.'

'Like light from a broken vessel,' my mother said. 'Two weeks late and suddenly in a terrible hurry so I had to stop where I was.'

And that's the end of the story.

Norma Cohen

Director of Ship of Fools Theatre Company, Norma Cohen is a writer, performer and creative arts teacher. She has written sketches, a short story for radio, a stage play *My Federico,* and ***Theatre Works: a Guide to Working in the Theatre.* She is currently working on a memoir *Karl Marx was a Scouser,* and she is editing *Bouquets for Flying Lovers: celebrating a life.***

'I have never felt British, simply Liverpudlian, which sings as its own autonomous state, and is the nearest thing to being Jewish—inheriting a similar whirlpool of radical ideas, political dissent and a crocheted quilt of food, family, comedy and culture. I can span the divide between fashion, the arts and international politics, acting as a galvaniser, a prism for looking both in and out. Responding to a restless internal dialogue, writing comes from a unifying desire to connect with people as I do as a performer and teacher, seizing the moment and transforming it.'

A Violent Tale

She was a very violent little girl. For instance, whenever she was sent out to buy a pound of sausages she demanded to know how the pig had been killed: whether the process had been slow or quick; had the animal screamed; did the blood slide neatly down the neck or spurt out like a fountain from a large hole? These questions were bound to silence the butcher, especially if other customers were present. He often slid her an extra pound to keep her quiet, hoping she would keep her relentless curiosity to herself.

She was also spiteful. If a friend slid over in the winter rain, she would stare blatantly at the swollen knee for five minutes before running off to gloat. She had hardened eyes. The kind that never closed, even in daydream.

One day she met a boy, a few years older than herself, but still with that air of innocence she had shrugged off long ago. He was idling round the square, the one where her grandmother lived, where the ferret mucked about behind the back garden fence, giving out its sickening odour. As she stared at this beanpole who stood between her and the mean patch of grass in the centre of Abacus Square, she thought of the ferret skiddling around at the lingering scent of white raspberry bushes in hot summer.

Sensing her attack, the boy stood his ground, his legs blocking her path with their knee-length school socks, his brown leather lace-ups clubbing the ground in a mixture of fear and determination. He had a sling in his right hand, and as she threw back her shoulders to jerk her chin up, he took aim. Right between the eyes he marked her with his bull's- eye stone, levering back the sling elastic as if it were a longbow.

She could feel herself frowning, her toes curling to keep balance as, ever so slightly, she keeled towards him. He staggered back, on the turn, ready to shout at the top of his voice and run, exhilarated, into the safety of the street. But she was mad, mad enough to swoop forward, to claw out her hands and go for him with a fierceness she could not contain.

Taking in wild gasps of air to steady herself, she started to run and fell on him with both hands and teeth, clawing her way through his body as though it were candy floss. She grabbed his hair and wrenched his head backward, she bit his neck, she forced his mouth open and punched him like a staple gun hitting paper. He wrenched his right leg under her knee and threw her onto the spiky ground.

'I'll get you for this,' she gasped. 'I'll get you,' remembering that time she had stood in the entry and her friend Valerie had dared her to kiss Tommy McKnight straight on the mouth. She had taunted him then, screwing up her face in distaste at his wet lips, his soft mouth hanging ever so slightly open, daring her to come closer. She had jeered at him for being a boy, surrounded by gangs from Class Nine at Corinthian Avenue Primary School, and she had taken the punishment for cracking his pride: an orange squashed in her face. He had jumped at her with a high, bloodcurdling scream, whipping the half-eaten orange from his pocket and rubbing it into her eyes, over and over. She had smarted as they ran off laughing, her eyes wincing at the sharpness and humiliation of it all.

Standing alone, she had longed to unclench, to let the fierce liquid pour out of her body, but she had held back, turning on her heel and going for it when the coast was clear. Just inside the prefabs, she felt the heat of it streaming down her face and legs. She could only stand and let it all tumble out, the salt tears and the shameful waterfall. She was wearing her school scarf, the one she had knitted herself in navy, green and maroon stripes.

He had always 'had a thing' about her, Tommy McKnight. He had always lain in wait for her at the same spot, the prefab entrance. Once he had grabbed hold of both ends of the scarf that was wound twice round her throat and pulled hard, stifling even her screams.

Tottering home, she had resolved to pay him back, if it took years. But Tommy McKnight moved away to the other end of Old Swan, far enough away for her to keep the memory out of danger—until now, when she grappled with this bony boy from the Square, for slinging his stone between her eyes.

Rolling onto her back, she caught sight of the sky, a faded afternoon blue with a racing cloud frittering into drops. In the distance, an ice-cream van tinkled. A motorbike roared past. The jangling tune came nearer. The familiar drear came across her, the dissolving cloud mingling with her memories. Her throat felt dry, like it did when she was in hospital, aged seven, having her tonsils out and the nurses had brought her ice cream and raspberry jelly to soothe it. She felt frail, as though she had undergone an operation, and huddled into her own arms for warmth and comfort, though the ground was hard and scrub-like and this unknown boy breathed hotly in her face.

'I… I'd like an ice cream,' she whispered. 'A Raspberry Ripple. A really cold one.' He looked up at her from far away.

'I've only got tuppence halfpenny,' he said. 'They cost thrippence.'

'Let's try and nick it, then,' she replied. 'Let's say we'll have it on tick till we fetch our mum.' He bared his teeth in a huge grin.

'Yeah. Let's go and nick a lolly ice. And then make a run for it.' She creased over with the mirth of it all as she leant to stand up.

'Don't you try any more of that!' she yelled. 'cos if you do—I'll kill you.' She felt suddenly free, released from the burden of holding back. She ran across the grass, yelling up at the sky.

'Gertcha, gertcha,' he shouted after her, stumbling along with those thick leather boots, the laces falling undone at the last knot.

'Ha ha ha!' she shouted, dipping her head like a toreador's bull and doing a quick flip somersault into the hollows of her own body. She was an acrobat, slicing the air, diving as a Roman gladiator, performing her tricks across a long beanpole strung between the trees.

'Let's do a circus,' she dared. 'Let's dress up and do dangerous things. Hold up the traffic. Aim pot shots at the glass door of number thirty-five. Stake out booby traps. Chuck arrows into the schoolyard. Break down the fence behind the caretaker's lodge.'

'Yeah!' he screamed again. 'Yeah!'—liberating the air with his wild laughter. 'Let's jump down from the sycamore tree and frighten Mrs Wilson from number ten, and scare off the snobs from round the back.'

'I've got a better one. Let's go and kill the skunk,' she shouted, aflame. 'Let's go and kill it off.'

'Yeah…' He tumbled, ripping up dandelion stalks in anticipation of the slaughter. 'Let's do it now.'

They raced off, snivelling at their own ingenuity, legs slowing down as they neared number thirty- six. It was the corner terrace, folding in on the square like a Victorian screen, protecting the squat square of grass overlooking the school fence. Tentatively, the girl stretched up on tiptoe to map her grandmother's movements. She would either be taking an early afternoon nap in the one comfortable velour sofa chair, dividing up a Battenburg for tea, attempting the easy crossword in the *Liverpool Echo* or doing the ironing—the endless pile of slim, fawn blouses and heavy duty skirts, even the odd cardigan—avoiding the welts. It was the ironing that took pride of place this afternoon, the strains of *Woman's Hour* floating through the walls and out into the front garden as the two Stealths prepared their route. Climbing over the back door that stood permanently locked, barring entrance and exit even to skunks, they skirted the few narrow yards of wall and jumped onto the back path outside the kitchen window with a spring, bending both legs as they fell, to break the sound.

'Put your shoes on, Lucy.' The girl could have sworn she heard her grandmother calling out as she sneaked past the kitchen door, but perhaps it was just a trick of the wind. Beckoning to the boy—she did not even know his name—she led him, nose in the air, towards the right hand hedge, skirting the musk of white raspberry bushes, past the brambles, the mint, the bit of old wooden trellis hanging off its hook and towards the ferret's lair down the back garden of number thirty-five.

Mouse-like, their noses shrivelled to accommodate the smell—a dry, dank, piercingly foul odour that got you by the throat and threw your entrails into a flat spin. She held onto the wall for comfort, careful not to show too much flesh, for fear a skinny, boned claw would come and rip it away. They were canny, these skunks. A man down the way had taunted them once, and was suddenly struck down with a fever. Some said it was the thorns the animals kept hidden in their claws; others their venom. She shuddered with the excitement of it all.

The boy was carefully constructing a new lasso from an old woody bit of raspberry bush, rolling mint leaves round a stone for bait. She felt her tongue go loose and moist. They could have skunk pie for tea, like in that silly songbook. It would taste more succulent than pigeons.

The air grew hazy with buzzing afternoon flies; an aeroplane threaded its thin line of vapour overhead; there was a grating of a tin plate being washed up after dinner. Leaning over into the jungle of number thirty- five, they held their breath. Better that Mr Bateson, Old Batesy, and his croney wife, Old Missus Batesy, didn't smell a rat. They laughed to themselves, hugging the pungent joke to their stomachs.

'Sssh !' The boy stopped dead. They heard a quick scuffle, a trace of leaves rustling at the bottom of the wall, just a few inches of sandstone brick lying between them and their quarry. Without acknowledging their plan, she cupped her hands into a stepping stone, nodded to the boy and with a one- two- three—over he went, into Old Batesey's garden, landing with a soft jump onto the debris of rubble and weeds and discarded bits of bacon rind.

He inclined his head over the wall, inviting her across, needing her to come. He sounded frightened and alone, and his legs were scratched to the thigh. She looked up at the six-foot wall. There was no one to give her a piggyback, a quick push up. She ducked.

Woman's Hour would be over soon—the first bit, the interview. It was time for her grandmother to visit the outside lavatory before settling down to the cookery and gardening bits, and then the serial. Better keep low and get away quick, before she sat out with a tin basin on the back step, to peel the potatoes.

Casting around, she came across an old shrimping-net. She must have got it for that day- trip to Hoylake to catch the jelly-fish. Holding it in two hands, she bent its bamboo pole into a bow. It was not strong enough to take even her slim five-and-a-half stone. She harpooned it into the soft bed of earth containing a few straggling primulas dwarfed by the raspberry bushes, its green net swinging jauntily like a pixie's cap.

Taking a foothold on the crumbling wall, she dared herself to lean against the flutter of netting which boomeranged her against the strip of wall bordering the two gardens. Winded, there was nothing for it but to climb. Pulling in her chin, she stuck out one plimsoled foot and like a mountain goat, scaled the wall with three nimble steps.

'Put your shoes on, Lucy.
Don't you know you're in the city?
Put your shoes on, Lucy.
Don't you know it's such a pity...'

Perched for the first time in her ten-and-a-half years on top of this ancient, sweet-and- sour smelling wall dividing the territory between danger and safety, she caught the faint sigh of her grandmother singing her old baby tune, willing her to tap-dance across the red lino-tiled kitchen floor. Looking across, there was not a sound, save the faint hiss of steam rising from the damp teacloth folded crosswise over her grandmother's best blouse.

Looking over the horizon, she caught sight of a bus, a number seventy-three, flashing past Queen's Drive down to the Pierhead. The kids would be out to play now, the teacher scouring the houses for her. The easiest thing would be to drop out of sight into the squelch of skunk's mess alongside the boy, still looking up at her with beseeching eyes.

'Come on, then. It was your idea. It`s scurrying around down there inside its cage'

She was a giant with the world in her hands, whiter and wider than that man carved into the hillside she had seen in Geography, taller than her grandmother, taller even than the boy. She towered over him, holding out her poaching net like a trident. 'I'm coming to get you,' she said with satisfaction and dropped, holding out her arms like bats' wings to steady her flight.

She was dropping, dropping, falling through her store of memories: Tommy McKnight squashing the orange in her face; choking her neck in the woollen school scarf; her mother shouting; her teacher shouting, the others running away; everyone running away: she screaming with the smarting of it all.

She tried to stamp her foot on the mud but a sudden pain arched her back and brought her, scissor-like, facing her stained plimsole. Agh ! She'd twisted her toe, the big one. Stiffly she pulled herself up. He was tugging her.

'Come on ! They'll be out from school soon. Let's do it and run.' She shivered.

‘Where is it? ’ He pushed her forward, towards an old metal cage screened by ferns.

‘Go on, then. Look.’

Her nose had begun to quiver again. The smell was reeking out towards them like a signpost, curling round their heads, invading the threads of their jumpers, the cracks behind their nails. She bent forward without taking a step, and gently, as if not to disturb its sleep, she pulled back the fronds.

A slimy, pale-brown thing, over a foot long, lay there sweating, its pink eyes fixed beadily on her. She pulled back in revulsion. The thing stank. She looked to the boy, appealing for absolution. He stifled a laugh.

‘Go on, then. Stick your finger in. It won’t bite you.’

The moment had come. She was going to kill the skunk.

Reaching back, she fetched the bamboo pole with its skinny net and gently prodded it through the iron bars of the cage. She would batter the animal to death like she had seen on the Saturday pictures, and then she would take the tail home for a trophy. Breathing in, she summoned all the bloodcurdling yells she could manage into one huge scream as she brought down the stick between its legs and prodded hard.

The thing didn‘t move. She shoved the stick through its claw like a barbecue fork and rolled it over. No resistance.

‘You’ve drugged it ! You’ve bloody drugged it!’ she shouted.

‘No, I haven’t, I swear. Try again.’

‘Yarrgghhh!’ This time she yelled in fury and frustration, bringing the stick down hard and flattening the animal with the net. It emitted a faint trickle of blood between its teeth and lay still, steaming.

‘You‘ve killed it! You’ve bloody killed it !’ she screamed, going at the boy, robbing his pockets, searching for the boomerang that had caught her and her rightful trophy between the eyes.

‘I couldn’t help it! It was asking for it. I couldn‘t stand it sitting there, grinning at me. It was the only way to get through the bars. I thought you’d be pleased. You wanted it dead after all.’

‘Yes, but I wanted to kill the skunk. It was my idea. It was my game. I just asked you to come along.’

'Well, you didn't have a lasso. You'd have got bitten. They're vicious when they bite.'

'An' I'm vicious when I bite too,' she screamed, going for him like she had wanted to go for Tommy McKnight all those years ago.

She scratched out at his face, clawing her way through his skin and jumping on his back, throttling him in spite of her twisted toe and Old Batesey about to come out with his big stick, and the school whistle about to blow, and *Woman's Hour* well finished by now, and her grandmother coming out past the raspberry bushes to search out the noise.

'I'll get my own back on you!' she shouted, steering him towards the parapet of the wall, grabbing onto it with her knuckles, lassoing the raspberry bush with her fishing net, pushing off his shoulders like a diving board and shouting, gloriously shouting, as she fell into the nettles, leaving the boy moaning,

'Wait for me ! Wait for me ! Gi's a leg up. Wait for me !'

'It's your own fault. You'll have to deal with Old Batesy now. After all, you killed the skunk. Not me.'

She could hear him trudging around in the muck, trying to find a foothold as she tripped back across the patchy lawn towards her grandmother's kitchen.

There she stood, looking out of the window, craning her neck for a glimpse of the fuss, while faintly, in a neat row along the garden path, like smoke lifting, emerged a chorus of young voices.

'Queenie, Queenie,
who's got the ball?'
'I haven't got it,
It isn't in my pocket.'
'Queenie, Queenie.
Who's got the ball?'

In and out the chant faded, as the pale childhood faces loomed out of the bushes and painted themselves against the back wall.

Hesitating, she turned back to Old Batesy's garden. The scuffling had stopped. She'd silenced even the boy. The potato went back and forth, back and forth as the game rolled on, as she tiptoed past the singing line of children and into the house, where her grandmother still stood looking out, a potato in her hand.

Tamar Yellin

Tamar Yellin grew up in Leeds. Her mother was the daughter of a Polish immigrant and her father a Jerusalemite. She studied biblical and modern Hebrew with Arabic at Oxford. Her short fiction has appeared in numerous periodicals and anthologies, including *Stand*, *London Magazine*, *The Jewish Quarterly*, and *The Slow Mirror: New Fiction by Jewish Writers*.

'Woman, Briton, Jew—all these are identities that have been imposed upon me. 'Writer' is the identity I have chosen for myself. To be a Jew, a Briton and a woman means to live in a vortex of contradictory forces: loss, longing, pride, guilt, exile and alienation. Only by writing is it possible to harness these forces and make my contradictions whole.'

The Newspaper Man

Within three days of my arrival I had found a room on the fourth floor of this decayed tenement block, on Simon Peter Street, in the old tanning district. It was one of those buildings missed by both bombs and the demolition ball, which still stood intact while all around its neighbours were having their guts removed, in the cynical way now popular with town planners: their fragile frontages propped up by matchsticks of scaffolding against the empty air. It had a facade of tall solemn women and art nouveau flowers, and had probably been beautiful and exclusive once, but now its days of elegance were over; until some property magnate chose to renovate, it remained a cheap means of living close to the heart of the city.

The landlady, a sharp, shrunken woman wrapped in bombazine, seemed suspicious of me at first. A large sum of money up front, which I thought extortionate but which I was later assured was usual, helped to set her mind at rest, and she contented herself with watching my comings and goings from the small grilled window of her boudoir on the ground floor. I had the privilege of watching her too, or at least her kitchen, across the inner courtyard from my hallway. She rarely appeared there, but a maid, dressed in traditional black-and-white uniform, spent hours preparing vast quantities of food, I could not imagine for whom: it seemed enough to feed an army of old ladies.

My place lay at the top of eight flights of dim steps, whose cleanliness declined with each floor, and whose only daylight came through a grimy dome of glass high above. On closer inspection I found this to be a once beautiful confection of green and red and blue panels, their patterns now obliterated by dirt. The banister, too, was a trelliswork of leaves and flowers, broken off in places and covered in dust. My top floor apartment was probably not as grand as the lower rooms, but it still bore evidence of more stately times, in the tall windows, the classical architraves, and the traces of stencilling below the cornices.

The mistress of the house, who soon changed her mind and

decided just as arbitrarily that she liked me, explained that the property had been put up by her father, in the days when this was a fashionable part of town: she had lived nearly her whole life in the apartment on the ground floor, had married and raised a family there, had seen the area and tenantry decline, and remained there, now alone, enlivened only by the visits of her grandson (an expensively suited, beautiful young man) and his brood of children, for whom, apparently, she provided those mountains of elaborate food. The fortunes of the district mirrored her own. She had, like the building, an air of faded glamour and, in her ripped lace, carried herself like one of the fallen aristocracy.

I quickly learned to take account of her foibles, a skill essential to a quiet life. It was necessary to acknowledge her face at the window, with a dignified nod, every time I passed; to allow her to look over my shoulder at my mail, whenever I came down to collect it from the box in the hall, and never to indicate any feeling of impatience or hurry if she chose to detain me in conversation. Questions about my personal life, or about my fellow tenants, must be negotiated with a diplomat's finesse: she always had a distinct purpose in asking them, and would not be fobbed off with obvious evasions. In return, I received from her information to which I did not always wish to be privy, knowing that she would discuss me with the other residents with just as little discretion and fully as much relish as she discussed them with me.

As things fell out at first I did not see a great deal of them. A face passed me on the stairs occasionally, or a hunched overcoat; and sometimes, in the dead hours after lunch, the sound of a violin rose mournfully from several floors below. I would pause to listen to it while I studied or prepared lessons. But clearly my habits did not fall in with those of the other occupants. I often went out late, when evening was already falling, and wandered the streets of the city as it grew dark; stumbling on hidden alleyways and sudden squares, and emerging time and again on the edge of the river—the broad, grey, doomy, phlegmatic river which cut through town like an emblem of history. There was in these labyrinthine lanes with their abrupt glimpses of life something which drew me on, always the stranger and observer, as if in pursuit of some discovery: some extraordinary building, perhaps, crouching among the others like a cat, or the luminous face of a child as she looked up momentarily from her play; snatches of music or argument, occasional laughter, bits of existence in which I had no part. As night thickened I would head inevitably for the brightly lit bridge where people gathered in summer, and where the oblivious crowds milled back and forth above the stream of black water; where sometimes I would meet and talk to those I knew. Many nights I was drawn off by the lights and music to the resurrected quarters of the city, striding there in the wake of energetic companions whose sole ambition was to drink and dance: pursuing that buzz of lights and jungle of music which had settled over the city like a cloud, a bright, precocious, evanescent cloud hovering over its gloomy monuments.

More often than not I would delay the return to the silent darkness of my room by a late visit to the Simon Peter Bar, just along from my aristocratic building. Like many such places it did not advertise its presence, and some weeks passed before I first noticed it. A modest sign indicated its establishment in 1782, but nothing was left of the original hostelry. It was as plain as a five-and-dime store, brightly lit, full of red banquettes and melamine, and at one in the morning it served a decent cup of coffee. A few desiccated sandwiches sat under a plastic dome, and if one was really desperate one could order a plate of French fries; its greatest advantage was that one could sit there for as long as one liked without feeling under an obligation to order more or to move on. It was, inevitably, popular with a regular coterie of lonely and sleepless people.

The proprietor, a man of very few words, seemed to bear these regulars no grudge, supported as he was by a dour, large-bicepped assistant. One in particular I noticed, an elderly man of untidy appearance, who would sit a good hour in front of a glass of mineral water, reading the newspaper with minute attention: not his own newspaper moreover, but that provided by the establishment, which he would at the end of his session carry away, for all the world as if it was his by right. I often watched him, his tangled silvery head bent above the broadsheet, turning the pages carefully one by one, and occasionally, with magisterial deliberation, picking his nose. He read as though he made a study of it, as though not one word should escape his most particular scrutiny: a man pursuing the clues of a holy scripture.

The Simon Peter Bar, once discovered, became my salon. There can be something addictive in such places, especially when one has nowhere very comfortable to retreat to. Before long I was going there every day, and so, I soon found, did the newspaper man. I never saw where he appeared from or where he went to. The fact remained that he was always there, already seated in his usual place, or, if I arrived unexpectedly early, creeping in soon afterwards, never acknowledging the silent proprietor, who wiped the table hastily and set down his glass from which he took two or three sips at the most, before departing. Sometimes I glanced up from my book to find that he had vanished, and only the glass remained; sometimes I dragged myself wearily off to bed and left him still tracing the hieroglyphs of the late edition.

It happened on one occasion, around two in the morning, that we left simultaneously. No sooner had I paid my bill and risen, than he stood up likewise, packed his paper into an untidy bundle and pulled on his deeply unappetizing coat. I glanced in his direction: he was absorbed in tying his broken belt, which held his distended form together in the same way as a piece of string might bind a bundle of hay. Our eyes did not meet, and immediately after I left I heard him follow.

It was a dark night, and at this hour, either through municipal penny-pinching or as a result of some oversight, Simon Peter Street was not lit. To tell the truth it was pitch dark: it was all I could do to feel my way along the pavement. Close behind me—I was unable to guess how close—the shuffling footsteps of the old man followed, accompanied by loud sniffs and frequent mutterings, and involuntarily I quickened my pace. Fortunately my building was not far, though far enough for me to imagine I was being trailed—to what end I did not dare to think; but it was with some relief that I dashed into the lobby. My relief was short-lived. The old fellow was still behind me, his viscid snufflings now echoing in the high stairwell. My heart started. The thing was, above all, not to look back, not to lose ground, I told myself, as I began to race up the steps, taking them now two and three at a time, too flurried to search for the light which had popped out, plunging us once more into almost palpable darkness. I hardly knew how I made it to the fourth floor, or with what trembling ham-handedness I fitted the key into the lock, my knees buckling— only to hear the clash of an apartment door down below.

Oblivious, he had gone to bed; and it was only after a moment's fraught realisation that I collapsed laughing onto mine. It had never occurred to me that the newspaper man and I shared a building. Yet a few minutes' reflection made it seem preordained.

I had never seen him under that roof before, but now, as if some spell were broken, he was everywhere—on the steps, in the hallway, in the corridor that led out back to the trash; I met him on the way to the train, on my way upstairs, or collecting letters from my box in the hall: a small, hunched, unobtrusive man, whose name, when I tried surreptitiously to read it on his own mail box, was so worn and faded as to be illegible. But I recalled the landlady's bilious complaints, against 'that man, that old devil, Cacik, or Tzatzkes, whose disgusting personal habits she insisting on describing. I had never understood who it was she meant, and had even wondered sometimes whether he might be a figment of her proprietorial imagination, but I decided now that this must be the Cacik she so resented.

He did fit the part: was tattered, malodorous, and carried with him always, like a permanent prosthesis, a small transistor radio on which he listened to the world news. In his ancient slippers with zips, whose disintegrating soles flapped under him, he shambled back and forth between the mail box and his room on the third floor; for he lived, apparently, in constant expectation of a message, though from whom, and of what nature, I could not ascertain. His daily visits to the back yard puzzled me at first, until through my own observations and the landlady's garbled testimony, I established that he was not taking out rubbish but bringing it in, for he was a champion of thrift and a natural searcher through dustbins. This was I suppose, the least harmless of his preoccupations. His coat, in which by daylight one could detect the faint traces of a Burberry check, was one of the more mildly objectionable things about him, but it seemed to inspire the old aristocrat with a kind of shamanistic horror.

I tried to extract more information from her, but it was impossible to ask her questions: she simply did not answer them; she had her own agenda. She talked and I listened, picking up (amongst a bewildering plethora of facts about people I had never heard of) the disclosure that he had lived in that flat for a long time, a very long time perhaps; that he had lived there for a very long time alone; that she couldn't remove him, much as she wanted to, because he lowered the tone of the whole building and frightened potential residents away. Oh, do not ask her about that devil Cacik! It wouldn't be going too far to call him the bane of her life. A good apartment, too, a big one: she might get twice what he paid her for it now. Only last week she had sent her grandson up there to speak to him, but it was no use. Good heavens, the state of the place! Her grandson had barely been able to set foot inside the door. So the litany continued; and when I pressed her further on the subject, it seemed only that she couldn't evict Cacik because she couldn't; she must be tormented by him because she must; this was a state of affairs which had always existed, and must go on existing, for the simple reason that she could not now imagine any other.

As for Cacik himself, he seemed quite content for matters to continue as they were, and for whatever standoff was rumbling between himself and his landlady to endure, if necessary, until death should end it. He had an air of obliviousness, and went about his daily activities with the serene attitude of a monk, for whom nothing short of earthquake or insurrection would disturb the even tenor of his devotions. Only once did I see him exchange words with her ladyship, and then he responded to her shrill red-faced hysteria with the mild contempt of a husband who has been through it all before: an alienated husband who sees no point in divorce, so long as he can slope off with a shrug of the shoulders, a muttered 'Silly old bat,' and shut the door to his den.

I knew better than to interfere between them or even to pass comment. The one time I did so, remarking in the gentlest of tones that he seemed, after all, an innocuous old gentleman, I was blasted by such a storm of protest I feared I had lost my landlady's goodwill for ever; in fact it was some time before she deigned to speak to me again. Such an incorrigible gossip could not resist me for long, however; though I was now cast, despite my most strenuous attempts at neutrality, as a confirmed crony of Cacik.

A crony of Cacik's I was not: we had never spoken to each

other, and for all my tourist's curiosity, I had not obtained more than a glimpse into his dingy apartment, the door of which sometimes stood ajar when I passed by on the stairs. He must have been aware of my existence, though he didn't acknowledge it, and though I now nodded to him when I entered the Simon Peter Bar to find him sitting there in his usual place, he never returned my nod. Instead he looked at me fiercely for a moment and, I thought, not approvingly, with his black beady eyes, and returned to his newspaper with an air of having been unnecessarily distracted.

This did not bother me, since I fully expected to be beneath his notice— I along with the rest of the human race. He was a vagabond emperor, a trashcan king, rigidly dedicated to his royal routines, from which long tradition would not allow him to deviate by one iota. Those around him, too, were drawn implicitly into the rhythm of his ceremonial, from the waiter who set down his glass of water before him, to the landlady who, it seemed, existed solely to be his penitential scourge. I myself played no part in this ritual, except perhaps as one of the vassal host whose vices would one day earn them a rightful comeuppance.

It amused me to read these things into his appearance and demeanour, while hearing nothing from the man himself; but I didn't think I was wrong— though I may have been influenced by the general atmosphere of that decayed city, which had lain asleep on its history for so long, and which was being shaken awake so late and so inappropriately into a world of decadence. I felt it in the solitary streets, where I walked pursued by ghosts on the edge of dusk, and in the high-ceilinged coffee-halls where the trapped echoes of a century ago still bounced, and my own voice sounded thin, light and unimportant. It was easy to imagine that he, the denizen for so many years of a place like this, should be possessed by secrets more ancient and earth-shattering than any I might discover, traveller, visitant, will-o'-the-wisp that I was.

Yet I was conscious of a certain romance in these musings. And if there was a threadbare regality about Cacik, the truth of the matter was he led a miserable, lonely existence. Nobody ever came to visit him; I never witnessed him in conversation. He descended twice a day to examine the contents of his mailbox with pathetic eagerness, so much so that on several occasions I inserted my own unwanted circulars for the sheer pleasure of seeing him gather them up. It was obvious that there was no one from whom he might expect a letter or message. Yet while he stirred neither hand nor foot to break the glass dome under which he lived isolated from the world, he was ready to welcome whatever the world chose to slip beneath it like billets-doux from a distant lover.

In the same way, he listened constantly to the radio, whose interminable drone must have filled, for him, the void of an annihilating silence. I heard it sometimes in the small hours, the disembodied voices arguing back and forth from his room immediately under mine; for there was a late-night political discussion programme he never missed, and being a light sleeper, I never missed it either. Occasionally, waking to the sound of its measured question and answer, half-listening, half-dreaming (I never could quite make out the words) I thought I shared for a moment his peculiar nightlife: that in some preternatural manner I had become him. I was filled then with a sense of unfathomable sadness, an almost intolerable burden of despair.

How could I know that the force which drove him was not despair but uncontainable hope, a hope so huge that it swept away all other considerations, was almost totally consumed by itself; that his life reflected one ruling philosophy of expectation deferred, to which he retained a dogged faithfulness?

Be that as it may, I was losing sleep on account of his obsession, and the time was approaching when I must do something about it. A number of options lay before me: either to continue as I was, which was impossible, or to complain to the landlady, which would be suicidal for both Cacik and for me. A third option remained, though one which hardly appealed—to tackle Cacik himself. I wondered how on earth I should go about it. But I decided to honey the bitterness of the occasion, so that in some way it should be pleasurable to us both; and that if I was to be cast in the role of a crony of Cacik's, I should at least throw myself vigorously into the part.

Attack is the best method of defence. I knew there were few things Cacik longed for more than a letter. So I wrote him one—a proper letter sealed in an envelope—and left it for him in his cubby-hole. I can honestly say that I have rarely experienced a greater feeling of well being than when I saw him pick it up. I had no idea what he was expecting, and knew he was certain to be disappointed, but the moment of anticipation seemed to me to be worth that. His face literally sparkled. The letter read as follows:

Dear Mr. Cacik,

Since we are near neighbours, and since we have not yet had an opportunity to introduce ourselves, I would be delighted if you would have tea with me tomorrow at four o'clock. I look forward very much to making your acquaintance.

Yours sincerely...

I seriously doubted whether he would turn up. Having rearranged my meagre furniture as comfortably as possible, and having raided the nearby bakery for its excellent pastries, I was startled to hear a knock on the door at three minutes past four. He was there; he had combed his hair. He wore a patched black jacket in place of his Burberry coat. He resembled nothing more than a boy who has been summoned to a Sunday tea party and has done his very best to look respectable just after some rough-and-tumble in the playground. He apologised for being a few minutes late, but he had paused to listen to the four o'clock news.

Indeed, the little transistor hung at the end of his arm, mercifully turned off now, but still available, I supposed, in case of any lull in the conversation. I invited him to be seated. In his dark clothes he had the air of someone visiting the bereaved household after a funeral, and the mountainous plate of pastries seemed thoroughly appropriate. I thought: he has not done this for a long time. And he suddenly appeared to me in an utterly different light, as one in whom the traces of a gentleman were still evident, who had had manners once, and could dredge up, even now, the gestures and etiquette of a social being: the required forms which had been stamped on his memory. More than this, he seemed to me to be a gentle man, a naïve, sweet fellow, as if behind the fierce brushwood of his outer defences there lurked not a lion, but a timorous mouse—a mouse decoyed by a monstrous appetite for pastries, all five of which he despatched without reprieve.

No doubt there was some sentimentality in my assessment. He had his boorish moments after all, as he questioned me without much tact about my own lifestyle, and seemed to take it for granted that I was rich—I suppose because I was a foreigner. Then, too, it was hard to tell how much of his talk was over-larded with lies. He also boasted of being rich himself, very rich, if anyone cared to know it: he wouldn't say where all his money was, but he could put his hand on it when he needed it. As the afternoon progressed he seemed as if drunk on sugar. I plied him with plenty of tea, and listened attentively to the strange, disjointed comments and observations in which, after years without conversation, he expressed himself.

What can I recall of his ramblings now, which would make any sense— which would create in any meaningful way, a picture of Cacik? He was not what he appeared; he appeared as he really was. Such paradox is the only adequate means of describing him. He came through to me as an image broken in pieces that did not wholly fit together: a man behind whom the possibility of another man always lurked—someone who might have lived a very different life. Perhaps it was true to say that this potential was the real Cacik, and the person before me—hollow, wasted as he was—had not led any life worth mentioning, for the sole reason that he was still waiting for it to begin.

This much was evident from the things he told me: that he always kept a packed suitcase sitting on the top of his wardrobe in case of emergency, because one never knew when one might have to travel on; that (examining my cheap tableware) he had never bothered to acquire china, since plates were unnecessary and difficult to transport. I could only attempt to imagine how he dined. But eating, too, was a frivolous luxury, or so he implied as he swallowed another cake: a needless distraction from the main business of life, the next item of awaited news.

It was this preoccupation with news that was his chief characteristic—to attempt to draw him out on the subject was to miss the point—he simply could not separate himself from it. He could not regard it with that detachment necessary to discussion. He fell silent when I mentioned topics of the day, as though these were things too personal to be talked of. And yet he did tell me, with great feeling and nostalgia, of his father's habit of following events almost as though his life depended on them; a habit that, he supposed, had been influential, and that he might say he had inherited from him.

At this point he rose, and, brushing the crumbs of pastry from his best jacket, walked over somewhat awkwardly to the window. I watched him for some moments as he contemplated the view. Eventually he remarked that I had a better view than his; and he admitted that in all the many years he had lived here, he had never ventured up to the fourth floor: that it was to him in a sense, a foreign country. He continued to look at the city for a minute in silence, scanning its rooftops as though really seeing them for the first time; and then, as if speaking to himself, he murmured: Once in a while it would be nice to hear some good news. He turned to me, his eyes shining. 'We interrupt this bulletin to announce the coming of the Messiah,' he said, softly. Just once— we interrupt this bulletin to announce the coming of the Messiah.

I thought this would be an opportune moment to cut to the main business of the visit, though there seemed to be no easy way to do it; and reaching into my pocket I brought out the little plastic earphone I had purchased. In the gentlest of terms I explained that, while I had invited him up for tea mainly in order to make his acquaintance, I also had to confess an ulterior motive: that although I fully sympathised with his compulsive listening, it sometimes interfered with my sleep a bit; and that perhaps this simple device might help us both. He looked surprised, and a little taken aback, and came over to the table somewhat flustered. I hastened to show him how it worked. There was fumbling as he attempted unsuccessfully to fit the plug into his rather large and misshapen ear, and awkwardness as I tried to assist him. We got there in the end, but it seemed that some ineffable moment had passed. I was aware of having missed an opportunity, and when he left soon afterwards I sensed that he, too, felt in some way cheated.

Nevertheless I did congratulate myself on having broken the ice between us; and though we never properly conversed again, I felt myself admitted to his recognition as an honorary stranger. I was now worthy of acknowledgment, and received a nod of greeting when we passed in the hall or laid eyes on each other in the Simon Peter Bar— a major achievement, if you consider that even the proprietor did not merit such a token of friendship.

It was strange that by an almost intangible adjustment such as this I should begin to feel myself, for the first time, a genuine resident of that aged building and of Simon Peter Street itself, if not of that city in which I never thought my stay would be anything other than transient. The bonhomie was brief, however. Not long afterwards we lost our landlady; perhaps she turned apoplectic when she found me to be a true crony of Cacik's. I heard from her well-dressed grandson, who had taken to haunting the stairwell in vampire fashion, that she had had to be removed to a nursing home.

The rest of the story might have been predicted. The morning came when, glancing into Cacik's cubby hole, I saw what I had never expected to see: an item of mail, a real letter for Cacik—perhaps the one he had always waited for. Or perhaps not, for an identical envelope sat in my own letter-box, and, in fact, in the box of every resident: an unequivocal notice of eviction. The grandson's schemes had come to their fruition, and the old leviathan of a building, in which his grandmother had sat so stubbornly and for so long, was to be converted and sold off at last for a mountain of money.

We were all given three months' grace, the news being greeted, by some, with a resigned shrug of the shoulders, by others with loud and ineffectual complaints. I could not imagine how Cacik would react. Nor did I have a chance to question him. That same day I returned at noon to be asked if I knew 'what Cacik had done'. What Cacik had done was to scarper without paying his final month's rent. The packed suitcase had finally come in useful: he had left his keys in the lock and disappeared.

I was sorry, but not surprised: sorry not to have had the chance of saying good bye to him; not surprised that he had reacted quickly to a circumstance for which he had for so long held himself in readiness. He imagined it, perhaps, to be a piece of persecution directed solely at him, and did not realise that the rest of us were included. Touched by a barb of real or imagined danger, he had been stung into action and had run for some place of safety, who knows where.

On my way upstairs I noticed that the key of his room was still sitting in the lock. I was unable to resist the temptation to look in on the apartment to which no one, so far as I knew, had ever been admitted, and where even the grandson himself had not dared to enter. The door was unlocked, but when I tried to open it, met with resistance and it only gave way a few inches. I managed to slip through. The obstacle, I found, was a pile of newspapers: a monstrous pile, almost as high as myself, and only one of dozens that filled the room. The air was fetid: one seemed to breathe newsprint, along with other less salutary smells. The blinds were half-closed over the dirty windows, and the light was dim, but it was easy to see that the place had not been cleaned or decorated in years. Spare as it was, it was difficult to manoeuvre because of the rubbish. The whole table was covered with the empty packages from which, no doubt, he had eaten his food direct. I hardly dared glance into the tiny bathroom, in which brown stains ran down the crumbling walls. Everywhere were heaps of newspapers—on floors, on furniture, strewn on the bed itself: the sacred newspapers he was sworn to scrutinize, to save religiously and never to discard, for the sake of the small advertisement lurking somewhere—the one that announced the coming of the Messiah.

I stood in silence and took in the enormity of that place, and it seemed to me that this was the true testament of Cacik's life, a life of such minimalism that these newspapers surely recorded its only landmark, and to that effect might have been rightly treasured and preserved by him. I thought of him arriving here as a young man, fleeing from who knows what chaotic trauma, to crouch, to hide, to wait until it was safe; I thought of all the years he had remained here, holding his breath in fantastic expectation. In such an existence one might feel justified in hoping for transformation through some cataclysmic and unearned event; one might well be sustained by such a vision. But the place that had sheltered him would give shelter no longer: soon that too would be nothing but a facade: the new city dancing in the old one's garments, the thin guise of history on a mansion of ignorant air.

Elizabeth Stern (nom de plume)

Elizabeth Stern was born in London, and lives there with her husband and children. She qualified as a doctor of medicine in the 1980s, then as a specialist in child and adolescent psychiatry, training and working at the Tavistock Clinic. She began writing short stories in her forties and creative writing is now central to her life. This is her second non-medical publication.

'At times I am profoundly, instinctively connected to 'Jewishness'—fiercely protective of it. At others it burdens, irritates, alienates me. It always surprises me to be thought of as British, as if many British characteristics have nothing to do with me. Yet many inspire me with admiration, affection and gratitude. I am fascinated by the ways that the life-changing experiences of women are reflected in small, seemingly mundane, observed details. Unsurprisingly, it is 'outsiderness' in any form that draws me as a theme.'

Cherries

Since you stopped walking, Dad, I visit you every week in the big house with grilles on the windows where I grew up. You are confined now to the first floor. You sit in a specially adapted chair in the bedroom that used to be mine. There are always new, unread copies of *The Times* and *The British Medical Journal* within your reach. They lie neatly on the veneered shelf unit from MFI that runs along the wall where my bed used to be. I kept my Janis Ian records there and an exercise book for my poems, covered in waxy kitchen drawer-liner patterned with pale blue flowers. I had a turquoise beaded jewellery box too, with a mirror inside the lid. I was only a teenager; I didn't have a lot of jewellery. Bluebird earrings, three wise monkeys dangling from a neck chain, and a brooch in the shape of a cigarette butt that I bought from Camden Market.

Each time I come I wonder if this will be the day that you don't recognise me any more.

I always bring you something to eat. A piece of plum strudel, which I break into pieces for you to have with your coffee, or some poppy-seed cake. I never ask if you want them. You told me once that, where you come from, you don't *offer* somebody food because they would never decline it unless they were ill. You just put it on their plate.

Today, I brought you a pound of shiny red cherries in a brown paper bag that got soggy in the rain. It disintegrated when I lost my balance on the slippery path. Most of the cherries fell onto the York stone paving and lay in puddles.

London is full of young people from your part of the world now. You can't get a table at the Cafe Mozart on a Sunday. You'd think everyone had been brought up on veal schnitzel. But when I was a child there were only a few places that smelt of mocha coffee and served a dry, swirly *kugelhopf* with waitresses in black skirts and starched white blouses and aprons, their blonde hair tied at the nape. They stayed long enough for us to learn their names. The other customers must have been displaced and 'continental', like you. Men with your high forehead and clean cheekbones. Purring women in beige cashmere with two-tone leather handbags and navy hats with little nets. But you spoke better English than anyone, with a wider, more subtle, more carefully chosen vocabulary. I never even realised that you had a foreign accent until I was grown-up. It wasn't something that people showed off about in those days. Anyway you didn't. I had to have two parties when I got married, one for my husband's noisy relatives to dance the *kazatska* and one for your consultant colleagues and their wives, with a string quartet and 'Coronation chicken'—people you'd worked with for thirty years, who'd come for dinner at our house, and didn't know that we were Jews.

When I visit you, we sit in my old room, underneath the dark Baroque paintings that you moved there when I left. I'm always surprised by how much smaller they are in reality than they have become in my mind. They show wounds trickling with blood and people with startled, frightened eyes. Pallid children crouch over empty baskets on a moonless river bank. Cattle roam in godforsaken forests. I live in a house with gingham at the windows and a herb garden. I've typed homilies on my word processor and put them up around the place: *A man is only old when his regrets outnumber his dreams* sits next to the hand basin in the toilet. *Go placidly amidst the noise and haste and remember what peace there may be in silenc*e is on the door of the fridge.

You lean over with an effort and beckon to me. Your filmy eyes are full of uncertainty.

'I'm very tired,' you whisper. 'I was on a train last night, crossing the border, and there was a woman telling people all about me. A patient of mine, saying things she shouldn't have known. I've had no sleep.'

I'm almost used to it now. Once, as my heart sank, you took my hands in yours and asked me if I hadn't thought of getting married, although I've been married for years to the father of your grandchildren. Sometimes you warmly wish me *mazzel tov.* 'It's marvellous,' you say, glowing, as if I'm getting recognition for some great work. You ask me who is to make the speech at the ceremony in my honour and whether we can rely on him not to let us down. Why would I take that away?

I've learned not to tell other people that you say these things to me.

'I haven't noticed anything,' my sister rebuked me when all this started. It was as if the issue was my own perversity. 'He's old,' she said. 'He tires easily. Stop looking for problems.'

You tell me that my mother won't give you any money. It's your money, you've earned it all your life and she's keeping it from you.

'You don't need money, darling,' I've heard her say. 'You can't manage the stairs yet. You have nowhere to spend anything. It'll just go through the washing machine because we'll forget you have it.'

You spit with indignation. 'What do you mean? It's my money. I have things to buy at the chemist. I need a haircut. How will I pay to come home in a taxi?'

But she won't go along with it so I slip you £40 without her seeing, because it comforts you to pat it in the pocket of your cardigan. My mother is considerably younger than you. She is waiting for you to get back to normal so that you and she can have ordinary conversations and go on holidays in the sunshine.

'But you never had ordinary conversations,' I tell her on the telephone.

'You only ever agreed about how difficult I was, and Dad hated holidays. You hardly took any once we'd left home.'

I can understand, now that I have given it some thought, why you were never one to travel. You travelled when you were fourteen. Your mother sent you to England when she heard that the Nazis were coming for Jewish boys. She got hold of false papers so you could leave. Since I've begun to wonder about you, I've imagined her and your sister waving you off at the bus stop, snow falling silently on to their winter coats; and you taking your seat on the bus when you rounded a bend and they disappeared from view. I've thought that you might have felt terrified because you were only fourteen and you'd never been away from home, but you might have been excited too. I've imagined you knocking at the door of your house, years later, jaunty in your British army beret. It's not your mother who answers but a shorter, harder-looking woman: a complete stranger.

'The Jews are back then,' she shouts over her shoulder to someone inside that you can't see; then turns back to face you for the split second before she slams the door.

I've been able to wonder about you since you've stopped being able to tell me.

My sister went back there with you when you could still travel and remember and explain. She took the baby. She saw the house where you grew up, with apricot trees in the garden replacing your mother's roses. She visited the wasteland where the Jewish cemetery used to be. Your father is buried somewhere there. She held your hand, she said, looking at the graffiti and the rubble and the grubby children kicking an empty Coke can among them. She picked up a pine cone for me and brought it home. She took pictures of your house, number eighty-one, which has an archway at the side for a horse and cart, and of the street with its backdrop of mountains covered in cornflowers and vineyards; and of the synagogue where you went to school and read your *bar mitzvah* portion. There are birds nesting in its derelict webby corners and planks nailed crudely to board up the windows. There are rusting bits of agricultural machinery and cleaning rags propped against the peeling frescoes. My sister wrote captions on the back of her photographs and arranged them for me in an album with dried grasses pressed into its cover. I put it away in a box

that I had been saving for something special.

I had to wait until you lost your grip.

It was imperceptible at first. It was just easier to be with you. You were less easily provoked, less willing to follow through your bitter argument, more mellow. Your speech became generalised, uncharacteristically littered with vague, all-purpose pleasantries. You forgot where my children went to school, and asked them why they weren't there on a Sunday. When you went into hospital with your broken hip and lost all points of reference, you wanted to know how long we'd been waiting at the garage. You said that we should go back home on the tube and let them telephone us to collect the car later. They called you by your first name, the nurses, chiding you on the commode. Thirty-five years earlier, you'd taken us in with you to the same hospital on Christmas Day to carve the turkey. You'd worn your work suit and a tie as you did even when we went shopping in case we met your patients or another doctor. How people welcomed us, gushing and shaking you by the hand, patting us girls on the head and showing us the glittery tree. Pronouncing your foreign name perfectly.

I had to wait until you'd stopped calling the shots.

Then I bought a tourist guide to the region where you lived. I read: *Svaty Jur, a small and ancient town on Bratislava's northern edge, named itself for Saint George, the hero of legendary fame, who galloped into the Town Square to save a distressed maiden and her village from a ferocious dragon.* I looked at my sister's photographs of you, a little shocked by how small and bowed you are. Shuffling from the taxi, knocking bravely on the window of your old house after all those years away, when you only ever wept in your sleep. My mother is behind you with her fists clenched.

I bought a book about the Holocaust and smuggled it into my study so that the children wouldn't see. It is on a shelf with its spine against the wall. I read that: *'At Auschwitz, the gas chambers and crematoria were not yet ready. The first deportees, 999 Slovak women, were therefore kept in barracks after their arrival.'*

I feel familiar with where you come from now, as if I have done a correspondence course. But there are things that you don't find in books, which are lost, because I am the only one who would have thought of asking about them: *What did you call your mother? How am I like your sister? Did you hope that one day you might be able to bear it?*

I've only got seven cherries clutched in my hand, mixed with the pulpy shredded remains of the bag that fell apart. I uncurl my fist when I get inside and give them to you, like a child back from the beach with treasures. You seem to be enjoying them, you've even offered me a couple. We sit eating in silence, careful with the stones, looking at the grey rain streaming down the window.

Wendy Brandmark

Wendy Brandmark is a writer and reviewer who directs a creative writing programme at Birkbeck College. Her short stories have appeared in anthologies and journals including *Critical Quarterly*, *Writing Women* and *The Jewish Quarterly*. She has reviewed fiction for *The Times Literary Supplement*, *Literary Review* and *The Independent*. Her novel, *The Angry Gods,* was published in 2003.

'I grew up in New York, but have lived in London since 1980. In the States I felt ambivalent about my Jewishness. Maybe it was too comfortable to be Jewish there. In Britain I have become more committed to my religion, but I am still an outsider. Even in Liberal Judaism with its egalitarian ideals and questioning spirit, I find much to doubt. This uneasiness seems the most Jewish aspect of my fiction.'

The Book of Life

Lucian had been cast out of the creative writing class.

'Why do you care,' Elaine asked. 'They're all ugly old women and men in strange hats?'

You yourself are a strange old woman. But Lucian's thoughts, unlike those of his characters, remained invisible.

He knew Elaine would never take an evening class. She believed herself a virtuoso in all she had not done. His ex-girlfriend of thirty years whose gossip bruised even his ears. If Dorothy Parker came back to life she would have been Elaine. Only she did not finish anything; she was a paragraph woman.

Lucian had met Elaine at an immigration study group at Conway Hall, she newly divorced, he as ever between and betwixt girlfriends. Why, after sex had ended and he went on to someone else,why she had remained, he could not explain. She was bold, critical; she talked too much and too loudly. Somewhere inside her was a proud Jewish girl from North London whose parents sent her to private school so she could marry well:'I learned to fence, but they couldn't make a *mensh* of me.'

'We're family,' she liked to say:'We're allowed to hate each other.'

But there was only one meal they always ate together,in a crimson-draped corner of the Cafe Budapest.

'To what?' she would say, pushing herself up from the soft chair and raising her glass. But it was always the same: 'May God in his ignorance inscribe us for a good year.'

Wasn't it enough to ask for more life? Did it have to be blessed? Lucian drank his Bulls Blood and smiled at her.

Every *Yom Kippur* she must draw him into her transgression, her rebellion against her 'Mittel Europe' parents. They ate three courses on the day of fasting. And she paid.

He did not tell Elaine what the creative writing tutor had actually said to him. For weeks the tutor had endured his sceptical air, his wounding criticism, but after he read aloud his story about a Bahian priest who enchants his women followers and then makes love to them, she said the class was not right for him. Maybe she had already heard about him, for he was dreaded in the creative writing classes, the elderly elfin man who always knew more than the tutor.

But she could not deny the distilled beauty of his language, how he fashioned each sentence, his stories set in fantastical South American villages, his characters' lives like filigrees. The real South America he had never visited nor did he wish to.

The tutor told him women in the class were upset by his sexual references. 'Gratuitous,' she called them.

'But I don't understand. What sexual references?' He looked her in the eye. 'Tell me then.'

'You know,' she said, 'You know what they mean.'

What did she think, that a man approaching seventy should not have wet dreams? He played with himself constantly while he wrote; it was the way he wrote. But what would a little girl like her understand?

He remembered the first time he had been cast out, the only boy never allowed back into *cheder*. The old man had told him to shut up, but he kept asking: 'Why did Isaac just lie there like a *nebbish* waiting to be knifed?' When he wrapped the *Torah* scroll around another boy, the Hebrew teacher took Lucian by the shoulders and pushed him so hard out the door that he fell into the street.

At first Lucian did not try to find another creative writing class. He did not need the circle of students clutching their words against the night windows. Yet as the months passed, he became like those men talking to themselves on mobile phones. Only there was silence when he listened in the early morning, his hands on the page, a silence that swallowed his words and the life of his people.

Lucian found a short story writing course in a college where he was not known. It meant travelling through central London, then down past Waterloo to a large building whose corridors twisted and turned upon themselves, so that it seemed he had to go back before he went forward. By the time he found the room, a chilly rectangle lit by bands of fluorescent lights, the small group of students had begun to introduce themselves.

He recognised the pretend actor. Old fool in his cape and broad brimmed hat who played himself over and over again. A woman with a stick arrived just after him. Lucian heard central Europe in her voice and saw in her soft round face and mournful eyes, the desire to write about her past. She might even cry as she read her work. The others, the young unformed ones gleaming with ambition, would be full of pity for her. He knew he could always leave at the break.

A dusky woman, large mouth, dark heavy eyes listened with one hand against her tragic face. He imagined she had Spanish blood and he became aroused. As they introduced themselves, she gave each of them a searching look, almost pleading. Was she worried the class wouldn't have enough students to run? He sighed. He would stay and it would all end badly.

He held back in the first weeks of the class. For Serena's sake. How could he scorn someone whose smile seemed to say that each of them was incubating some rare and wonderful creature. Even he began to think that he must, he would soon, begin not just another novel, he had had so many beginnings, but *the* novel, the one he been waiting for all his life.

Serena pointed to the paper he covered with his hand. 'Don't hold back on us.'

It was his Bahian priest piece, revised. He had begun, but stopped before the first sex scene. Serena was not fooled.

'Yes,' said Hanna, the woman from central Europe or as it turned out Belgium. 'You must not worry. We are all friends.'

He shrugged. They had asked him after all. At the end he saw bewilderment in Hanna's eyes. The actor smirked, but the others, the young ones, were cool, methodical as they pounced. He was just being clever, but not clever enough.The characters were ciphers, the story derivative. Nobody seemed to notice his exquisite descriptions of vaginas except for the young man writing a gay novel of manners on the net, and he called them 'pseudo porn'.

At the break, Lucian wandered down the corridors till he found the cafe. He would have sat over his coffee and not returned, if it were not for Serena. She sat alone smoking, staring out at the darkness till she saw him in the window; then she turned and beckoned.

'Don't be such a lone wolf.'

He stood before her unwilling to sit down.

'They were hard on you.'

'You were one of them.'

'Someone must stop you. You write so well but why always, always you write about nobody? Do you never think of starting from flesh and blood?'

He wanted to say that he had been writing for more years than she had lived. Had he not heard this facile advice? Real people were predictable, and most boring of all was your own self.

'Are you so above us?' What Elaine used to say. She once called him 'Mr God'.

'Why is there such a need for reality? Don't you get enough in your life?'

She sighed at this. 'Sure Lucian.'

He imagined Serena confiding in him about a boyfriend who could not satisfy her.

But she looked at her watch and got up. 'Try being a bit less godly.'

She asked them to develop a conflict between two characters: 'a dialogue of strain.' He thought of his mother and father picking at the minute details of their lives, the atmosphere in the kitchen so dense with words that he could not breathe. It was too easy, as if he were not writing at all, as if both parents were alive in his brain, their voices raised higher and higher till his head ached from them. Their former selves, not the corpse of his father dead for fifteen years, his mother dulled in a nursing home.

Serena said what an ear he had. But there was no art in it. If his mother heard the dialogue, she would say: 'Lucian stop imitating us.' Would it be cruel to show her, for once find out why they had needed each other? Was their arguing some complicated form of lovemaking like the ministrations of his Bahian priest? But when he went for his weekly visit, his mother seemed to ignore him and the nurse said she was lapsing more and more into uncomprehending silence. He felt strange as he stood there before her wheelchair, as if the mother he knew had stolen into his pages, leaving the silent figure behind like a decoy.

Serena asked the class to write a monologue; someone they

could not bear to hear, would speak. Hanna said she hated no one. Lucian chose the actor who might listen in class to his own voice played back to him, with all his follies amplified, but never know because he was so vain.

During the break the actor came over to the table where Lucian and Serena sat. He put his face close to Lucian: 'I see you have acquired me.' Lucian stared at him and for once could think of no retort. His creations were so true that even fools could see themselves.

'I know. It's all made up, isn't it Lucian? And we're fellow travellers.'

'You are wonderfully cruel,' Serena said when actor moved away. 'But can you be loving as well?'

He had never written so easily, the characters' words rushing from him as if they, not he, were writing. He wrote about his younger brother's vanity, the loud mouth newsagent he had patronised and disliked for years; an aunt who lived on boiled onions and spite. There seemed to be no end to flawed humanity, to the figures who sauntered across his mind, paused and spoke words. He had become an old fashioned copyist: Bob Cratchit on a high stool, a stenographer of lives.

He began to notice something almost out of the corner of his eye. Those he wrote about did not flourish. The first was the actor who came down with the flu, but he always blighted a class for weeks before leaving. Then Lucian saw his mother grow more removed from the world and begin to refuse food. His brother's wife threatened to leave him, and the newsagent was robbed. Even Serena. After he'd written her into a story which he kept from the class, he could see no change in her. Then she read aloud a section from her novel—the lament of a woman whose lover steals what she would have given him—and Lucian could not look at her for the rest of the class.

He worried about Serena even if he could not have her. Not just because in his story she had been sexually kind to him or that she flirted with an old man like him. She drew each of her students into her fold even as she herself was abandoned. He stopped writing about her, even threw away the page, but she seemed no longer a playful woman.

He thought of returning to his South American fantasies. They had never hurt anyone, his gorgeous impossible figurines. Then Serena asked them to write a caricature, and Elaine came into his mind, a fully formed cartoon character. Hunched over, hoarse-voiced Elaine who never bored him but never changed. She was invincible.

Serena said how true his Elaine sounded, but the others called it 'acid attack'. They were jealous because without doubt his was the best. Elaine, a living one-dimensional character, stepping from his pages like some paper doll.

'Don't you pity?' Hanna asked. If Elaine saw Hanna in her long dress and cardigan, with her hangdog face, she would say how much she hated old women. And if she saw the piece, she would either shrug or pretend not to recognise herself. Even so he would not show her. So what if he had borrowed from her without asking, put back without telling? All the time she sat by the window of her Swiss Cottage flat, smoking as she stared down at the street.

He thought he might phone Elaine that weekend, but didn't. Had she phoned last, had he promised anything? The writing had consumed him after all. Serena put his Elaine piece into a class booklet. He was trying to extend it into a story he could send somewhere. It had been years since the rejections and small successes in magazines that fluttered briefly into life.

When she phoned him, he felt disappointed. She did not sound like his Elaine; behind her voice he heard voices, the distant sound of phones ringing. 'Believe it or not I'm in hospital. I fell,' she said. 'Tried to get off a bus before it stopped. I'm such a fool. You don't fall at our age.'

'Elaine. You're all right?' He heard himself stutter.

'Of course I'm not all right. Would you be in this hell hole? They keep saying, you're on the mend. But I'm thinking they'll never let me out. '

She looked small and somehow younger sitting in the hospital bed. He bent over and kissed her and she seemed to brighten. He wanted to ask her just when she had fallen. Was it when he had started to work on her, giving her a new name, masking his feelings in laughter and scorn. Was it then? Or in the middle of his reading of the piece when he felt such mastery?

She looked at him. 'What's wrong with you?' she asked.

He was remembering the lines he gave her to say in his caricature. Had he made them up or stolen them?

'Will you wipe off that pity, or whatever it is besmirching your normally cruel wizened face?'

'My face is my face,' he said.

She lay back. 'I'm going to die here. You can't smoke. There's a hideous woman who will not stop talking about her hernia. Speaking of which, how're your night writers?'

Just coincidences. That Elaine was foolish, her bones brittle. Was it his fault his brother had married a woman too young for him, or that his mother forgot who he was?

He had wanted to ask Serena what she meant by 'godly', but the class ended before he could catch her alone. He put away his Elaine story. It was too late to destroy it and re-form her broken bones, but he would not continue.

Elaine left hospital but complained that she couldn't stop smelling the place. 'I'll never be the same. Never,' she said. Maybe he'd taken so much from her that she could not mend properly.

Who do you think you are Lucian? His mother's scorn. As a child he rolled the poems that he had written about werewolves and uncles into little scrolls and hid them around the house, so that even he could not find them. But his mother had discovered 'his droppings', as she called them.

He tried to write one of his South American stories. A market woman sold discarded sins. Bloodless writing. He was like some animal who had to have live prey. He wrote about dead people and was bored, even attempted a poem but saw his words harden into abstractions and crumble. Then silence from his pen. He unplugged the phone so that Elaine could not reach him. What had he done to her? Not done. Not done.

The characters would not stop running across his brain, gesticulating at him. But they were not themselves were they? We are never ourselves. Always one self removed from who we are. Half brothers.

He could write his own life on the page, what he had always scorned in the fiction of others. Only his self would be detached from him; like Peter Pan's shadow, he could hold it out and examine. He wrote about his child self, and saw that he could have two child selves, even three, sometimes in the same story. His teenage self, his schooteacher self, his declaiming poet self, his army self, his sad-eyed lonely self. Selves wearing bell-bottoms and berets in flats he occupied for six months, a year; selves wandering through Regent's Park and gazing at women in the National Film Theatre cafe. Some he could barely discern, others came willingly to the fore of his mind. He was father and son, sometimes several sons, the stories like ballads in his singsong voice.

One night he stayed up to write a story in which he was both lovers, man and woman. He held and was held, entered and was entered. He wrote till the muted darkness of early morning, fell asleep and woke to a hard-edged sky, daylight washing through the hollow he had become. And there was no more desire in him.

A buzzer sounded once, twice, three times. Then deep in the building he heard footsteps, slow, ragged. He was reminded of the mangled ghost son in the *Monkey's Paw* story, whose parents wished him alive and then wished him dead again. But these footsteps would come and he imagined not one person, but a multitude of himself trailed down the stairs like a cubist painting.

He tried to rise when the knock came but was too dizzy: Let them go, all of them. I have had enough.

Someone was turning the key, then calling his name. He remembered exchanging keys with Elaine. She had said 'When I drop dead I'd rather you find me than one of my idiot sons.' He tried to call back. He could not remember when he had last eaten or allowed liquid to pass through his mouth. His throat was so dry that he could not speak.

'Lucian. Are you all right?' She moved in a large soft bubble, she and the stick she said she would never use. She came closer. 'I've been ringing for days. I began to think.' She sat down on the edge of the bed and wiped her eyes, an old woman smelling of tobacco and lemons.

She looked hard at him. 'What's wrong? Will you speak? Lucian.'

He pointed to his throat.

'You've laryngitis? *Meshuggener*. You made me so.'

She fumbled a cigarette out of her bag but seemed to forget to light it.

'But you're coming to lunch. Aren't you? You must.' She watched him smile and shrug.

'You've forgotten?' She actually looked hurt.

'Don't you even know what day it is?'

He shook his head.

'How could you? The holiest of holiest.' She waved her hand about, still holding the unlit cigarette. Her Bette Davis routine but today he did not mind.

'Are you all there?'

If he listened hard he could hear him, the self who escaped his pen.

'Lucian. It's *Yom Kippur*.' He stared at her. She seemed to gather all the light in her bent body.

'I booked our usual table. They've the goose, but not smoked duck.'

She grabbed his arm. 'You hear me? You forbidding old fool. God opens his book today and we're not going to be in it.'

Rivkie Fried

Rivkie Fried was born in Israel and raised in Tel Aviv and New York. After a career in journalism, including several years at the BBC World Service, she turned to creative writing. She has published poems, short stories, and has recently finished a novel. She lives in London with her husband and son.

'Because I began my life in Israel and was raised in an ultra Orthodox home, Jewishness is an intense part of my identity. This is not merely rooted in historical or cultural continuity, but in something deeper; a primal sense of one's place in the world. It also informs my writing, which is frequently preoccupied with Jewish themes. My fiction is often set in foreign locations (Israel or the US), perhaps reflecting my lingering sense of being an outsider in England. When I write of the *haredi* world, it is with a woman's eye for domestic detail, but with an instinctively restrained, protective hand. The *haredim* are sometimes portrayed harshly by writers and filmakers who cannot slip through barriers and share the intimate life of a closed society. I can—and feel it is my duty to cherish and defend it, with some reservation, rather than to criticise.'

The Glamorous Aunt

Part I

She was just ahead of me, astride a massive white horse with elaborate gold-painted carvings. That's how I remember her, riding with me on the carousel as it dipped and glided through the sharp brightness of the Toronto autumn, the air like polished gold. A scarf covered her hair, because of the breeze. She kept looking back at me, waving and laughing: the laughter of a child so delighted and aroused it can scarcely contain itself. The tail of her scarf—pink, her favourite colour—flapped in the wind, and her lips were pursed, as though she was kissing everything: me, the bright day, life itself. I was only six years old at the time, and found the carousel somewhat overwhelming: a frantic blur of colour and very loud, insistently cheerful music that numbed my mind unpleasantly. Yet I smiled, aching to please her because she was so beautiful; more capable of raucous fun than I ever knew myself to be.

Not many years later, when I encountered the word 'glamorous' for the first time, I knew it described her, belonged to her by right. She was my glamorous aunt, striking, extraordinary and beyond the rules—the rules that lent to adulthood a leaden and trapped quality that, even then, I began to sense but not to understand. My aunt Rochel appeared to escape this unhappiness by remaining somehow child-like, even as perceived by a sombre and over-sensitive boy who instinctively sought to protect her. Yet these same rules later caused her great anguish: rules which, in summing up a complex situation, ultimately offer only cold, heartless terms like 'cuckold' and 'harlot'. Or the Yiddish for the latter—*kurve*—a damning word I was to overhear repeatedly in the years to come.

That day, when we arrived home from the carousel, Uncle Solomon shouted at Aunt Rochel for buying me forbidden *treif* sausages at the fun fair. Solomon is my mother's brother, a loud and nervous man who always frightened me. He was prone to bursts of ebullient generosity, like inviting me to stay with them, because my mother had become weak from the birth of my brother. Solomon drove all the way to New York to fetch me and take me to Toronto. We stayed at a motel near Niagra Falls, and he was very kind to me, even when I had difficulty falling asleep because I'd never slept away from home before. But that day he was furious—with Aunt Rochel, that is. 'I wasn't thinking,' she kept repeating in apology. 'Malcolm just seemed so happy. I wanted to make him happy.' Solomon only shouted at her some more, calling her a thoughtless idiot, a child. I felt guilty because, unlike Aunt Rochel, I had fleetingly wondered if the sausages were *kosher.* But the windy, invigorating weather had given me an appetite, and I consumed them with great relish.

****

Somewhere a telephone was ringing. Malcolm glanced up distractedly from the letter he was reading. He rose from his bed, automatically straightened the bedspread, and began crossing the room, only to sink into a chair instead. An untidy pile of newspapers—mostly old copies of the New York Times sent by his mother already occupied the chair, causing him to perch uncomfortably, but he was loathe to move a second time. Let someone else, he told himself, answer the telephone for a change. His eyes went to the window. It had rained steadily all morning, and the grounds outside the university dormitory were a gloom of mud and strewn leaves. Malcolm felt dispirited. In the rain even Jerusalem was a melancholy sight.

Suddenly he heard a knock at his door. It was followed by a bellowing voice. 'Telephone! Feldman, telephone!' Before he could reply the door was flung open. Saul Miller, an American like himself, stood on the threshold. Saul occupied a room across the hall.

'Telephone, Feldman.'

Malcolm rose to his feet with a groan. 'I heard you, for God's sake. I heard you the first time.'

'It's a woman.'

Malcolm meant to scoff, but instead heard himself blurt out, 'Israeli?'

'American. Definitely American. Too old for you, if you want my opinion.'

'Cut it out, Saul,' said Malcolm irritably. 'It's too early in the day for your—' But his neighbour broke in, saying, 'You don't want to keep the lady waiting.' His pale, bespectacled face was friendly with curiosity, so that Malcolm did not attempt a further retort as he proceeded toward the telephone.

They had easily formed a close group: Malcolm, Saul, and perhaps a dozen other young men and women at the university who were both American and Orthodox. These friendships were driven by necessity, a need for the intimately familiar. They had been raised in similar homes, attended Zionist religious groups and summer camps. Yet, in Israel of all places, they felt doubly foreign: from abroad, and also *datiyim*. Not that Malcolm and his compatriots experienced hostility; far from it. If anything the secular Israelis he'd encountered were excessively friendly, as though seeking to demonstrate a lack of prejudice he had not even begun to suspect. And the girls! The girls were the worst at this; odd and strained—even if he'd merely approached one to ask for directions. The girl would study him intently, eyes scurrying from his skullcap to his face, as though seeking clues to his surreptitious intentions.

The telephone was mounted on a wall next to a window in the dormitory hallway. Malcolm peered outside as he took the dangling receiver in his hand. The rain had turned into a downpour. Urgent drops pelted the windowpanes, obscuring his vision, causing him to blink away an imagined dampness as he began to speak.

'Hello,' he said.

Immediately a female voice replied in English.

'Hello. Hello'—the word was repeated a second time, then a third, although he'd scarcely had time to reply. 'Hello, is that Mr Feldman?

'What?' His gaze left the sodden landscape beyond the window as he spun round, convinced Saul was eavesdropping. The hallway was empty. 'Yes. Yes, it is.'

'Mr Feldman, is that you? Is that you, Mr Feldman?'

The woman on the other end sounded agitated, and was apparently in the habit of repeating everything she said. Gradually Malcolm realised her voice was dimly familiar, like a vanishing image or sound when one wakes from a dream. He couldn't locate where he'd heard it.

'Yes, this is Mr Feldman.'

Malcolm! Malcolm, is that you?'

The voice was warmer, and more familiar still. All at once a strange thrill gripped him. Outside, rain drummed on the window incessantly.

'Yes, this is Malcolm. Who am I talking to, please?'

'Malcolm, hello. Malcolm, this is your—'

Abruptly the voice broke off. Only silence followed. An urgent unease seized Malcolm. He called out, 'Hello, hello', and, wrenching the receiver from his ear, scrutinised it intently, as though to conjure an image of the unknown speaker.

'Hello,' he shouted into the mouthpiece.

Somewhere close at hand a door opened. Malcolm sensed questioning eyes on his back; heard footsteps. Then Saul loomed behind him. Malcolm spun round in annoyance, then noted his friend's grave expression.

'What's going on?' whispered Saul. 'Is it bad news?'

'I don't know,' Malcolm began. Then a sound reached him from the telephone receiver. It was repeated a second time. The woman at the other end was crying.

'Malcolm…Malcolm…' the woman managed at last. He was in no doubt; the woman sobbed as she uttered his name. He lowered his eyes in embarrassment. Behind him Saul retreated a few paces.

'Yes? Yes, who is this?'

'Rochel,' came the reply after a pause, 'Rochel, your aunt. At least I used to be your aunt before—' There was a catch in her voice, followed by a sigh 'Before I divorced your uncle. Your uncle Solomon...'

'Oh,' he breathed, finding himself speechless. And again, 'Oh.'

'Your Aunt Rochel. From Canada. Toronto. Toronto in Canada.'

'Yes, of course. I know who you are now.'

'Your Aunt Rochel. From Canada.'

Malcolm listened in dismay. Had she always talked so nervously, repeating everything she said? It was difficult to associate this jarring voice with his image of his attractive aunt. But then some years had elapsed since he saw her last; seven years at least. Somewhere Malcolm heard a door close. Saul had retreated, and returned to his room.

Suddenly a glimpse, a fragment of memory, surfaced in his consciousness. Somewhere a lovely woman in a pink dress floated across a lawn. The dress was of a thin, sheer material. He recalled feeling a delectable sensation as she drew near, the pink dress billowing about her. How beautiful she was. Always so beautiful. Then other details crowded Malcolm's memory. His parents were also present at the scene which, he now realised, had taken place outside Grossinger's Hotel in the Catskills. His younger brother Howard, still a small child then, was in his mother's arms. Malcolm stood between them and his mother's sister, Sally. Of course Sally did not share his pleasure at the vision of Rochel proceeding toward them, her smile at once gracious and merry. That was the thing about Aunt Rochel: she was such fun. But Sally had long harboured a dislike for her Canadian sister-in-law. 'Take a look at that dress,' Sally breathed to Marilyn, his mother, so he could not help but overhear. 'Just take a look.' Although she'd spoken in an undertone, the mean-spiritedness clouding her face did not escape Uncle Solomon who, coming up behind Rochel, stared askance at his two sisters. 'Would you kindly,' hissed Marilyn at Sally, 'shut up.' But Rochel had already noticed. She paused, suddenly wild-eyed, and waited for Solomon to reach her side. Malcolm fixed her with a gaze of desperate love. He silently urged her forward, determined to protect her from unkindness. But Rochel only tightened her grip on Solomon's arm, her face downcast. Malcolm felt something cut through him. It was as though cracks appeared on his heart, a child's impotent pity oozing from them.

But now, in his Jerusalem dormitory, her voice resumed in his ear. 'Malcolm, do you still remember me?'

'I...yes. Yes, of course.'

'Your aunt,' she repeated once more, as though seeking to impress upon him an irrefutable fact, 'your aunt Rochel.'

'Yes.' He was, it seemed, incapable of saying more. 'Yes.'

'I want'— her tone was still agitated, although no longer tearful—'I want to see you. I...I need to talk to you. Talk to you about something.'

He nodded, then foolishly remembered she could not see him.

'It's important, Malcolm.'

'Yes. Yes, of course. Are you staying in Jerusalem?'

She mentioned the name of a hotel unknown to him.

'Don't worry, I'll find it. But when?'

'Tomorrow, in the evening. No, not tomorrow; I have to be somewhere tomorrow. On Tuesday— is that okay? Tuesday evening?'

'Tuesday evening,' he repeated after her.

****

Most of all I recall the light. A shimmering radiance, like pale gold spilling from the sky. If only the carousel music, with its forced cheer, were not so loud. I'd chosen a small horse—a grey pony, I think—battered and missing half an ear. Its vulnerable air restored some measure of my confidence. But Aunt Rochel seemed so high and out of reach. Her horse, tall and monstrous, appeared fully capable of breaking into a sudden gallop and vanishing with her. Don't vanish, I prayed. Turn and smile at me some more. Each time she did I waved and shrieked, to please her. To elicit her aroused, gleeful laughter. Lips kissing the air, kissing the world. Kissing me.

****

They've forgotten me. Although we're in the kitchen together, they—Marilyn, my mother, and her sister Sally—are at the other end, leaning against the counter and murmuring softly. Between them is a tray of freshly baked cake—a cheese cake, I think—which they're pretending not to eat. Yet they're scooping up crumbs and straightening edges of the cake, all the while whispering inaudibly. Sally lives across the street from our Manhattan apartment and is practically a permanent fixture in our home. She and my mother frequently visit one another on Friday afternoons, when their preparations for *Shabbos* are behind them. Over coffee and a rapidly diminishing cake, they ruminate at length over the latest news, repeating opinions already cited during hasty encounters and telephone conversations over the course of the week. But today there's a different air in the room. My mother appears downhearted, while Sally is visibly giddy with excitement.

As I was saying, they've forgotten me. When I was very young—I'm thirteen now—I perfected an eavesdropping technique. I realised that if I remained motionless, eyes averted from the adults around me, they soon ceased to remember my presence. And so, although I've long finished my salami sandwich and coleslaw, I dare not stir. My gaze is fixed on the *Shabbos* tablecloth, over which a thin sheet of plastic is temporarily spread to keep it clean. I know they're discussing the shocking events in Toronto last week. A few hissed words reach me now and then. *Her. Poor Solomon. The shameless kurve.* Most of these words are spoken by Sally. My aunt Sally is not a very nice person. In fact she's downright vindictive, without a kind word for anyone. I've never fathomed the reason. Uncle Srol, her husband, is a travelling salesman who works very hard, and is rarely home. Their daughters, my cousins Phyllis and Beatrice—they're much older than Howard and myself—are always well behaved and mute as shadows. They're intimidated by their mother, and never open a big mouth and talk back. That's what Sally often says to us: 'Stop opening a big mouth and talking back.' But what's the point in living in perpetual silence? I think that in tidy, quiet homes such as Sally's, the very air hums with unspoken hatefulness. It presses against your side in the corridors, causing you involuntarily to hold your breath. Maybe that's why Uncle Srol travels so much.

Our home is a more outspoken and cheerful kind of place, although quite messy, because Mom prefers her charity and fund-raising work to housekeeping. Dad doesn't mind; I don't suppose he even notices. If Dad were to come home one day to find an elephant in the hall, he'd only remark that it ought be given some water, or a refreshing shower. Dad is like that—always busy and distracted, but a thirsty, misplaced elephant would prick his conscience. He is a lawyer, and works in a practice that represents survivors of the Nazi death camps. He's even bit famous: the newspapers call him the 'Holocaust Lawyer.' In the evenings he's often exhausted, and although Mom says, 'Kids, leave your father alone tonight', he still sits with us on the living room carpet, listening to the unremarkable incidents and details we offer him. When I'm troubled, he questions me patiently, despite my convoluted accounts that meander with gathering incoherence until I'm in tears with surprised grief. Dad is familiar with grief.

He appraises me with sadness, or holds me, despite my resistance, until I'm calmer. 'It's a tough world for sensitive people,' he often says. This phrase offers me succour. Later, in bed, I repeat it to myself: *it's a tough world for sensitive people.*

Sensitive like Rochel, I now think. The whispered voices across the room—silent for some minutes—have resumed. That word again. *Kurve*. Each time Sally utters it my mother hisses, 'Sshh.' Sally repeats it nonetheless, eyes bulging with loathing and relish. Although I'm staring down at the *Shabbos* tablecloth, I'm certain of her expression. *Kurve*. They're still talking about Aunt Rochel's separation from Uncle Solomon. It happened only a week ago: Solomon telephoned from Canada with the news. 'Thrown her out of the house,' Sally now says aloud. She obviously has forgotten my presence. 'Thrown her out of the house.' This is blatantly untrue. It was Uncle Solomon who left, in fact, late one night after an argument.

What Sally says next is so shocking that I'm hurled against the back of my chair with surprise. 'The *kurve* with her boyfriend,' Sally said. I collect myself and straighten surreptitiously, holding my breath. The two women take no notice. 'The *kurve* with her boyfriend,' Sally repeats. *Kurve* is Yiddish for whore—according to Beatrice, the younger, and less cowed, of Sally's daughters. She even, to my sickened disbelief, provided the word's definition.

What boyfriend? I want to shout. The room is so hushed I fear I involuntarily had, and peer hurriedly to my right. Sally is sucking cake crumbs from her fingers while my mother looks on, indignation and sorrow in her features. As I lower my gaze, Sally loudly draws breath and repeats the phrase a third time. 'The *kurve* with her boyfriend.'

What boyfriend? Glamorous Rochel—with a boyfriend? But that's preposterous. It's obvious she's terribly attached to Uncle Solomon, who scolds and reproaches her as though she were a child. How could Sally concoct such vindictive lies?

Yet my mother does not appear shocked, or even disbelieving. She only silences her sister with another hissed 'Sshh.' Their voices drop to an undertone once more.

****

On the afternoon of his meeting with his aunt Rochel, Malcolm wandered through the centre of Jerusalem, aimlessly peering at shop windows. To lift his spirits, he went into the King David Hotel and treated himself to an exorbitantly priced cup of coffee. He savoured the beverage while gazing nostalgically at the tourists, mostly Americans, scattered about the lounge. Then, as evening drew near, he slipped into a nearby synagogue, prayed hastily, and boarded the bus that would take him to his aunt's hotel. Jerusalem sped past, all cold white stone and green cypress hurtling into darkness. The bus entered an unfamiliar neighbourhood and he looked around, surprised at the shabbiness of the buildings he passed.

Jerusalem—that is to say, Israel—had not been his first choice. When Malcolm grew restless in his second year at university, and craved a change, Israel was not on his mind. The place of his yearnings was undefined, a blurred, sigh-filled dream: a dream that nonetheless clamours loud and deep, disturbing his peace in waking hours. London, Paris—they beckoned to him. Even India, China—why not? This was the hippy era: many of his contemporaries interrupted their studies for a semester or year and, with slender means, slipped off to Kathmandu or Bali.

Malcolm did not wish to cause his mother further distress. 'India?' he could hear Marilyn's anguished disbelief. She was always less open-minded than his father, who had been dead now for almost four years. Marilyn, seeking guidance and authority, often confided in the rabbi at their synagogue, a singularly myopic but kindly man who undoubtedly would have informed Malcolm that no Jewish communities remained in India—nor China, for that matter. Further advice would have followed from Uncle Solomon in Canada who, since his divorce, increasingly hungered for family involvement, devoting Sunday evenings to long telephone conversations with his widowed sister in New York. So, after some listless, irresolute months, Malcolm compromised and opted for a year at Jerusalem's Hebrew University. The move drew hardly a murmur from the family. Israel was familiar, trusted, an extension of home—*the homeland*, after all. It would not lead him down alien paths or cause him to wander astray as might India's ashrams and Goa's amoral beaches.

****

'It's all because of that Sally,' Aunt Rochel was saying.

'Who?' he asked, although he'd understood.

'Sally—his sister. Your Aunt Sally. She poisoned Solomon's heart against me.'

Malcolm nodded without speaking. Images of Friday afternoons in the Manhattan kitchen rose before his eyes, his mother and Sally, picking at cake and murmuring softly. He shifted uneasily in his chair and nodded a second time, hoping Rochel's voice would not rise further. She was becoming agitated.

'Poisoned his heart against me,' repeated Rochel in a gentler tone, as though guessing his thoughts. 'That's all there is to it.'

She had greeted him in the hotel lobby—dimly-lit, with seedy furniture—and led him to a small dining room. The room's dingy décor dismayed him. Clearly Rochel was living in reduced circumstances. Did Solomon not allow her a sufficient alimony, despite the acrimoniousness of their divorce? Rochel appeared abashed as she motioned to a table at the far end of the room, behind two large plastic plants. He said he'd already eaten; she ordered tea for them both.

'Malcolm,' she suddenly said, breaking into his thoughts, 'stop looking at me like that.'

'Like what?' he blurted in surprise.

'Like—I don't know what. Like you're looking at a photo album or something.'

She gave a sharp laugh, fingers tugging nervously at the linen napkin on her lap. Malcolm also laughed, to put her at ease. She was still very attractive, with the tender, smooth skin of a much younger woman. Her eyes bore traces of sadness, their dark blue hue reminiscent of a remote and rarely glimpsed lake that had tired of its solitude. But it was her mouth, generously daubed with the pink lipstick he recalled from his youth, that drew him most. Pink was always her favourite colour—although this evening her dress was navy blue, and of a stern cut. Her expression, too, was stern, despite the occasional nervous smile—like a woman, weary of her playful image, who now strove for sobriety.

As he continued to appraise her, a stunning thought struck Malcolm. He'd always been in love with Aunt Rochel. *In love.* The realisation made his head go empty and numb, so that he couldn't hear what she was saying. *In love with her*. Maybe only a little, he consoled himself: the remnant of a childhood infatuation. Presently the numbness had gone, and instead he felt himself blushing. In love. Could it be? Malcolm's gaze dropped to his hands, tightly clasped on the tablecloth like some grubby, overly-intimate creatures. There was dirt beneath his fingernails. In love. How preposterous. But the silence within him told him it was the truth.

She was addressing him once more.

'I can't get over you, Malcolm. You're an adult, so sophisticated.'

'And you,' he replied, face burning, 'look exactly the same.'

'No,' she giggled, poking him with one elbow, ' no, I don't, you're lying. But that's very kind.'

Their tea arrived, as well as a plate of chocolate biscuits. Malcolm pretended to appraise the other diners in the room as he struggled for composure. Rochel passed him the biscuits. Then, with a rapid intake of breath, she said, 'You're probably wondering why I wanted to see you—'

'No,' he protested. 'That is—'

'But why should you wonder?' she broke in. 'An aunt comes to Jerusalem; she has a right to see her nephew, no? We always got on well.'

'Always,' he echoed. Those dark blue eyes disconcerted him. Perhaps she'd guessed. In love? In love with her? A woman of middle age—*his aunt*, for God's sake.

'Do you remember, Malcolm, that time you stayed with us? In Canada?' Then, her face sagging, she said, 'No, how could you remember? You were just a small boy.'

'But I do remember,' he blurted urgently. 'I remember very clearly.'

'And the day I took you to the fun fair?'

'Sure. I remember going on the carousel.'

'You do?' she cried out, then clapped a hand over her mouth.

'Don't worry,' he said gently, leaning forward. 'No one heard you.' She was so beautiful... Still so beautiful.

'You don't mind sitting here? Maybe it's nicer in the lobby; there are couches,' and she made to rise.

'No, it's fine.Really.'

She sank into her chair once more. 'But you really remember that day? You're not just saying so?'

'Every detail,' he nodded vigorously.

'You wouldn't get off the horse.'

'Pony. It was a pony, I'm sure of it.'

'Pony,' she murmured, suddenly radiant with recollection. 'Every time the ride ended, you begged 'Again, again.' We rode that carousel at least ten times. Do you remember, Malcolm?'

'Of course. And you bought me some snacks; hot dogs, I think.'

She grimaced. 'Yes, I wasn't thinking. Your uncle was so angry when he found out. He said they weren't *kosher.*'

'Oh.'

'Then you got sick. You had a temperature and we had to call the doctor. Solomon said it was all my fault.'

'Your fault?'

'Do you remember? Getting sick—do you remember?'

He searched her face. 'Not really. I'm sorry, I was very young.'

'Then he blamed me. Because it got cold, and I kept you outdoors too long. He was always blaming me, scolding me.'

He nodded in agreement, wishing to calm her. In love with her. Was it possible? And she so beautiful. Maybe his imagination was playing tricks. Because of this place: the shabby hotel with its abominable décor. They didn't belong here. They were still outdoors, riding that timeless carousel, dipping and gliding in the crisp Ontario sunlight.

'Always,' she was saying, a catch in her voice. 'Always scolding me—treating me like a child.'

She paused and, blinking rapidly, began sipping her tea awkwardly. He had an impulse to reach over and stroke her face. But the gesture seemed momentous, terrifying. Like ripping through time, space; breaking some law of nature. He was losing his mind, he told himself, and groped for a biscuit instead.

'Aunt Rochel,' he said, 'maybe let's not talk about all that. It's upsetting you.'

She glanced up, eyes red-rimmed. 'I'm making you uncomfortable, probably.'

'No. No, you're not.'

'Yes. Yes, I am; I can feel it. You're wondering what I want from you.'

'Well, I—'

'Let me be frank with you. Let me talk straight: wasn't that what Solomon'—she flinched momentarily—'always said? Maybe not to you, but that's what he'd say on the telephone to his customers. Let me talk straight. Then'—with a hard laugh—'then he'd lie like a *goy*, without even trying.'

He regarded her mutely.

'Tell me, Malcolm, what do you hear of him?' Suddenly her voice was low, pleading. 'Forget what I said about Sally poisoning his heart; it's only that I was feeling this…bitterness. But what do you hear of him? Is he healthy?'

'Oh, he's fine,' offered Malcolm cautiously. 'Still charging along the same as ever. In fact I saw him just a few months ago, on *Rosh Hashanah*.'

'Here?' Rachel gasped, 'in Jerusalem?'—and she patted the front of her dress, then her hair, as though grooming herself for the arrival of an unexpected visitor.

'No, not here. In New York. I went home for the holidays; and he stayed at our house.'

'Of course,' she replied matter-of-factly, 'we often came to stay with your family for the holidays.' To his surprise her hand touched his fleetingly. 'You know, Malcolm, I was always sorry for not telephoning you after your father…after he went like that…'

'Oh. Well, that's okay.'

'He was a prince, Robert was. The kindest man that ever lived; all his good work for the Holocaust survivors.'

'Thank you. I know.'

'He—he was the only one in your family who didn't treat me like a half-wit. A prince he was.'

'Thank you,' he repeated.

She paused, fixing him with a wild gaze, as though mentally phrasing words she dared not utter. What? he thought. Now what? He longed to be gone, away from the depressing hotel, and the woman who'd stirred in him such hopeless and unspeakable emotions. She wanted something. Not him—but something.

'And Solomon?' she managed at last. 'How did he look on *Rosh Hashanah*?'

'Fine. He looked fine.'

She nodded expectantly. Malcolm thought back to the week he'd spent in New York, ransacking his brain for details. Solomon had seemed unusually subdued, that was what struck him now—sleepy and muffled, with dark pouches under his eyes. When, at one of the holiday meals, Aunt Sally tried to provoke him with the usual banter about finding him a new wife, he scarcely mustered the vitality to respond, so tired did he seem.

All at once a memory visited Malcolm. He recalled an angry scene that erupted at their dining room table some years previously, also during *Rosh Hashanah.* Sally had sat beside Solomon, and throughout the meal attempted to interest her brother in descriptions of various divorcees and widows of her acquaintance. But each time Solomon waved her remarks aside with a plump, exasperated hand. Finally—Malcolm was unsure of the exact reason—Solomon lost his temper and began shouting at his sister. Sally leapt to her feet in a fury and blurted, 'The trouble with you, Solomon, is that you're still waiting for your whore to come back.' She used the Yiddish word—*kurve*. A cold ripple of agitation skated along the table. 'What,' Solomon bellowed, 'did you call her?' Suddenly Sally appeared chastened—frightened even. 'You're waiting for her. You're still in love with her'—and she fled the room.

Now, in the Jerusalem hotel, Malcolm grew aware of Rochel's waiting silence.

'He looked fine,' he offered lamely. 'Really, much the same as always. Maybe more tired.'

A small sound, like a stifled sob, reached his ears. He glanced up. Tears glistened in his aunt's eyes.

'Malcolm,' she said. At her tone, dread clutched at his heart. 'Malcolm,' she repeated.

'Aunt Rochel.'

'Malcolm, I want to ask you something. I—it will give you a shock.'

'Oh,' an involuntary sigh escaped his mouth.

'Does he still...do you think he still hates me?'

'No.' He sighed a second time, steeling himself. 'No, of course not.'

'How do you know?'

'Well. I mean, he never remarried...'

'Malcolm.' Her voice shook. 'Malcolm, I never did anything wrong.'

'Of course not,' he muttered, suddenly exhausted. On his skin was the clamminess that normally follows physical exertion. 'Of course not.'

'You don't,' she went on, 'believe me. No one believes me. Maybe I was...maybe a bit wrong. But I didn't do anything.'

'Aunt Rochel, all this is none of my business.' Then, when she did not reply—'Tell me, what do you want from me?'

The words spilled from her rapidly. 'Malcolm, talk to him for me.'

'Me? What...'

'Ask him.' She leaned forward avidly. 'Ask him if he doesn't miss his Rochel.'

A pause followed. Malcolm's clenched fists pressed into his eyes—seeking darkness, oblivion. Oh God, to be gone, escape this nightmare. Why had he agreed to see her?

'Why not?' she queried in a mild tone, as though merely negotiating some trivial matter. The sound reassured him, restoring a sense of normality.

'I don't know,' he struggled for words. 'It's not a good idea, coming from me. He'd think I was interfering, like Sally-'

'Is she still interfering?'

Unthinkingly he blurted, 'She's always trying to interest him in marriage proposals.'

'Hah! I knew it.' Her fists hammered the table with grim triumph. 'I knew it.'

'Rochel, you call him. Call him up and talk to him.'

'Me?'

'Yes.'

For some moments there was silence. Rochel stared hard at the table, her mouth working. Finally she nodded, face rapt with something like admiration.

'Call him up and talk to him,' she murmured, as if rehearsing. 'Call him up and talk to him.' Then she said to Malcolm,' You really think so?'

He felt somewhat crazed, as if at the culmination of a harrowing ordeal.

'Sure. Sure I do.'

Rochel nodded some more and peered into the distance, a small, expectant smile on her face. She then resumed drinking her tea. He did the same, although the beverage was tepid and lacked any identifiable taste.

Suddenly she said, 'You really don't remember getting sick that time?'

'I beg your pardon?'

'In Toronto. After the fun fair'

A disconcerting sensation of unreality returned to him. Perhaps Rochel was indeed somewhat unstable, as some members of the family always maintained—even his usually generous mother. 'I,' he murmured apologetically, 'only remember the carousel.'

'Yes'—peering into her cup— 'yes, you were so happy… More; that's what you said. But then you got a temperature. Solomon was furious. He kept blaming me. But you don't remember.'

She was so beautiful; her face tender and pensive. *What was he going to do?* Still so beautiful. Aloud he said, 'No, I'm sorry. I don't.'

But her thoughts had already darted elsewhere. 'Call him up and talk to him,' she said, half to herself. 'I'll call him up and talk to him.'

'Yes. I'm sure he'll be happy to hear from you.'

'Happy,' she echoed.

****

She's crying. She's in the next room, and through the wall I can hear her crying. Broken sobs; loud, ragged intakes of breath. Then more sobs. I can't move. I can't go to comfort her, make her laugh. She's so pretty when she laughs. But I'm ill; my head is so hot. Vivid, extravagant pictures jerk and hurtle behind my eyes. She put me to bed earlier—or maybe it was yesterday—and told me I had a fever. She, my pretty aunt. The fever makes me shake. I'm burning and shivering all at once. In a minute, I keep thinking. I'll go in a minute. Then sleep grabs me again. The sleep of illness, so I'm both asleep yet awake. Radiant images leap about in my head. Dreams, only dreams, I reassure myself, even in my sleep. She's still crying. Loud sobs come through the wall. One minute, I try to say.

But now she's calmer. Someone is talking to her—softly, but in an urgent tone. As though rushed for time. Perhaps it's Uncle Solomon, scolding her again for some misdemeanour. He's always scolding her. But no—this voice is different—unfamiliar, low, with a pleading and gentle quality. Then there is silence. I am relieved. I need not go to comfort her. I can relax, succumb to the sleepy heat in my limbs.

Suddenly there's movement in the next room. A door opens. Now I can clearly hear the unknown visitor. He sounds distressed; he says he's leaving. Goodbye, he says. And again—Goodbye. I wonder who he is. His accent is odd, foreign-sounding. But now Aunt Rochel is upset again. She's rushing after him; her strides are audible along the carpeted hallway.

Oh no—she's crying again. Now I must make an effort; go to her. But wait, no— she's stopped crying. Her voice is muffled, as though something is pressed against her mouth. Now they're returning to the room next to mine. The door must be ajar—I can hear them. I can hear them kissing; I think it's kissing. They must be good friends, to kiss so much. Now I'm certain the man is not Uncle Solomon. I've never witnessed Solomon kissing my Aunt Rochel.

Part II

'Adam, take my hand. Adam!'

'All *right.*' The small fingers curled reluctantly round his. 'All *right*. You're always afraid, Dad.'

'You bet I am.' Malcolm paused to zip up his son's jacket. 'You don't know the drivers in this country. They're maniacs.'

Adam strode along moodily. With his free hand he unfastened

his jacket once more.

'You always say that, too.'

'No, I dont.'

'You do, Dad. I've heard you.'

'Where? Where did I say that?'

'In Rome. Last week in Rome.'

'Rome—well, that's different. Italians, they're crazy drivers.'

'Crazier than Israelis?'

Malcolm scrutinised the Jerusalem street. The morning rush hour gave so sign of waning. All manner of vehicles streamed chaotically past, amidst an unceasing honking of car horns. The light turned green and two taxis raced forward, followed by an equally impatient army truck. Behind them the honking continued unabated. 'It's an even contest, I'd say.'

'You're always so afraid, Dad.'

Malcolm did not reply. He was not afraid, only mistrustful, a mistrust born of too much grief. His father's early death; then Solomon and Rochel; the bleak years of Susan's countless miscarriages. Then, at last, Adam arrived. When Adam was born Malcolm's mistrust turned to panicky love. It was he, not Susan, who sprang awake several times in the night and leaned over his infant son's cot, to listen for his breathing. The panic lessened with time. But Malcolm, now in his forties, was shadowed by a wariness he couldn't shake off. There were times he envied his confident eight-year-old: envied his ease, a quality he had never possessed. Many of the law students Malcolm taught appeared to have it as well: a youthful, arrogant assumption of immortality. Someday they too will die, but they seemed not to know it.

'Why,' asked Adam, 'did Mom stay in the hotel?'

'She's tired. She's just having a nap.'

'Are we going to the pool?'

Malcolm studied the overcast skies. 'Soon as it gets really sunny. I know—how about a hot chocolate?'

Adam appeared to reflect, then scratched his nose. 'You mean you want another coffee.'

'Don't you want a hot chocolate?' He heard the disappointment in his own voice. 'What about that place near the pool, with the juke box and stuff.'

'No, it's boring,' said Adam. Then, abruptly—'I know, that place.' He pointed to a café across the road.

'There? You're sure? It looks dingy. Not your kind of place, if you ask me.'

'Let's go see,' said Adam, lengthening his stride and approaching the kerb.

'Adam! Adam, wait, take my hand! *Adam!*'

'You're always so afraid, Dad.'

An hour later they were still at the café, both reading contentedly. Adam had consumed two cups of hot chocolate and a sandwich; now, over a bowl of ice-cream, he was engrossed in a book Malcolm had optimistically stuffed into their rucksack at the hotel. The morning remained cloudy; they'd postponed their swim until later. Despite Malcolm's reservations the café was decidedly pleasant. It had old, smoky walls on which were hung photographs of Israeli politicians and celebrities. Now and again, looking up from his newspaper, Malcolm felt a rare well-being as he sneaked glances at his son. Now, he resolved, they would take more holidays. The university had given him tenure; there was more money. He recalled the restless yearning of his youth, which first brought him to Jerusalem.

Suddenly Adam spoke.

'That lady,' he said, 'keeps staring at me.'

'Lower your voice,' admonished Malcolm automatically. He turned toward the table his son indicated, where an elderly couple was seated. 'And don't point like that—it's rude.'

'But she keeps staring at me.'

Malcolm examined the woman at the neighbouring table without interest. All at once an unpleasant sensation shot through him—a kind of shock. The woman resembled his late Aunt Rochel. Malcolm froze, as if submerged underwater, thrust into a cold and silent place. The sounds of the café dimmed. The woman was elderly: all pale, rumpled pink. She wore a dress of pink linen, and her creased but still lovely face bore traces of a florid tan. Malcolm finally wrenched away his gaze.

'Stop staring,' he whispered again to his son, feeling the need to speak, to jar himself from his unpleasant reverie.

'*She* started it,' Adam shrugged, returning to his book.

After some moments Malcolm peered furtively at his neighbour. As his shock faded, he saw the resemblance to Rochel was only superficial: a similarity in colouring and bearing. The woman blinked slowly, in the curious manner of a cat, yet her gaze lacked expression. Malcolm wondered if she were blind, or had impaired vision. Her companion was a very old man whose hands shook uncontrollably. He grimly attempted to pierce a slice of cake with a fork, while the woman watched expressionlessly. Finally the man addressed her and she leaned forward, clumsily taking the fork from his hand. Malcolm tried to return to his newspaper, but a morbid feeling had seized him. He peered out at the street instead. Just then a brand-new Mercedes, a sport model, drove past. It was a silver vision, streaking across his consciousness like a memory.

Had Rochel once driven a Mercedes, he wondered? She was always a superb driver. When he was in her car—even in Toronto, as a child—her relaxed expertise had impressed him. Just as some people discover in themselves an innate grace and skill when swimming, or riding a horse, Rochel's love was cars. Raised on a farm in Ontario, she'd boasted of learning to drive at the age of fourteen. So how to explain her death in a car crash—or was an explanation even required?

She was driving a rented car the evening she and Solomon came to Harvard to visit him. His uncle had telephoned unexpectedly a week earlier, to invite him out to dinner. It was the first time he'd seen them since they remarried a year earlier—very quietly, in California, without telling anyone. And although Malcolm had long recovered from his infatuation with Rochel, he was wary of the meeting, recalling the tormented months he'd spent in Jerusalem, thinking of her obsessively, grasping any excuse to mention her name. Hence it was with some relief that he spotted Rochel's startlingly bulky figure striding toward him at the assigned meeting place, one hand seeming to support Solomon's arm. Although still a handsome woman, she'd put on a great deal of weight. Gone forever was the girlish, injured air that had haunted him for many nights in his Jerusalem dormitory.

They dined at an expensive hotel restaurant. As the evening progressed he noticed other changes in the couple. Rochel, unusually, did most of the talking. Solomon, by contrast, appeared thinner and somehow diminished, on several occasions breaking off in mid-sentence to gaze at Rochel appealingly. They inquired after Malcolm's career plans; described their recently-purchased cottage near Toronto, where he'd always be a welcome visitor. Malcolm relaxed, drank some wine, congratulated them on their new-found happiness. Then Solomon complained of tiredness, and they parted at an early hour. The encounter disturbed Malcolm. He came away with a feeling of some unspoken trouble or grief.

A short while later news of Solomon's illness emerged. He was suffering from advanced cancer, and had not long to live. Aunt Sally, malevolent to the last, predicted dire suffering and neglect for her brother, now at the mercy of his wayward, *kurve* wife. Not that anyone paid her any heed. Malcolm, although preoccupied with his bar exams—and his early courtship of Susan—often reflected, with compassion and mounting dread, about the ordeal confronting his reunited relatives.

Rochel proved exemplary in her devotion to Solomon, clearly desperate to find, if not a cure, some means of keeping him alive as long as possible. Apart from chemotherapy treatments, she cajoled him to try all manner of alternative remedies. Malcolm heard this from Marilyn, his mother, who anxiously telephoned Toronto several times a week. 'She takes me to witch doctors,' Solomon reported to his sister in weak but jolly tones. 'My house is full of crystals and herbs, smelling of incense like a church.'

Yet the cancer progressed. Solomon lost weight, lost his hair and confidence. At night he couldn't sleep; he and Rochel went for slow, nocturnal walks along Toronto's deserted streets and parks. When April came, Rochel was adamant they drive to New York for a final Passover with the family. It was there that Malcolm—home on a spring break from Harvard—saw them for the last time. The sight of Solomon's wasted body was more than he could bear. Instead he focused on the extraordinary vision of Aunt Sally who, contrite at last, sat on the sofa stony-faced, holding hands with Aunt Rochel.

The manner of Solomon's dying in early autumn was known to Malcolm. His mother and Sally were present, having flown to Toronto to bid their brother farewell. Rochel remained with Solomon at all times, at night sleeping on blankets on his hospital room floor. Solomon was terrified of death. Heavily drugged with morphine, he fought against unconsciousness and lay gazing up at his wife and two sisters, whimpering with fear. Finally Rochel climbed into bed beside him and took him in her arms. She remained thus for two days without sleep, whispering words of comfort and crooning songs. 'She sang to him,' said Marilyn later, 'that corny song in Yiddish, the lullaby called 'Raisins and Almonds'. God knows where she learned the words. Solomon liked it; when she sang he wasn't afraid to close his eyes. That's how he finally slipped away, listening to that Yiddish song.'

With Solomon's death something in Rochel snapped. She left the hospital with her sisters-in-law, pale and staggering from lack of sleep. Depositing them at her home with instructions for the funeral preparations, she said she was going out briefly to tend to some chores. A short while later her car was found, crashed head-on into a garage wall nearby. She had died instantly.

The shocking news of Rochel's death was broken by Marilyn to her two sons, who'd arrived in Toronto that same evening for Solomon's funeral. Malcolm recalled they were in the empty house that had belonged to his aunt and uncle. At his mother's words, a fog of darkness enveloped him. He made some excuse about needing to use the bathroom and groped his way upstairs, to the first room he could find. It was small and dark, containing a narrow sofa and little else. He hovered in the doorway for some moments, blinking dazedly at the room's dim, somehow familiar, contours. All at once he found himself crumpled on the sofa, wracked with sobs, a cushion pressed to his mouth. Malcolm wept for some time, astonished and almost frightened at the grief flooding him. Later, as he lay quietly in the dimness, he knew this was the room he'd occupied as a child, when he stayed with his aunt and uncle.

Some days later, at Rochel's funeral—delayed because of a police inquiry—Malcolm looked up at the clear skies. He was reminded of another autumnal Toronto morning; that sharp, bright, radiant morning long ago, the carousel dipping and gliding through air that was like polished gold. Now, as Rochel's coffin vanished into the ground, he felt he was bidding farewell to something within himself: innocence, longing; childhood, perhaps. The carousel music stopped;

the radiant morning dimmed. Only grief lingered. Even many years later, if Rochel came into his thoughts at unguarded moments, he'd feel a sudden pricking of tears.

Suddenly a voice returned him to the present. Someone was speaking to him. It was his son, Adam.

'I'd like to go to India one day,' Adam said.

Disoriented, Malcolm looked up. 'India?' he echoed vaguely. Slowly the present flowed into focus: the Jerusalem café; a sputtering espresso machine. A huge portrait of Ben-Gurion dominated one wall, his features somewhat obscured by a wreath of smoke. Had Ben-Gurion smoked a pipe, wondered Malcolm distantly. His gaze shifted to Adam's face. It was a lovely face, with huge, intelligent eyes—the eyes of his father, Robert, the human rights champion. A prince among men, Rochel had once said.

'What,' asked Malcolm, 'made you say that?'

At the neighbouring table the elderly woman in pink was wiping the chin of her companion. Her movements were awkwardly tender. Perhaps, mused Malcolm, she wasn't blind after all.

Adam held up his book. 'I was just reading about it. The girl in the story, she comes from India.'

Malcolm examined the book's title. 'The Secret Garden,' he read aloud. 'Hang on, I know this book. Who gave it to you?'

'Grandma. Grandma Marilyn.'

'She did? My mother gave it to you?' He opened the book. 'How do you like that? It's still got my name in it.'

Adam snatched up the book. 'But now it's mine. Grandma said I could have it.'

'Fine, okay, it's yours.' Malcolm reflected for a moment. 'India,' he murmured. A rare sensation visited him: an expansive rush of liberation; of promise.

'Sure, we'll go there. And China, too. I've always wanted to see those places.'

'And China,' said Adam. 'We'll go there too.'

Elisabeth Russell Taylor

Elisabeth Russell Taylor was educated at the Sorbonne and at King's College, London. She has received numerous awards, including a Wingate scholarship and grants from the Arts Council and the Authors' Foundation. She was short-listed once for the 'Mind' Book of the Year and twice for the Jewish Quarterly/ Wingate Prize for Fiction. Her fiction includes two collections of short stories, *Present Fears* and *Will Dolores Come to Tea?* and novels including *I is Another,Tomorrow* (translated into French and Dutch), *Swann Song,Divide and Rule,* and *Tomorrow*. Virago Classics is to re-issue her novels *Mother Country* (in 2004) and *Pillion Riders*. She has also published literary criticism, journalism and children's literature and has written the new introduction to *In a Summer Season* by Elizabeth Taylor (Virago), as well as writing for film and radio. She is married to the painter Tom Fairs and lives in London.

'I am a secular Jew married to a non-Jew. I was born in England but do not live here from choice despite my affection for the language, literature and landscape. I believe in equality and am uncomfortable in a country in which the gap between rich and poor is widening: three million currently have to choose between heat and food and half the children in London living below the poverty line. The history of the Jews has led me to abhor all froms of prejudice, to understand asylum, and to respect learning. If my Jewish background has contributed to my identity this is best revealed by my writing.'

The Sin of the Father

'Put me through to the doctor.'

'I'm afraid the doctor's still with a patient.'

'Do you know to whom you are speaking? This is Mrs Grossman! Put me through at once!' Dr Grossman's secretary knew better than to demur.

'Joseph! I want you home at once! Portia is out of control. She's been rude to me!'

'Sybil, I'm with a patient. I shall be at home at the usual time.'

The doctor put down the receiver carefully and turned back to the young woman who lay on the examination couch in the foetal position, her face to the wall. She was fully clothed but for her French knickers that were pulled down round her knees exposing her naked bottom. The doctor drew on a pair of gossamer-thin rubber gloves and as he gently explored the woman's rectum for a possible growth Dr Grossman found his solace. Here was something with which he could cope: a physical diagnosis. He felt well pleased with himself. Only that morning Sir Barnes Fitzpatrick, the royal physician, had rung him, Joseph Grossman, a mere South African Jew twenty years his junior, for a second opinion. And only last week the organizing secretary of the London Cancer Convention had written asking him to elaborate on his article in the *Lancet* on varieties of rectal carcinoma. As Joseph's fingers probed the diseased cavern, somewhere from the back of his mind the thought seeped into his consciousness: some varieties of birds shit over their feet to keep cool.

Joseph Grossman had not wanted to be a doctor. He had wanted to be a geologist.

'And what sort of a profession is that for a nice Jewish boy?' his father had bawled, adding that it was sheer lack of gratitude on his son's part so much as to suggest such a thing. He would be made a laughing stock at his Lodge.

'What am I to say? "Joseph? Oh he's studying stones." Stones, my boy, we Jews know enough about stones without studying them. We've been the target of stones for two thousand years: big stones, small stones, sharp stones, blunt stones.. . .' Baruch developed the theme with all its variations until he was satisfied he had exhausted its range.

'So, go ahead, my boy, break your old father's heart.' And when that elicited no opposition he delivered the *coup de grâce:*

'There'll be no money for studying stones!'

Joseph studied medicine. But to spite his father he failed his first MB. He regarded the humiliation his father suffered as worth the personal inconvenience of having to resit his second year.

Baruch Grossman's pride would have been best served had his only son stayed in Johannesburg, bought an architect-designed house in Houghton, recruited a minimum of six servants, put in a larger swimming pool and a tennis court, married Baruch's partner's 'lovely' daughter, and become a brain surgeon. In the event he settled for Joseph's removal to London, England, to take up a houseman's job at Barts, to prepare for his Membership. Baruch was still in something of a dilemma, however. Should he give Joseph all the material assistance his son expected, or keep him short, show him who was master and thereby lure him back to South Africa and the prospects of wealth? The compromise he settled on was like most compromises, a disaster.

Things might have been different for Joseph had his mother lived but she died when he was an adolescent. His father raised him, taking good care that Joseph never became attached to a surrogate mother. Indeed, it seemed that Joseph became suspicious of women after his mother died. When invited to parties he tended to search out the younger children of the household and, rather than dance, he played with them or read to them. He never mentioned his mother's name. She was lodged in his heart and he did not dare dislodge her to examine his feelings.

In 1927 Joseph and his fellow examinees sat for their Memberships. On receiving news of his success Joseph put in a call to his father, and Baruch, over an admittedly faulty line, was predisposed to understand that, out of sixteen examinees, his son alone had been successful. Drawing himself up to his full five feet and three inches he looked down at his personal servant who had been polishing his master's shoes under his office desk, and communicated the news. The bemused African, realizing his pay-master was expressing extreme pleasure, and knowing which side his mealy-meal was seasoned, rose from under the desk, plastered a smile from ear to ear across his face, and jumped from his left to his right foot and back several times.

'Masser Joseph right fine man, baas!'

Joseph had met Sybil Young at a dance given in Bayswater by a pollarded branch of the Rothschild family. By making astute enquiries he had been able, throughout the London season, to weave his way in and out of dances and dinners to which Sybil had been invited. His relations with the haughty young woman were straightforward enough—he placed her on a pedestal and sat at its feet, an attitude she approved—and worshipped her. Sybil had one London season behind her, and had had to come to terms with the unpalatable realisation that no member of the Rothschilds, the Sebag-Montefiores or the Waley-Cohens had shown serious interest in her. English Jewry knew her provenance. Whilst unanimous in their agreement that she was as beautiful as she was accomplished, they were as snobbish as their hosts, the English, and Sybil's father was a travelling salesman. For her part, Sybil was determined not to marry out, however persuasive Sir Avon Smythe, and she was certainly not making herself available to trade, and although a South African cut no figure in London society, a rich doctor of South African extraction (she would do something about the terrible accent in due course) *was* a possibility.

Sybil had been blessed with an abundance of auburn curls, a straight back, a slim figure and somewhat above average height. She had cold grey eyes and thin lips and unless she remembered to appear interested in what she was being told, or at what she was required to direct her gaze, her mien was expressionless. She had been taught at dancing class that it was *comme il faut* to eschew enthusiasm. And so it was she affected indifference and a languid pose towards life, and directed her gaze, particularly towards men, from lowered eyelids. Within the family circle no one ever crossed Sybil. Her very presence was regarded as a privilege; she performed as it was deemed correct to perform and was gracious in accepting praise for so doing. Her mother and father were aware of her coldness but interpreted it as a sign of good breeding and therefore an essential ingredient for social success—and a good marriage. It had been their greatest pleasure to indulge her.

Sybil had to contend with the none too agreeable fact that her family originated in central Europe ('thank God not from Poland, though'), and was neither rich nor educated. Fortunately, her parents had had the good sense to send her for a year to Aunt Rosie in Paris to 'finish' her. 'Finishing' expressed itself in the acquisition of a variety of accomplishments with which Jane Austen's heroines would have felt well satisfied. Sybil sang sweetly to her own skilled accompaniment, embroidered exquisitely, and was able to reproduce a likeness from nature. 'Tante' had married for love and notwithstanding achieved an enviable position in French society by judicious dealing on the Bourse. Sybil's cousins were generous in sharing with her the benefits they had reaped. Sybil's finely tuned ear helped her with her French pronunciation and her eye, assisted by her cousins' fashion sense, led her to dress more stylishly than her English rivals. Her doting parents mortgaged themselves to the hilt to equip her with the extensive wardrobe 'Tante' indicated was the minimum required by a young woman looking for a husband more privileged than herself.

Not long after his return from Paris Joseph's cup was to overflow. He was in Sulka, poring over swatches of shirt materials, when he bumped into Sir Avon Smythe, a young man whose father was one of the directors of the Bank of England.

'So sorry you won't be at the Applebys' on the 14th, old man,' Sir Avon mumbled over an adjacent swatch. 'And I hear the beautiful Miss Young is otherwise engaged! I've got tickets for a show—Naunton Wayne and Millie Sim—I'm sure she'd love it but when shall I see her?' Sir Avon whined theatrically. But Joseph was not listening to that part of the conversation. The word 'engaged' had startled him and he saw no reason to account for his own absence from the Applebys' to Sir Avon, who attended many of the same parties as he and Sybil and was a rival for her attentions. But should he be relieved that Sybil would not be there? At least Sir Avon would not be sitting at her feet. Would someone else, however? And where? Joseph would not be at the Applebys' because he would be in synagogue observing the Eve of the Day of Atonement. Could it possibly be that Sybil would be likewise engaged? His pulse raced; he selected an unsuitable silk, and in a loud voice ordered a shirt to be charged to his account. He almost ran up Bond Street back to his flat in Portland Place; he went straight to the telephone.

'Lenny, will you do something for me? Ring Sybil Young and ask her to dine with you on the 14th.'

'My dear Jo, it's the Eve of *Yom Kippur*.

'Precisely!'

'I don't get you.'

'It'll establish her credentials.' With the help of Lenny, whose call to Sybil concluded with some embarrassment and not a little colonial ineptitude and did not convince *him* of her religious affiliation, but only that she did not want to dine with him, Joseph satisfied himself that Sybil's background was remarkably like his own. While his family had been leaping on a boat in the Baltic to avoid the attentions of the murderous Cossacks, hers had been jumping on an ox-cart somewhere south of Sophia.

Joseph asked Sybil for her hand in marriage and Sybil, her eyes lowered and her expression impenetrable, nodded her assent. It had never crossed her mind to marry for love.

For the first two years, Sybil enjoyed the status marriage to a doctor assured her. For his part, Joseph enjoyed the unexpected achievement of having acquired an accomplished and elegant wife who did not remotely resemble the vulgar South African girls with whom he had been raised and with whom Baruch had expected him to share his life. Sybil's taste led her to furnish the Nash house in Regent's Park strictly in period. She disdained the fashionable Art Deco, feeling much safer with style that had been long accepted. Joseph never tired of listening to the compliments showered on his wife by everyone who entered the house. When Rubinstein came to entertain some dinner guests and Gerhardt to sing, Sybil was so overjoyed by her conquests that she came to Joseph when the guests had gone and told him that without him she could never have achieved such heights. Sybil had traded love for power and found it deeply fulfilling.

Had either known, Joseph was no more than head-over-heels in awe of Sybil and Sybil no more than satisfied to have added to her accomplishments that of wedlock. But neither did know.

And this was the climate into which their daughter Portia was shortly born. Sybil's pregnancy started as a pleasure—her latest accomplishment—but its inevitability and tendency to disfigure made it unpalatable after three months, when Sybil was overwhelmed by the sense that with the swelling of her abdomen came the withering of her youth. Unable to accept or offer social entertainments, Sybil was entirely dependent upon Joseph's attentions, which were absorbed by his patients. It was during her pregnancy that Sybil started her monthly letters to her father-in-law. She described the house to him; she elaborated on Joseph's remarkable career; she sent him photographs taken on holidays they took abroad. And the result of her regular and long letters was another conquest.

In her mother's estimation, Portia was born six weeks later than nature intended, thus incommoding her from her conception. Unlikely though this reckoning was, Joseph knew better than to question Sybil on the matter. The baby was certainly advanced; she emerged into the world pearly-pink and unwrinkled, with a head of golden curls and ten perfect fingernails. The midwife remarked on the baby's first cry; it was one of sheer joy to be alive, she said to the gynaecologist. Joseph, who counted his relations with little girls the most satisfactory of all, was delighted to have a daughter.

'She's exquisite!' he murmured to Sybil on first sight of Portia.

'And me? Am 1 not exquisite?'

Sybil was shocked to discover that the nanny she had engaged to look after Portia expected to take a day off a week as well as every Sunday afternoon; she solved this inconvenience by asking an infertile friend to take over on Tuesdays, explaining that she was not going to entrust her own flesh and blood to any of the maids. On Sunday afternoons, when Sybil habitually attended a concert at the Queen's Hall, Joseph cared for the baby.

In the early stages of her life, when Portia was confined to pen, cot or pram, she presented few problems and Sybil was able, largely, to ignore her. But by the time she was three, Sybil found her presence all too burdensome. The joyful baby metamorphosed into a sad, disturbed little girl with straight hair, bitten finger-nails and a nervous stutter. Furthermore, she was obsessed with the vision of a night visitor; an old wizened woman who, she insisted, stole into her nursery dressed from head to foot in a green cloak that concealed all but half of her decomposed face. She sat bent forward on the wicker chair (that creaked), until Portia went to sleep, and then slid over to the child's bed and strangled her. Because both Sybil and Nanny dismissed the visitor, 'there's no such person, Portia', because each responded, 'you're imagining things', frustration and fury against Sybil and Nanny were added to her terror. The child often woke from her trauma at two in the morning and screamed until dawn. Sybil's reaction was to buy herself ear plugs, banish Portia to the room over the garage and give Nanny a bedroom in the attic.

It was late 1935. Baruch signalled his intention of visiting Europe the following summer. He would stay with Joseph and Sybil before going on to Germany where he would try to persuade two of his deceased partner's relatives to get out while they still could. Storm clouds were gathering. Perhaps they were easier to see from afar. Joseph wondered whether Sybil would manage a measure of warmth towards his father who had in the past been disorientated by her manner; his father mistook her elegant letters for a greater interest in him than Sybil felt.

At the same time as Baruch was making his plans Hitler was making his. Joseph and Sybil were sitting in the dressing-room, Sybil working a tapestry and Joseph reading *The Times*. Most uncharacteristically, for she could not bear being read to, Joseph quoted out loud: 'Nothing like the complete disinheritance and segregation of Jewish citizens now announced has been heard since medieval times.' Sybil replied that she had been approached to lend the house for a fund-raising luncheon to bring out from Germany (she thought) some Jewish children but had not really wished to get herself involved: 'I've enough on my plate with the musicians' charity,' she added by way of explanation. Joseph stopped reading out loud. It was not that his wife had silenced him but that a lump had risen in his throat and he was incapable of speech. He was reading a report about a Jewish doctor in Berlin who had been sent to a concentration camp for 'race defilement'; in order to save the life of a non-Jewish patient he had given the man a transfusion of his own blood. The lump in Joseph's throat was the first he had experienced since the death of his mother. Unless he was careful his mind was going to flood with memories and pains. He rose quickly from his chair and said in an unexpectedly loud voice,

'I'm not having Father visit Europe. We'll go out to Jo'burg.'

'Oh, must we? I'd far rather drive down to Nice.'

'There's going to be a war,' Joseph told his wife.

'Really?' she asked, dipping her needle in and out of a bunch of flowers, 'and when will that be?'

It was Tuesday afternoon. Sybil's infertile friend had been called to her mother's sick-bed and Sybil found herself in the alien and unwelcome position of having to supervise her daughter. On reflection, she judged it would be less of a strain to take Portia shopping with her than to entertain the child in the nursery; and so it was mother and daughter found themselves together in Cattlaya, the florist's shop owned by Miss Pym. Miss Pym invariably remarked on Portia's beauty. On this occasion she did so not only because it struck her but because she judged it would flatter the mother, and she accompanied her words with a bunch of violets she pressed into the hands of the little girl.

'How kind! Say thank you to Miss Pym,' Sybil murmured, as unenthusiastically as her grasp of graciousness demanded. Portia looked at Miss Pym, snatched the violets and in a loud voice said,

'Ta!'

Sybil was stunned: where did the child pick up that sort of language? She must impress upon Nanny that Portia was to be kept out of the kitchen. Meanwhile Portia disappeared under the eucalyptus foliage, into a corner where she sat concealed on an upturned box. Sybil took it for granted that Miss Pym would always come forward to serve her personally, and would not delegate her assistant, Valerie, to receive her. Miss Pym judged that Valerie might not treat Mrs Grossman with the servility owed to so healthy a bank balance. Whereas Valerie knew a species rose from a hybrid, she did not have an equal talent for distinguishing between the highly valued and the less valued customer. Sybil was gratified to be served by the same Miss Pym who had served Clarissa Dalloway with flowers for her celebrated party in the days when Miss Pym was merely an assistant in Bond Street, saving to open her own premises. Sybil identified with Clarissa; she too liked to give parties, bring people together. She too, after seven years of marriage to Joseph, wondered whether she might not have achieved more by marrying out, by marrying Sir Avon Smythe. He might have made a more stimulating husband and assured her of the central position in his life and not insisted upon parenthood. And now there was all this trouble in Europe in which she was going to be involved. Joseph was clever, at least in his professional life. But he was not commanding in his private life, and would never show the panache and social case Sybil regarded as a necessary accompaniment to her own gifts.

'Yes, Miss Pym, white lilacs; masses of them, if you please. I want a white May in all my rooms!'

Miss Pym, said she would have the delivery boy cycle over with the flowers that evening. With a piece of white chalk she deftly marked three green jugs containing lilac with the letter 'G'. Sybil watched Miss Pym lean humped-back over the book as she wrote out the order with her left hand. Sybil was suffused with a desire to be particularly solicitous to poor Miss Pym, a woman who not only had that nasty disadvantage of left-handedness but many others too. Who would ever marry a stick insect with so pasty a complexion, so flat a chest, so curved a spine, and hands wrinkled and red as if they had been stood in cold water with the flowers?

'We must go now, Portia. We mustn't keep Miss Pym; she has work to do.' A rustle in the eucalyptus leaves heralded the re-emergence of Portia, clutching her violets.

'Say goodbye to Miss Pym. And thank her—nicely this time—for the violets.'

'I don't want to!'

The two women looked at one another. Miss Pym indicated by

her expression that 'children will be children' and that it was quite natural for a child of Portia's age to behave as she was behaving. Sybil indicated by her expression that children were a mystery to her, that she despaired of Portia, and that somehow it was seemly for a woman in her position not to be able to control a child; it was an expression that indicated, moreover, how exhausting child rearing was and what efforts she had to make to conceal the fact. And as the two women exchanged their unspoken points a green tin jug filled with madonna lilies fell from its perch, bringing down in its wake several other green tin jugs crammed with roses, carnations, stocks, and branches of viburnum and deutzia. The child watched fascinated as water cascaded down the plinths and over the floor.

Miss Pym's sensible shoes and overall were some protection against the flood; Sybil's chiffon ensemble, white silk stockings and shoes were not; her soaked dress and jacket clung to her body as if in fright. She wondered whether she should apologize to Miss Pym but quickly dismissed the idea as being unfitting. Miss Pym wondered whether she should comment upon the incident but dismissed the idea as being unfitting. Meanwhile, Portia slopped happily on the stone floor, kicking up the pools of water, and murmuring over the scattered blooms,

'Poor fflowers!They're swimming Mummy! Poor fflowers!'

It was half a mile from Cattlaya to the Grossmans' house. Sybil led Portia back through the park by the scruff of her neck. She dragged the child upstairs and threw her into the nursery and locked the door behind her.

'You'll stay there until Daddy comes home. And then he'll give you a thoroughly good hiding.' Portia sat down at the child-size table on a child-size chair and had a tea-party with Edward, her bear.

'Do you take Chchina tea, Mr Bear, or would you brefer Indian?' Leaning toward the bear, who was seated in a second child-size chair opposite her, Portia placed the bunch of violets between his paws,

'I bought you these from the jjungle, Edward Bear!'

No sooner had Joseph put the key in the lock than Sybil appeared in the hall ready to launch into the drama in which she would play the victimized heroine seeking justifiable redress from one who owed his all to her.

In the early months of their marriage the ice-princess had melted just sufficiently to permit her husband's admiration to express itself in occasional acts of desire. But following the birth of Portia, Sybil's narcissism and her determination to avoid further children combined to reinstate her frozen image more impermeably than ever. Although determined to keep Joseph's admiration at arm's length, she calculated that she might have to submit to his desire from time to time. But the intervals had lengthened and Joseph had sought out Cissy.
It was only when her husband became physically incapable of making love that Sybil started to reflect on her marriage and Joseph's love for her. She judged that the two matters were independent of one another. The marriage was a social contract and, as such, worked well. Joseph's love for her, on the other hand, was wanting. According to conventional wisdom, admiration on the part of the husband for the wife should find its expression in acts of passion. It was not enough for Joseph to say he admired her, he should demonstrate the fact. She did not wish to subject herself regularly to his sexual appetite but, she felt, he should show gallantry, and impotence fell short of that. He had no problem expressing his love for Portia; he positively slobbered over the little girl, and spoilt her outrageously. She could do nought wrong in his eyes. There was something obscene—unnatural—in his love for Portia.

And it was only when Joseph realized that he was physically impotent with his wife that he reviewed his marriage and his relationship with Sybil. So far as the outward form of the marriage was concerned he was well satisfied. He was proud of Sybil, she was beautiful, she dressed elegantly and it was a joy to load her with jewellery. He could confidently lay claim to the most scrupulously maintained house, presided over by the most gracious hostess in London. Sibyl gathered illustrious company to her dinner table; she served impeccable food, faultlessly cooked, and kept an exceptional cellar. As a couple, they enjoyed the same plays and the same classical music—a recent visit to *Glamorous Nights* at Drury Lane, in which their friend Ivor Novello appeared, had been a particular success. And now that the purchase of modem art was becoming so fashionable, he enjoyed as much as Sybil being courted by the art dealers. He might not have chosen the Picasso drawing himself but the Eddy Woolf portrait pleased him; he liked knowing the artist personally. Joseph thought back to Baruch and Johannesburg: he had come a long way in a short time. It did not enter his thoughts that he might, en route, have stubbed his toe on the pedestal he had made for his wife. However, it was somewhat embarrassing to find oneself impotent with one's wife even if, over the years, she had shown precious little enthusiasm for sexual congress. Perhaps his problem was actually a relief to her? But if that were the case, why did she pout and look forlorn as if offended? He made a note to pop into Boucheron and buy the sapphires he had noticed in the window when last he ordered shirts at Sulka. And he resolved to show more interest in Sybil's fund-raising for the Home for Aged Musicians.

On the whole Joseph was well pleased with himself. He had a successful practice, a consultancy at a teaching hospital; he had been made President of the British Cancer Committee. The wives of his colleagues were flattering in their attentions and so too were his women patients; they made him feel entirely desirable. Given half the chance, he was confident that he would be well able to satisfy them all. From time to time he had been the butt of some anti-Semitism but he could honestly say that it had never affected him emotionally. Meanwhile, Cissy never complained—unless to regret that he only found two hours a week to spend with her. Perhaps he would organise a surprise for Sybil: drop everything, take a week off to motor up to Scotland. Soon there would be war and no question of holidays.... Meanwhile, there were queues of young doctors waiting to do a locum for him. Sybil liked that vast Edwardian hotel ... and the soft air in Scotland in summer was particularly suited to her constitution, being neither too hot nor too cold and always moist for her complexion. Yes, that was what he would do. And he would astonish her with the sapphires there, in the moonlight, on the terrace....

'The child's impossible! She's uncontrollable and she's insolent. She takes not one iota of notice of any instruction 1 give her. She's wilful. She does these things to test me, to annoy me and to humiliate me. You've got to show her once and for all, you won't put up with me being treated in this way!'

'Sybil! She's five!'

'She may well be five but she knows perfectly well what she's up to. And if you don't make it clear now who's who and what's what, you'll have a little criminal on your hands by the time she's seven. She's no respect for authority, that's her trouble. She'll end up with no friends and no school'll keep her. I'll wager that before long we'll find ourselves with a so-called "difficult" child on our hands and I'll be spending three afternoons a week at the Tavistock Clinic!'

'I'll have a word with her.'

'No you won't! Words are not what are needed: you'll give her a sound thrashing! That's what she deserves and that's the only language she understands!'

Sibyl unlocked the nursery door. Portia was on her bed, asleep; she had her right thumb locked in her mouth and her left arm round Edward. Without warning, Sybil pulled the child's arm free of the bear and dragged her off the bed. Portia was still with fear.

'You're hurting! You're hurting, Mummy!' she screamed.

'Nothing like the hurting you're going to get, you little beast. Daddy's here.'

What was intended as a threat spelt relief. Portia tore herself free from Sybil's grasp and rushed towards her father's outstretched arms and kissed him:

'Ddaddy! Ddaddy! Ddaddy!' Joseph caught his daughter in his arms and hugged her to him.

'Mummy tells me you've been a very naughty little girl, my darling,' he said, kissing her face.

'Yes, I bbeen very naughty, I sssplashed Miss Pymy and Mmummy in the jungle.'

'Did you do that on purpose?'

'The water did it on purpose. It just jumped out of the jugs', Portia waved her arms about to illustrate her point, 'and made a pond.'

Joseph was entranced by his child. Sybil stood by, silently observing his seduction. She could bear it no longer and stamped her foot.

'Joseph, this child is incorrigible. She may be only five but she understands perfectly well what she's up to, and she's got to be disciplined.'

'Ddaddy, I'm hungry.'

'How's that my darling? Didn't you have your tea?'

'She most certainly did not and she won't be having her bed-time drink.' Joseph took a bar of chocolate from his pocket.

'Green peppermint cream. Your favourite! And don't forget to give Mr Bear a piece,' he whispered in Portia's ear. Portia turned to retrieve her bear from where he lay on the floor; he was lying face down where he had fallen when Sybil had pulled him off the bed. Portia picked him up and kissed him and said 'I love you Edward Bear' three times, and pressed chocolate against his leather lips.

'You're such a good bear, Edward,' she added emphatically.

And while she was absorbed in play, Joseph ushered Sybil into the drawing-room. But he left the nursery door wide open; he made a point of doing so.

'You'll do it tomorrow morning, first thing, before you leave the house!'

'No child of that age would remember what she's being beaten for by then. She almost certainly wouldn't know if I did it *now*!'

'The trouble with Portia is that she knows she can get away with murder with you. She believes you love her so much that you don't mind how she behaves—particularly to me.'

'When she's with me she behaves quite beautifully.'

'That's because you spoil her.'

'If spoiling leads to good behaviour I would prescribe over-doses of it. And if she murdered Mr Bear I'd still love her.'

' Don't be frivolous, Joseph! One of your troubles is that you won't take a firm stand.' Sybil had not chosen her words with conscious care; nor were they ones she would ever utter in another context. They had risen unbidden, but encapsulated her resentment with uncanny precision.

That evening, while Sybil talked at length to Boris Tchernickov about the charity ball he was to design and she was to organize as a fund-raising occasion for the old musicians' home, Joseph bathed Portia. He blew soap bubbles and promised not to use soap on the child's face, as Nanny always did, getting it up her nose and into her eyes where it stung. And as he lifted her into bed Portia begged him to stay, seated in the wicker chair so that the ghost wouldn't have room to sit down.

'I've told that ghost that she must never, never come again, my darling, so you won't have to worry about her. But now I've got to go and change for dinner. I'll leave the little light on ...'

When Joseph had changed and descended to the dining-room, he noticed that Sybil had left a note for Nanny on the silver salver on the hall table. He unfolded the note and read the instructions: Nanny was to bring Portia to the door of their bedroom suite at 7.30 next morning, and leave her in the corner until the doctor fetched her.

Sybil was seated before the looking-glass in her negligee giving her auburn curls their one hundred strokes when she caught sight of Joseph, sitting in bed, admiringly watching her. She turned to face him:

'Boris says he's sure you'll get a knighthood. I'd like that,' she murmured. 'Sir Joseph and Lady Grossman! It sounds right, somehow. You're so clever, Joseph, and I was so right to marry you.' She let her negligee fall to the ground, and in her slinky nightdress she approached her husband and kissed him tenderly on the face and ran her hand round his neck before slipping into the twin bed by the side of his. He really must find ways to please her, he thought.

Portia was dressed in a flowered Liberty print smock. In her arms she clutched her teddy bear. She stood in the corner, her face to the wall. She was shaking. When Sybil threw open the door she stood so near to the child that Portia had to throw back her head to get her mother and now father in view. Sybil was resplendent in her satin negligee trimmed with ostrich feathers. Joseph was immaculate in his grey pinstripe suit.

Joseph crouched on his haunches and took his child's hands in one of his. He looked into her eyes.

'I'm. going to punish you, Portia, for being rude to Mummy, yesterday, in the flower shop.' He spoke slowly, quietly, 'You were a very naughty little girl, you know that, don't you? You upset Mummy. I'm going to smack you very hard so that you remember in future that it is a thoroughly wicked thing ever to upset Mummy.' He felt the bile of treachery rise in his throat. 'You mustn't upset Mummy,' he repeated more firmly as he felt increasingly uncomfortable. Portia gazed, bewildered, at her father. But as he looked into the child's face he started to see what was a condensed version of Sybil's. He turned into his dressing room. Sybil followed, dragging Portia behind her.

'Lean over Daddy's lap,' Sybil ordered. Silently, obediently, the child did as she was told. Sybil drew down the frilly knickers that matched Portia's dress and exposed her pink buttocks. With his eyes fixed on his wife's face Joseph took the ivory-handled hairbrush Sybil held out to him and landed five blows across his daughter's bottom. Portia was so stunned by the first two blows that she did not react, on the third and fourth, she screamed deafeningly in pain and terror, and on the fifth blow her sphincter gave way and Joseph's immaculate Savile Row suit received the contents of his daughter's bowels.

Joanna Pearl

Joanna Pearl was born in London a third generation Jew. She has written part of a novel exploring Jewish female identity for her recent thesis for a Master's degree in Women's Studies. She currently works for Social Services in West London, developing services for adults.

'I am keen to write about the issues which I struggle to negotiate, in particular those of assimilation and 'belonging' in both a Jewish culture and a wider society, and the search for a coherent identity. I feel that I am at a crossing point between generations and how they experience being Jewish, and that to write about the world I live in needs a new fiction.'

The Woman Who Wasn't Elijah

Under the watchful eye of her mother-in-law she eats to quell the nausea, her body craving the carbohydrate that she crams into her mouth. She feels herself swelling like dough under that tepid gaze.

'More *charoset*…?' asks the woman who refers to her as 'the Pope' behind her back and shudders every time she is forced to address her by her 'Good Catholic Name', Mary. (Mary refuses to say her name, Ramona, too, on principle). The horseradish she has just eaten is bitter on her tongue.

She nods and David slides a large piece of *matzo* across the dinner table, topped with the sweet stickiness of wine, cinnamon and apples; he squeezes her swollen fingers in an attempt at solidarity.

Inside her, the baby clamours for space.

Auntie Dolly, who appears to be tenuously connected to the family through a series of distant liaisons, insists that the front door must now be left open for the prophet Elijah, the stranger, the wandering Passover beggar who must be welcomed; she is immediately shouted down by Uncle Stan, who has rabbinical pretensions, and says that part of the service definitely comes after the meal.

There is a stand-off during which David, fearing a skirmish, discreetly puts the door on the latch.

Uncle Stan mutters darkly into his napkin and vest.

Mary realises she has been holding her breath.

She wonders if it is like this every year—this frenzy of wine-drinking, random standing up, sitting down, songs sung in rounds dissolving into forced barks of laughter; she feels she has intruded on a private party, and wonders if it has been organised purposely to exclude her. (David has told her: No, it was always like this; she'll learn to love it. She has persuaded herself that he is right). She imagines it was fun when the children were young; now the rituals seem empty and slightly ridiculous. She wonders if he feels the same about her family's chaotic Christmases.

She tells herself that they'll have a laugh about this when this evening is over and they are in the flat his parents bought him; nestled dampty against his chest under the duvet, her David will be back.

For the moment he is on temporary loan to his religion.

When the young woman slips round the door, between the roasted egg and the chicken soup, she feels the vicious kick inside her, and wonders later what her baby knew.

He sees himself as a buccaneer: daring, defying convention, sallying forth through the oceans of life; then as a sneak-thief, robbing the people he loves and leaving them bereft. He can almost feel the ropes round each wrist as they pull and call him from each direction—David, David—his mother and his wife; he almost snorts when he hears the Passover words about celebrating his freedom.

She is the stronger of the two, Mary; she could reel him in with one jerk of the wrist, and he would be hers.

He is hers.

She is small and round like the rest of her family, like the Easter eggs she buys her nephews—with the baby well on its way, she is the same shape as her mother. Sandwiched between her and her parents on their torn sofa on Sundays after church, he is like an exclamation mark between two commas. They put their hands over their mouths when Mary's Uncle Si calls someone a Jew-boy in front of him; are they shocked or are they laughing?

He feels a twist of love for his mother who shops at Harrods to prove she has 'made it', and caters for ten too many at every 'do,' then another twist for Mary who buys her clothes at jumble sales and wolfs down pork chops with an anxious eye on him.
(Her aunt who lives in Devon finds a butcher who sells 'kosher' meat, probably the only one for fifty miles; she makes a trifle with 'pareve' cream especially for him—no milk after meat. He feels his cheeks burning as the rest of her family gape at him at every mouthful).

She seems to be listening intently as his Dad rushes full-tilt through the service, jumbling and slurring his mechanical Hebrew in an effort to reach the meal as quickly as possible. Her face is fixed and serious and her lips pursed; her hands are cupped around the baby, shielding it.

He notices that no one else is concentrating: his mother is inspecting her nails; Stan is peering at the 'matzo' box as if decoding an ancient Aramaic text; Dolly is rummaging through her handbag, scattering the debris beside her plate. They are together and alone.

The cup of wine sits expectantly on the sideboard, waiting to be claimed by Elijah, the Jewish version of Santa Claus. (How was it that when he was a child, the wine was always drunk by the end of the evening but he never saw anyone near it?)

He wants to catch her eye but he doesn't seem able to; she looks as if she is far away.

They dip their little fingers in and out of the wine ten times, symbol of the blood of baby boys murdered by the Pharaoh, one drop for each of the plagues inflicted on the Egyptians. He sees her lick her finger, and wants to tell her: No, that's bad luck!—but he stops himself.

When the young woman enters the room, he feels as if they have all been roused with icy water from a deep, warm sleep.

The door creaks as it opens and cold air rushes in; six heads turn, startled; six pairs of eyes stare. Hers meet theirs. She smiles.

Mary sees that her front teeth are chipped.

The woman says that she is the daughter of the new couple from downstairs; she came from up North to surprise them, but, unexpectedly, they aren't here.

There is a silence.

She shifts her large shoulder bag, looks at the table. 'I came for *seder* night,' she says, establishing her Jewish credentials, giving them no option.

Again there is a silence, until they are forced to invite her in. (No one dares to say that they left the door ajar—ajar but not open—because custom dictates that they must).

She takes her place at the table, between Mary and David. 'Oh, you're pregnant!' she says, and she reaches out and touches Mary's stomach.

Her hand is cold against the heat of the baby.

She is served chopped liver and eats it quickly, her head low over the plate.

Mary is aware that she is watching the younger woman devouring the food; waiting. Mary asks her where she lives, and the girl answers, 'The North side of Manchester. Do you know it?'

Mary replies that she doesn't. She, who is normally curious to the point of near-rudeness, cannot think of a single question to ask.

The girl asks Dolly and Stan about themselves, drawing them out; Dolly is reluctant at first, but is soon seduced into animation, waving her hands and talking fast as if she must use all her words before she is stopped.

There is a clatter of dishes as David and the girl stand together to help Ramona into the kitchen.

Mary realises that no one has asked the girl's name.

The baby is still.

She is sweating and there are damp crescents under her arms, marking the fabric of her dress. She notices that her cross is showing and she hides it under her shirt.

When the girl comes back into the room, she is holding the chicken aloft; it is a huge, brown, glistening bird, flanked with vegetables, and the guests clap their appreciation.

They wonder how they thought her plain when she arrived. As the plates of food are eaten, she tells them about the Passovers she has known, the stories she was told, and, gradually, they tell her theirs too. She holds her audience captive, and her face is shining and alive. Each feels that he or she is the central object of her attention; even Uncle Stan switches from monosyllables to full sentences in her presence.

Their elbows, fingers, forearms touch as they pass dishes between them; they feel the warmth of each others' bodies.

When she says her name—Miriam—David sees his mother nod her approval.

He is reminded of when he and Stevie and the cousins were young. There was laughing and joking round the table; most years they drank, giggled too much, and fell asleep in the tangle of legs under the table. He realises he looked forward to Passover, willing it nearer for days beforehand. The excitement started when he took his 'Pesach Haggadah' out of the sideboard, fingering the worn pages and pulling Moses in and out of the bulrushes on a tab; he thought of the wicked Pharaoh as a dog because Lucy-at-school had a dog called Pharaoh.

Now Stevie—his little brother Stevie—is at university and the cousins are scattered across the world. Aunt Dolly, who always seemed so vibrant and quick-witted, is old and hard of hearing; Uncle Stan, the wide-boy cabbie, is surly and reclusive. Suddenly he sees them as they were, as they really are, and feels a surge of schoolboy love for them.

When the sponge cake is passed round, they each take a slice, one for everyone, and they are united in a circle of togetherness.

Only Mary refuses a piece—it's just as well because one too few has been cut. This is one of the rare waking moments in the last month when she is not transferring food from sausage-fingers to mouth to yawning stomach; suddenly her hunger has abated.

The baby's hunger is gone.

She wonders at the rest of them, chattering and swapping tales, carried away on a wave of need, lured by this thin dark reed of a woman, her bony wrists jutting from frayed cuffs, her hands like claws.

Can no one else see that those hands have only ever taken?

And their hands reach back to hers, wanting to give, to trust her with their hospitality.

Who is she? Why is she here?

And where is David, her David, overtaken by this man whose face is flushed and whose voice has the sound of a happier time?

As she stands up, she feels the rush of fluid down her legs—*released not broken*, they told her at her childbirth classes—and she knows that the end is beginning.

Ruth Joseph

Ruth Joseph grew up in Cardiff. After working as a freelance journalist, she is now completing her M. Phil. in Creative Writing at Glamorgan University. A Rhys Davies prize-winner, she has had work accepted for *Honno Modern Fiction, New Welsh Review* and *Cambrensis*. She lives with her husband and two children in Wales.

'Although I come from a religious background, it is the cultural heritage of the Jews that inspires me. I revel in the diversity and vibrancy of our literature, art and music. However, I feel a responsibility as a Jewish woman to draw attention, through my writing, to the injustices of daily life, from bullying to the chaining of women and the treatment of asylum seekers.'

Patchwork

They have confined me to a hospital bed. They think I am ill. But they are wrong. I am content within my cell-like withdrawal. The alabaster whiteness of the walls and the bleached linen of the sheets have created a perfect cocoon. There is no sink, no toilet. No place where I can eliminate, evacuate. But I have my ways. The nurse in charge of me is not vigilant. She uses my toilet time to phone her friends. So far I have been lucky.

Every day a doctor comes to visit me. Although he's a he, he is not a man. He just wears man's clothes and a starched ivory coat—a bloodless arrangement of person, with a stethoscope around an anaemic neck and pewter grey hair. He is accompanied by a nurse. He brings a weighing scales and talks to me of food, of eating, of gaining weight, of the outside world, of my need to join these people. But I have no such desires.

Sometimes a window cleaner washes the outer contaminated glass of my window. He is man. I watch him as I lie in my bed. I see the tight T-shirt pulled over muscled shoulders pushing a chamois over the glass, the arms etched with dark hairs, the ligaments roped like strong twine, . He pretends not to see me. He is told to keep his eyes averted.

I have brought my patchwork. It projects my mind away from their constant nagging, and uses up a few calories. I was going to cut the pieces here. I would enjoy watching the silver steel of my tailor's knife lacerate and cleave seams carefully sewn. But they found the scissors concealed in my bag and removed them. Close with a suicide's bracelet? They do not understand.

I was allowed to bring the pieces, ready cut. My mother supervised the preparation. She said that it would not be good, not be perfect, for all the fabrics are different and for a patchwork quilt, each fabric has to be of equal density and of similar type. But flawlessness is not the object of the making. She always needs the ideal, strives for the unattainable that I, too, am supposed to crave. I like to mix the colours, palette bright, in my colourless cell, lying on my blanched bedcovers. They vibrate with their own violent energies.

I start with my brown, cotton, striped school dress. They do not understand the pleasure I derive slicing and bruising the fabric. There is a smell about it—a damp, sweaty, chalky mix of cooked cabbage and fecund bodies. A time when the carved wooden panels ached with the fears of the inadequate, and the ink-splotched desks held their young captives prisoner. 'We expect you to do well. We did not have all your advantages. Your mother and I were lucky to get out when the rest of the family perished. We have had to work, save, and sacrifice for you to get to that school.'

Cut it with knives. Blade its existence. Sew it into something that is mine. My design—perfectly imperfect.

Royal Blue is the uniform colour of the towels from my school showers—they reek with a nauseous smell of chlorine, foot dip and cheap deodorants. 'Please Miss. I can't do games this week. Can I be excused? Can I be excused showers?' The cream and dark green tiled walls shiver with the echoes of the misunderstood. I have developed early. I am a full-breasted woman with a mid-European bone structure, solid, heavy. My nipples are tight, erect with fear. Lithesome girls with tight, tiny breasts nudge each other, giggle behind my back. Some are staring. I run my fingers over the harsh terry cloth. 'It will spoil the patchwork,' my mother says. But it has to be executed. Cut it. Make it into pieces. It has lost its life.

Yellow is the seersucker tablecloth from my home. It lay on the kitchen table listening to the murmuring of the ancient fridge and the constant bubbling of a pot on the stove. Sometimes it is chicken soup, steaming with golden carrots, onions, and celery, creamy barley and beans; or green pea soup so thick that we would joke about having a slice for supper. My mother's tiny green glass vase from her first life sat on that cloth. It had been wrapped in a peasant shawl with her candlesticks and a few photographs when she ran. I'm sorry I broke it. Yellow is the cadmium colour of the wallpaper of my bedroom; of golden egg yolks and rich butter; of sticky dried apricots chopped with peel and moist bananas crushed with the zesty juices and rinds of sharp, knobbly lemons. Whip them together. Beat in the sugar. Fold in the soft white flour. Make a cake for Daddy for his tea… Not for me.

Pink is the nylon tulle dress from my Barbie. 'Why do you have to have such a doll? We never had such dolls in the old country. Such a strange birthday present for a child of thirteen!' But she is perfect. She is beautiful. She is thin with long, blond silky hair, shapely breasts, no stomach and no sex hair. I want to be her. She makes it impossible. Cut her dress. Finish it.

Purple is the colour of my cheap Lycra bathing costume. We sit together—a day at the seaside. But the parents keep their clothes on. My father rolls up his black trouser legs, exposing white skin and blue, cabled veins. My mother unbuttons her blouse a little. I see creases in her breasts. She looks at my father. They laugh and then, a little uncomfortable, they look at me. My mother's face goes pink. I do not like the feeling. I do not like the look my Uncle Saul gives me when I have to relinquish my towel from around my body, to run into the sea. When I am away from them, it is beautiful. I feel the smack of the wind hitting my face, the fingers of the warm sun—touching, loving, unconditional. But then I have to return. To Uncle Saul's eyes 'smirring' over my body, through the stretchy costume, to my secret places. Cut into slivers with the honed silver steel. It curls as it cuts. Decimate it.

Mamma does not fuss as we slice my old pinafore into neat squares. The background is cream with tiny green and pink flowers. Though she does not see why it has to go. It saves the good clothes…always save…keep for best. Help Mamma in the kitchen. We have to cook a special meal. Uncle Saul is coming for supper. Mamma is excited. *Gefilte* fish to start—fluffy, poached balls of fish lying cold on glass plates decorated with a slice of carrot. Then *borscht*, soup the colour of blood. 'Grate the beetroot darling. Uncle Saul loves a good soup.' Then Mamma takes the boiling chicken that has flavoured the soup and sets it in a casserole to brown with rice in its bed and more carrots. Dessert is my job. 'Make the pastry. You have such a light hand.' I enjoy rubbing the sticky margarine into the flour with a little vanilla sugar, and seeing the whole come to a pliant ball with lemon and egg. Mamma has gone upstairs to wash and change. Uncle Saul comes early. I have just finished putting the sliced apples into the pie with cinnamon and sultanas. I am putting the pastry on the top. I used to love the smell of cinnamon. Now I hate it. Cut up the apron. Get rid of its face.

Red is the colour of my best *Shabbat* dress, now a year old. I love its sleek velvet fabric and the garnet colour is reminiscent of autumn light through the synagogue stained glass windows. It is Friday night—the highlight of the week. We sit around the solid, dining room table laid with the best snowy, damask cloth. The polished silver candlesticks bear ivory candles; they cast a gentle flickering luminance over the waiting family. The *kiddush* cups have been polished bright and two vast crusty *challot* sit under their white embroidered cover waiting for my father's blessing. He trickles the blood-coloured liquid into the silver *bechas*. It is one of my favourite sounds. We stand for *kiddush*—the Sabbath blessing. As we rise, the white pearly buttons on my dress pop, exposing my new bra. My little brother giggles and my father mutters something to my mother about me developing and having a suitable dress for a woman, not a child. But I do not want…

Grey is the colour of my father's face. I have no fabric for his face. I hear him talking to the doctor outside my door—hushed sounds not words.

My mother is upset that I want to cut all these materials. 'It is a waste to cut up good things. They could be passed on and I could sell the red dress,' she says. But the doctor is on my side and says they have to indulge me. When he visited me this time, he wanted to examine my body. As he pulled back my nightdress, revealing my shrunken breasts and bloated stomach, he discovered the belt from my red dress pulled tight about my waist. 'What is this here for?' he said gently, as if talking to a small child. 'It keeps me safe,' I whispered. I dare not tell him that every day I pull it a bit tighter. It stops my appetite. 'But it is stopping your blood,' he said in his sing-song voice. Yes, my blood has stopped, the other blood, the woman's blood. When the doctor goes, his face too is grey like my father's. I pull off my nightdress and look at my body. There is no mirror in my room. It is not allowed. They say that I am thin—that I could lose my life, but I only see fat, bulges of blubber poured into skin, covered by a soft fluffy down.

My father returns. He has talked to the doctor. He says that if I would eat a little, I can go on a long holiday to Italy. Sit in the sun.

Drink coffee in a dusty piazza. Lie in a chair watching mists clear over slate-blue mountains with tall cypresses standing on tiptoe for a better view. Listen to cicadas sounding like old wristwatches being rewound, and gentle bird song in vast magnolia trees.

I am going to try to eat. My father's grey face upsets me too much. I do not want to hurt him.

****

I am sitting at the side of a glittering lake. Small ochre and terracotta-coloured buildings cleave to gentle slopes and the sounds of clinking church bells bless the sunlit landscape. The colours of my patchwork have found new meaning.

The brown and white striped cotton has been pin-tucked and transformed into an arch of reeds at the edge of the lake, safe-keeping grebes, mallards and a flotilla of swans. Below its ankles, rainbows of small fish arrow through craggy shards of granite and marble.

Blue is the lake water—navy and turquoise wrinkled silk sprinkled with sequins of sunlight basted to a muslin sky and pinned and tacked by tiny pen-and-ink sailing boats.

Yellow are the fields of sunflowers, rough cloth of *girasole* that point their seeded heads to the warming sun, and fields of maize, their spires golden as they ripen and climb to the light.

Pink is the polished marble of Verona. We feel its hardness and its history at our feet as we walk. Pink is also the colour of soft tulle sunsets on the lake when the sun is tired and waits for the silver attendance of the moon.

Purple is embroidered bougainvillea, hugging sunlit loggias with violet passion. And freckles of tiny scabious and wild cyclamen decorating, petit point, the hedgerows and cool, shady woods where blackberries and blueberries wait for the plucking.

My apron is now a sunlit meadow of light cotton organza which holds its summer flowers outstretched to the light. It is the host to ancient olive trees spreading convoluted branches, legend telling as they sit and wait for another harvest.

My colour red is still wine, but not the bloody, fortified stuff of religion. It is the light pourings of crushed grapes tasting of warm vineyards and laughter. Red is also the colour of my new cotton sundress. My mother is pleased. She tells me it is a good shape and that I look better.

My father has lost the grey from his face. He makes jokes with my mother and from time to time I see him look at me. They think that I am cured and this makes them happy.

Except Italy has given me a new way of living. I have discovered a way to eat which keeps them, and me, contented. They see me eat pasta with rich tomato sauce; relish pizzas crisp out of fire baked ovens; lick ice creams made of crushed strawberries folded with whipped cream; feast on peaches and nectarines from gentle orchards with the bloom kissing their skins.

But now I have discovered a trick. It is a conspiracy between my two fingers, the back of my throat and my stomach. I eat my whole meal. They watch and smile at each other. At the end of the meal, I excuse myself, and then it is done—a couple of minutes and all is eliminated. It is easy to check that everything is out. At last, I can taste and eat all the things I would never allow myself. Sometimes I eat just for the eating. I force down cold pasta waiting for tomorrow's sauces, ice cream and chocolate till my body will burst with the forcing. In the black velvet when they are asleep with only the rhythm of the fridge playing its music, I stuff...gorge... lust after food. But my woman's blood has not, will not, return.

****

We are home. Italy is past. Smudgy grey skies saturated with ice skewers of rain make stabbing autumn sounds on the outside of the house. They talk of my education. I must go back to school. I do not want to be with those people. Tomorrow Uncle Saul and Aunty Millie will eat with us. He is here now, staying the night, as he wants to go to our synagogue tomorrow morning with my father. We have been busy all day preparing a special meal for *Rosh Hashanah.* In the fridge are two fat balls of pastry, resting, waiting for me to attend to them. The one pastry is a light short-crust that I have to make into a pie; the other is richer, for biscuits.

All last night, I lay on my bed immobile, rigid with fear. It is now early morning and I cannot stay in my room. I need to eat to drown the furies. But I have to be careful now I am home. They watch me all the time. The doctor has warned them. He is suspicious about my condition—my little conjuring trick. As I walk down the stairs I feel my heart banging in my throat. My body shakes. My stomach is screaming. I go to the fridge door. What can I take? There is a whole chicken, intact—I can't touch that. We have made *kneidlekh.* I push them in my mouth, raw salty dough, putting others together so that they will not detect any disappearances. I go to the cupboards. I eat cereal, raw cereal without milk, dry so that it makes me cough; put fingers in golden syrup, strings, sticky over my body. Faster, faster. Two lumps of pastry—I cut pieces and force them in without tasting. My heart beats so fast. I feel dizzy and faint. I sink to the floor. The black and white ceramic tiles are cool to my throbbing, bloated, overheated body. I look across at the dog's bowl where my mother has left the spare pieces of meat from the soup flavouring. The dog has had enough. I look around. My father will be down soon. The day is about to start. The pieces of meat in the dog's bowl lie calling me. I take the bowl and force greasy pieces of meat into my mouth.

There is a sound at the door and Uncle Saul walks into the kitchen wearing an old faded silk dressing gown. I see his face drawn with horror.

Anna Sullivan

Anna Sullivan was born in 1939 in Hackney, East London, to a Jewish mother and a non-Jewish father who, as a communist, fought the fascists at Cable Street and served in the International Brigade. She taught Art and Creative Writing for many years and her work has been published in *Poetry Now(The Women's Press),* and in several journals. She has three children whom she has brought up mostly alone.

'Because my father was a communist and we lived in the East End, our house was always full of Jews, so I was very attracted to *yiddishkeit*, even though I had no Jewish upbringing. My younger daughter's life in Israel has brought me closer to the roots I had lost. Though I am a socialist and a feminist, as a mother I have sought common ground through my stories.'

Jerusalem Pictures

The sun dips and is gone. Terraces are silent, the shutters pulled down, and candles light the long journey into *Shabbat*. It is a time of resting, feasting and prayer. Men sway to the rhythm of words to God and sing high beautiful songs in praise of women—songs of love written long ago.

From the hills above, the Muslim call to prayer, carried on the hot tongue of the desert wind, rings out against the black sky. Over our heads the mosquito nets hang like bridal veils. I lie shrouded from such devotion, I am a stranger in this land. Love has brought me here—not for a lover's kiss, but to my daughter who has chosen to live far from me. She is slipping through my life like grains of sand.

'You could sell your clothes,' says my granddaughter, 'and buy new ones. You could cover your hair and then you could stay.'

'That isn't possible,' I say. She thinks it is as simple as changing my wardrobe, this contract with God.

'We could ask the Steiners to move,' she continues, unwilling to give up. 'Then you could come and live by us.'

'But my home is in England.'

'You could bring all your books and paints.' Her high voice relentlessly pursues the plan for my exodus to Jerusalem. I hold her close to me. We are lying under the net, hidden from the heat and I sing her to sleep; a song from the days of her mother's childhood.

It is so hot we will eat lunch on the *mirpesset*. I have learnt the Hebrew word for 'terrace'. It rolls around my tongue like wine. We are many at the table this hot *Shabbat*. Young men from the *yeshiva* far from home, seeking what is familiar in my daughter's house. Two of them are brothers. The elder, tall, handsome, with a witty tongue and a mind and soul that loves the *Torah*. His younger brother, I am told, is morose and difficult. He has been sent here because he is in trouble at home in England. His parents are in despair. The boy I meet is none of these things. Since being here, he has found his way. There are two others, polite, funny, and unbearded, learning to become like my son-in-law. Then we have an older man, new to this life. His finding of God came late.

The young men start to sing.Their voices weave together in words that I cannot understand. Some of the songs have no words at all, just ancient lines of melody. One of the boys translates a song for me. The language is rich, erotic, like the *Song of Solomon.* Their voices float across the hillside carried by the trembling wind. Bees hover over the bougainvillea, purple in the white light.

The older man is talking. 'When I find a girl to marry, we'll watch all the Woody Allen films and then never bother again.' No one watches television in this religious community, so he hopes to get such pleasures out of his system. He has been married before, has grown-up children, but now he is looking for a young wife. He hopes to start a new family and will not consider a woman of his own age. My daughter has told him of the lovely women she knows, older women who would suit him. He is not interested. In this world, where the matchmaker plays a powerful role in affairs of the heart, he has not yet found the right match. We think he never will.

Soon everyone will go, to sleep away the rest of the afternoon. It is too hot to read. I pace the rooms alone, lie down, and listen to the cicadas humming in the burning landscape.

** **

Bright light stripes the room piercing the shadows still there from the night. The sun rises early here. It grows over the hillside like tea spreading on a tablecloth staining the earth with gold. Heat spirals from the baked soil.

Voices of children invade the cool walls of the house. I hear my son-in-law moving around and then the low murmuring of his morning prayers.

There are sounds of frenetic activity outside. Important work is done early before the heat becomes overwhelming. The children carry water bottles wherever they go. They are in school by eight in the morning, and by one o'clock they climb the dusty hill roads, rucksacks on their backs, to shelter in their homes. They wait for the wind that comes roaring down the valley, to bring some respite from the wall of heat that keeps them from play.

There is a soft knocking on the door. Yesafa Malka calls to play with my grandson. She is three years old; he is a couple of months younger. She stares at me with eyes as black as night and as wary as a cat's. Children come to a standstill when they see me in the street, their curiosity unconcealed. Can my hair be real! My feet are bare, my toenails painted red. I am from the outside—another world. Yesafa Malka never speaks to me, but then she never talks to grown-ups, so I'm told. I talk to her anyway; offer her ice-cream, orange juice. She just looks at me.

I am sitting on the *mirpesset*, paintbrush in hand, trying to capture the brilliant landscape before me. Boychik, my grandson, is in the play tent with Yesafa Malka. I can hear their voices. She is speaking at length to him and ends every sentence with 'Okay?' 'Okay,' he answers. They are playing '*Abba* and *Imma*.' He has borrowed his father's black hat, his baby face glowing beneath it. They emerge from the tent and he takes her hand and leads her to his toy car, opens the door and helps her in. He sits beside her and ever so gently feeds her crisps left there from a previous visit. They are chattering, shrieking with laughter. Suddenly they realise that I am there, watching them. Boychik smiles at me and then becomes silent, punishing my intrusion.

One day Boychik asked my daughter, 'Can I go to look for Eli Sheva?' He was holding Yesafa Malka's hand at the time. Eli Sheva is her older sister. 'Yes,' said my daughter, believing her to be in the courtyard. But she wasn't, and sometime later, Eli Sheva knocked on the door asking for Yesafa Malka's return for supper. My daughter and son-in-law fled from the house, panic and fear giving them speed. They ran down the hillside, now covered in black-coated men going to early evening prayer. The words echo round the dusty roads. 'Yesafa Malka and Boychik are missing!' Everyone knows them. Images enter their minds that no one dare voice: stolen children; bodies broken, hidden by mountain bush; children in terror without comfort. In a country where hate and vengeance create terrible acts of human suffering these thoughts are ever present.

Men and women, their food left forgotten on tables, join the search.. Here people are not isolated from their neighbours. Older children run in all directions calling their names. Faces are white with anxiety; memories of loss. Yesafa Malka's mother and I stand at the top of the hill in case they should come back. We talk about everything except what is really on our minds. Forty-five minutes have passed.

And then we see them, still holding hands, in the middle of a slow procession making its way up the hill. Like the Pied Piper, my daughter walks in front; she is slowly shaking her head.

The children feel they have done no wrong. Their search for Eli Shiva just took them a long way—half way down the mountainside. They stand, flushed and solemn, as people surround them.

For a while they are confined to their own homes and balconies but it does not last long. Boychik and Yesafa Malka are soul mates.

* ***

'We should go swimming,' suggests my daughter's friend, Rachel. During their busy day the women visit each other's verandas to drink coffee and to devise ways to expand their lives. These women have a common bond. They are the returned ones. They have left their former lives where they lived without God. Now they have Hebrew names; they are the female defenders of the faith. Like women everywhere they find affection for and solidarity with each other in the difficult life they have chosen.

'We should hire a mini-bus and ask some others; share the cost,' she continues. 'It's in the Jerusalem forest,' my daughter explains to me. 'They have women-only days and it's in a beautiful place.' Any mention of a swimming pool sounds like paradise in these hills where white dust covers everything. A friend said to me once, on my return to England, 'So you brought Jerusalem back with you then, ' looking at my white covered sandals.

The bus is hired and the morning arrives as hot as a frying pan. Have we sun hats, cream, food and water? Yes, yes. Rachel is already out of her house, opposite my daughter's. The children are excited, ready in their swimsuits. The mini-bus arrives. The three of us stand and stare at it in disbelief. Rachel berates the driver. 'What's this? I asked for a ten-seater.' He shrugs. It is nothing to do with him; he is only the driver. The bus holds six, with room for one more in the front. Hannah arrives. She is heavily pregnant. 'Sit in the front seat and I will hold your little boy,' I offer. Reluctantly we set off to pick up the other women. First there will be Shula and her new baby. Rachel is shouting at the bus company on a mobile phone that she has wrested from the driver. She speaks fluent Hebrew, so we leave all such confrontations to her.

'Can you believe it? They said they had no ten-seater today so they thought anything was better than nothing! But I told them: we can't come back in this.' Cancelling the trip is not an option. This kind of thing happens all the time in Israel. Such things are seen as minor, considering what could happen at any time on any journey. Shula is waiting for us. Already we are cramped. The other two women and their children have not turned up. They are already half an hour late. The driver is getting impatient. 'Are we going or not?' he growls.

'Okay, go,' replies my daughter, 'you can drive past their street.' I think we are all hoping that they have decided to stay at home. Already I am welded to the seat with sweat, a wriggling child on my knee. Then we see them, strolling along, and they look at us in surprise as if we are too early. The bus stops abruptly at Rachel's command.

'I'm sorry,' she says to the women. 'They didn't send a big enough bus. We just can't fit any more in.' The women look upset. 'But we packed our lunch,' says one. 'Perhaps we could all try to fit in,' says my daughter. With a sigh Rachel gets out; we all follow her. Once again we try to arrange the seating. The driver is looking fed up and is talking on his mobile phone. Is he perhaps phoning the bus company to say that he will not drive us? Hannah tells me he is speaking to his wife. Rachel stands in the road and directs operations. The children are remarkably quiet and uncomplaining.The women fit themselves and their children into the smallest spaces possible.

'Right,' shouts Rachel to the driver, 'Now you can go.' The heat in the bus is suffocating. Hannah asks the driver if the air-conditioning is broken. With a grunt he switches it on. Cool air circulates around our pounding heads and sweltering bodies.

We leave the environs of Neve Yaakov. Leave the burnt hills

and move towards Jerusalem and the forest. We leave the valley and begin to climb again.

'Don't look down', says Shula, but my eyes are drawn hypnotically to the dropping landscape. The hills have had no rain for a long time. Bush and tree rendered naked by fire, stand stark and black in the orange earth. The driver rips along at high speed around the perilous bends and twists in the road. The colours of stone and earth give way to those of cypress and cedar. Ridges of emerald and dark green stretching high into the brilliant sky. The bus is very quiet now. The intimacy of such close proximity has silenced us.

The child that I hold has gone to sleep. We are driving through shaded avenues, roads cut through the forest. We stop on a high ridge. This is the place. A vast open-air pool shines below us, with many steps down to it. Trees shade the bathing area and all around are placed white chairs and loungers. We fall out of the bus, stiff. We pull out buggies and bags and the driver leaves.

'My bag, where is my bag,' cries Hannah. We look at each other then at the muddle of bags and children by the roadside. Her bag is not there. She starts to cry, her arms wrapped around her swollen abdomen. She stands rocking her body back and forth, choking on incomprehensible words. Her wild grief at the loss of her bag terrifies her child who clutches her leg and begins to wail. Rachel looks stricken.

My daughter puts her arms around Hannah and holds her close.

'Don't cry,' she says, 'It will be okay. We can get your bag back.'

'But I have all my things in it—everything,' she sobs, her weeping getting more impassioned. Anxiety shows on everyone's faces. Rachel, who feels responsible for this trip, feels guilty about the loss of the bag.

'I have a spare swimsuit that's big and stretchy; you can borrow that,' I offer.

'And I have trunks for Simy,' says Shula.

We all try to comfort her and gradually she quietens, and we set off down the steps.

Earlier on in Hannah's pregnancy, a neighbour came to my daughter's door and told her that there was a woman wandering around in the street who looked very ill, so could she come to help her? There was Hannah, by the roadside, sitting in the white rubble. Her eyes were dark, unseeing, her face empty of any recognition of her surroundings. My daughter managed to take her home. She would not acknowledge her husband. All night my daughter talked to her: about her family; about the first time they met in Jerusalem when they both decided that they wanted a different kind of life. Finally she asked Hannah if she wanted to go home and she nodded. She hadn't spoken for hours. Home for her was America.

Immigrants here often have no family network and life can become very difficult and lonely without the love and support that they grew up with. That is why the women form such loving friendships.

My daughter spoke to Hannah's husband.

'You must take her home. She is too lonely here, it's too hard for her right now.'

His response was that she would be okay.

'She won't,' argued my daughter, 'she will break down. Can't you see how ill she is already?'

He was not willing to admit how ignorant he was of his wife's unhappiness, but he took her home all the same, for a while. Now her baby will be born very soon and the women are afraid for her. They think she will be hurt too much by the difficult life here. One day they hope that she will be able to deal with what she really feels and not seek escape into madness.

I float in the pool. The water is sharp and cool. The trees weave dark patterns in the sapphire sky above me. If I close my eyes the sunlight shines dappled and golden behind my eyelids. My daughter is with me; the children floating on rings. We all hold hands and drift through the water.

****

The bus-stop is almost outside my daughter's apartment. The buses actually run on time and come every twenty minutes on the dot. We are going into Jerusalem. Once a week my daughter leaves the children at home with their father. Sometimes all she does is sit and sip coffee in one of the many cafes that line Ben Yehuda street. Only recently two bombs exploded amongst the parasoled tables. At the time she was in a second-hand bookshop on her usual search for books. The bookshop has an excellent system: you take in the books that you have read, sell them and buy back others. In England I trawl the second-hand shops for books to build up her library. Ever since she learned to read, she could never bear to be without a new book. How easy it is to take for granted the local libraries we have in London.

The bus is cool after the furnace of the morning's heat. It is a long snaking vehicle: two buses yoked together with a swaying, clanking central passage. It is the buses on this route that have been the target of suicide bombers, so getting on is like a lottery. If you live here you have to develop a facility to put such thoughts out of your mind otherwise you would never step outside the front door. But I have not attained this state of mind and I find myself scrutinising the other passengers. At the moment we are all right; everyone on the bus is Jewish, recognisable by their orthodoxy. But maybe they are in disguise. Didn't I hear of such a case? No, I must not think about it. Instead I look at the view.

We are climbing now to upper Neve. Apartment buildings of amber coloured stone made white by the sun, line the hillside. Brilliant flowers shine like jewels on the balconies and over the walls. Everything grows prolifically, if you can stop it shrivelling in the scorching sun. I have planted many things on my daughter's balcony, having to learn anew the techniques of plant survival. My grandchildren have grown giant sunflowers. They stand like golden sentinels facing the hills and the Arab village above. They live just inside Israel, with the border of the West Bank a snaking hillside away.

Upper Neve is home to a large number of Russian immigrants. Israel is a country of immigrants and people often group together according to national origin, as they do in most immigrant communities throughout the world. It is not easy to become 'Israeli' in a fragmented and fearful society impatient with newcomers. In Jerusalem there is a community of elderly English women who look like they have just stepped out of a senior citizen's club in Golders Green. Some are very old and come to spend their last days here. They gather together in the cafes and are deeply immersed in the cultural life of the city. Many do voluntary work in hospitals. I admire these women who have chosen to leave everything they know in order to live here.

The bus drives at high speeds and wastes no time at the stops. People will readily stand and give up their seat for anyone with a child or whoever else looks like they may need a seat. We are passing through an Arab suburb. The bus was stoned once, when my son-in-law was travelling home from work on this route, and I wonder if the bus will stop here. We pick up passengers, and I can't help feeling nervous. This is, after all, how it's done. No one else seems perturbed. Does one young man look particularly intense, or is it my imagination? My daughter is talking about a forthcoming wedding and all I can see are bodies blown apart; the gathering up of pieces for burial.

The Arab houses that we pass are old and beautiful, the wrought iron balconies painted turquoise. The shops spill their wares onto the pavements. Old men sit on chairs in the shade smoking pipes. As everywhere else in Israel, building works are going on and white dust shrouds everything.

A woman is standing up in her seat. She is shouting at the driver. My daughter translates for me: apparently the woman is complaining about the air-conditioning, saying that she is too cold. As it is hotter than hell outside, the other passengers look at her as if she's mad, shaking their heads in amazement.

'She's Russian,' observes my daughter. The other people nod in agreement as if this fact explains it all.

'You see,' she goes on, 'They moan about everything. Some of them came here and expected it to be America and of course it isn't.'

Getting no response from the driver, the woman has sat down. The persecution of Russian Jewry gained world notice and the *refuseniks* who would not abandon their Jewish identity attained heroic status. In Israel they are expected to live like everyone else and to get on with it. It is very hard to live here. Unemployment is high and state benefits are low. Wages are poor and there is a limitation on jobs for artists, musicians and intellectuals. But the Russians brought with them the richness and diversity of talent that flourished even under oppression. The streets of Jerusalem abound with musicians of concert standard. Where once they were forced to assimilate into a society that would not accept their differences, they now find it hard to fit in, in a country that treats them as ordinary.

The bus is now packed full of people and every time the bus stops no one gets off. All passengers are heading for the city centre. As the doors open, the bus utters a deep squelching sigh and a blast of fiery air comes in. We are approaching Mea She'arim, the neighbourhood of narrow streets and endless activity housing its *Hasidic* community which has been here for over a hundred years. We pass men in long black coats, black hats, white shirts and waistcoats, the dress of the *shtetl.* Their beards are full like my son-in-law's, only more so. The *Hasidim* are mystical, steeped in centuries of tradition. They pursue their way of life whatever the political situation and their singing and dancing is legendary for its joy and beauty.

The women and girls are dressed even more modestly than my daughter. They do not seek approval from those outside their community and are oblivious of what people think of them.

My son-in-law admires the *Hasidim* but he cannot become one. My daughter says the community is too old, too established for them ever to be a part of it. It is difficult for the 'returned ones' to find a place for themselves. All the time they are learning that a belief in God is not separate from the living of everyday life, which is why they live by the *Torah.* All the issues of life are there; the moral questions. I have no belief in God and I was told once by a friend who was a *Hasid* that it was not such a problem, just a matter of philosophy. I have struggled all my life to overcome the selfishness that besets us all when faced with hard decisions, and to live by the socialist beliefs that I hold. My friend was trying to make me see that the things that I hold sacred were not so different for him: family, love, freedom, equality and a love of people. But I still feel I am on the other side of the fence.

We are now reaching the junction with King George Street, the main thoroughfare in this part of Jerusalem, and where we get off.

The pavements shine in the bright light and the air is filled with the smell of exotic flora, spices, bad drains, petrol fumes and pine. How can people move so fast in this heat? I drag my daughter into a little shop selling hats. Beautiful hats. I choose one made of finely woven raffia with a large floppy brim, the crown covered in silk flowers and a green ribbon. The owner of the shop is very old, her skin as thin as tissue paper. She tells me that I am elegant but I am damp with sweat and my clothes feel like armour. I convince my daughter to let me buy her a hat and she chooses one that is smaller than mine but just as lovely. Her hair is covered by a thin cream snood and she places the hat over it. Now she looks like a 1930s film star. She wears clothes that cover her arms and legs from top to toe, but they are in rich colours and soft materials.

I want to buy her a new dress. She doesn't have much money to spend on clothes. This is one of the ways that I can show my love for her, clothing her body as I did when she was a child. We go into one of the shops that she likes and she chooses a long graceful gown, the colour of cream, with many thin layers which drift around her body like butterfly wings.

We are going to the Ticho House for lunch where we will meet my friend Leah and her husband, who are visiting from England. This is where Anna Ticho lived. She was an artist and the house is full of her work. It is a beautiful place and you can eat or just drink coffee in the lush, shaded garden. It is an oasis of peace in the middle of the hot dusty streets.

I first came to Israel many years ago with Leah. We had both come to visit our daughters. Mine was living on a kibbutz in the Galilee—the beginning of her journey. The old city was fairly open and safe then. Now you have to be careful where you go. I can get away with looking like a tourist, but my daughter can't. We stayed in an Arab hotel by the Jaffa Gate. My eldest daughter had joined us, so there were three of us in a room with long French windows that opened out onto a wrought-iron balcony. So there we stood facing King David's Wall, and looked out high over the city. Heat and dust hung over the golden stone and the Mount of Olives stood green and parched on the hot slopes. My first time in Jerusalem. I had never been anywhere like it. Much has changed since then.

There were three narrow beds in the room covered in brightly coloured nylon bedspreads. The shower and toilet were feats of ancient plumbing, rusted and cacophonous. But it was cheap and the view was wonderful. The architecture suggested grander times but it had fallen into an impoverished state. It still boasted a winding staircase which spiralled its way to the top of the building. Each floor had an array of old leather sofas and armchairs, but there were never any guests resting in them. Overhead fans groaned on the high ceilings and there didn't seem to be a lift. We saw few other people there except the man behind the front desk who wore a red fez and had the largest moustache that I have ever seen, and the cook who boiled eggs in a rusty billycan in the basement dining-room. In the street next to the hotel was an Arab cafe that served the best mint tea I have ever tasted. Mint leaves floating in pale golden liquid, nectar to a parched throat. Since the first *Intifada* the cafe has closed. Now the surrounding streets teem with missionary groups.

I once sat with my daughters, at the *kotel* to watch the setting sun. As the light slowly changed, it coloured the golden stone, first orange then pink then purple. Then the shadows settled on the great glittering dome of the mosque. The square in front of the Wall was full of people, Jews from all over the world, many *dovening* and others, like us, quietly reflecting as we watched the sun become an orange orb, then disappear. Everywhere you go in the old city you are surrounded by history. Stories of separation and anguish, joy and renewal, are bound up with the rock and foundation of this beautiful place. That it is so full of conflict and sorrow is tragic and I am sad that I can no longer walk there with my daughter in peace.

Leah and her husband have arrived. Leah and I have been friends since our school- teaching days. She is a small thin woman always on the move, and I have never seen her look so happy as I see her now in this garden. She loves Israel and has always wanted to live here. She has been visiting since the 1950s when there were hardly any decent roads,let alone fast food restaurants and night-clubs. I have only ever met him before in their home at their *seder* or to celebrate *Rosh Hashanah*. He came to England on the last *kindertransport* from Berlin.

We are all sitting under a large parasol and my daughter is talking about how children react to upheaval and displacement; her daughter grieved for the people she loved and left behind in England. Leah's husband listens quietly then starts to talk about his leaving

Berlin.

'First I remember *kristallnacht*.' He pauses and coughs as if deciding whether he should continue.

'I was ten years old. After it happened the pavements were covered in glass. Like crushed ice, streets and streets of it. And the great synagogue, just smoke and ashes, smoke and ashes.'

He told us that when the children had to leave their families as he did, they almost accepted it as normal—this separation from home and everything they knew, amid great terror.

'Perhaps that was the only way we could cope with it.'

His brother went on a different train that ended up in Holland. He was caught there in the German occupation and miraculously survived the camps.They found each other after the war and searched for their mother, but they never found her. She died in the camp at Riga; his father had been murdered earlier on during the Nazi reign of Terror.

He is nearly seventy years old now and it is only in recent years that he has talked of those times. He does so now without tears, in this peaceful garden. We do not need to know every detail for he knows that we understand what he leaves unsaid.

It is time for us to leave. Every Friday is a race against the sunset. I say goodbye to my friends until we meet again in England to resume our normal lives. Nothing in Israel is like normal life.

When my daughter speaks of her life here her face glows with happiness. Her eyes look incredibly blue in her tanned face. When she was a small child people would remark on the extraordinary colour of her eyes. Her hair is dark, almost black, but you can't see it, as she wears it covered all the time. I have photographs of her in her old life. Pictures of her working in the fields of the *kibbutz*, her face smiling at the camera, her long legs in shorts and boots. I do not understand her new life. She tries to explain it to me and because I love her I listen. I try to find reason behind the many laws that shape her life. Now I no longer ask questions. It only causes pain between us. What I do know is that there is an abundance of warmth and humour in her community. A sharing of problems and help given in hard times. I think that they suffer prejudice from secular society that they do not deserve.

We hurry through the crowded streets. One more stop to buy the *cholla*. My son-in-law will have done most of the *Shabbat* cooking while we were away. It's too late to go to the bookshop so we make do with the weekend Jerusalem Post. We do the crossword on the bus before *Shabbat* forbids all writing. The steaming streets are left behind as the sun sinks low in the darkening sky.

****

A wall of heat greets me once more as I step off the plane at Ben-Gurion airport. It is January and I did not intend to be here until my daughter's birthday, but events have overtaken me. She is very ill and needs me. You can disguise much in a telephone conversation but somehow I knew all was not well, just as my mother always knew when I needed her. She would appear at my door just as I was about to put a gun to my head. 'I knew you were in trouble,' she'd say.

I take a taxi that my son-in-law has sent so that I don't have to battle with Hebrew to make myself understood. My daughter and her husband left Neve Yaakov two years previously, when their baby died. It was the one time when I could not be with her. Her sister and I tried to comfort her but our phone calls were an agony of grief and weeping. She has another child now. He is nine months old.

When I arrive it is almost midnight and the house is silent. The rooms are empty of life except for my son-in-law who is studying at the long dining room table. He embraces me and I can see the look of relief on his face. He takes me to the bedroom where my daughter lies. She is paler and thinner than I've ever seen her. I put my arms around her and hold her close. 'I'm so glad you're here,' she whispers. I learn that she has been ill for weeks and now has pneumonia in both lungs. Neighbours have been cooking the meals for the family for two weeks as my son-in-law struggled to care for three children who are very distressed and frightened by the fragility of their mother.

As the days pass I get used to the routine again. Early to school, then home for lunch. Sometimes in the afternoon I paint with the children, and teach the baby my usual repertoire of songs. Often, when the weather permits, they play outside with their friends. Then I make dinner, before bath-time and bed. They seem to be happy with this regular routine and are becoming calmer. My granddaughter says that she hates it when things are messy. She doesn't mean the state of the house but the insecurity of days without her mother. I am a reasonable substitute. My daughter is beginning to feel better but it is a slow healing.

Two weeks into my stay there is a knock on the door. My daughter has been getting up for a few hours now and is lying on the sofa. I open the door and a man walks in. He greets my daughter in *Ivrit* and then she introduces him to me in English. He smiles. He is the man who delivers fruit juice. I later discover that he also lectures in music and is a school security guard. He is a tall man, not strictly orthodox. He has a beautiful face, deeply tanned and etched with living. His hair curls in a silver thatch on his head. He is a *sabra*, born in Jerusalem, and now he lives in the Judean hills. He is concerned about my daughter's health and talks to her about natural remedies that might help her. My son-in-law offers him a drink and they start to talk about music. This is obviously no ordinary delivery man. When he gets up to leave he asks me how long I am staying. I tell him that I will stay a while yet. He nods and then he is gone.

I think I fell in love with his voice as much as anything—rich and caressing and totally seductive. Love comes when you least expect it and in the most unusual circumstances. In this community there is not really any place for me except as visiting family. I am a woman from the other side and, however much someone may be attracted to me, nothing could ever come of it, unless one of us radically changed. Now I have met a man who has an amazing effect on me. I have lived happily alone until now. I discover that he has five children from two failed marriages. Well maybe it wasn't his fault. How foolish we are when we are in love.

I sit with my daughter on the patio. The sun at this time of year is gentler and will be good for her. The tall crane from the hillside opposite gleams red against the unclouded sky. Moni, the builder, sees us and waves across. He climbs the hilly slope, covered in lavender and rosemary, that leads to the garden. He climbs over the blue metal fence and stands before us. He tells my daughter how pleased he is to see her up and about again; that he has been very worried about her.

She smiles and introduces him to me. He takes my hand in both of his then says something to my daughter in *Ivrit* that I can't understand. She laughs and tells me that he is saying how good-looking I am. He doesn't say it in a flirtatious way and the warmth of his personality shines in his face. He is a secular Israeli who has an unusual friendship and business relationship with my daughter. When he goes, she tells me that he has a beautiful wife and children that he adores.' Ah, well,' I say. 'It would be too much luck to meet two attractive and available men in one week.'

The children are at school and the baby Yehuda Aryah is asleep. I have made some coffee and Rachel joins us. She also moved here from Neve Yaakov and now they live next door to each other. They both decided to move deeper into Israel and they now live in a valley that seems hotter and dustier. There is building going on all around them. Even so the air still feels cleaner than London. It looks a bit like the Wild West: half built white roads, the skeleton of a park, dust and diggers in the noonday sun. We are further from Jerusalem and nowhere near the sea.

My daughter and her friend ask me how I feel about my man from the mountains. I feel as shy and silly as a teenager and they act like they are my parents.

'He's a very charming man,' says Rachel.

'He could suit you,' adds my daughter, 'mind you, he has been married twice. That could be problematical.'

'You make sure he doesn't make you responsible for all his baggage!' exclaims Rachel.

'And he's bound to have plenty,' agrees my daughter.

'Right.' I say. What can I say when I hardly know the man?

I do know that we have a lot in common: we have both been teachers, we are both artists, we love music to a passionate degree and we have a very strong attraction for one other. I am ten years older than him, which does not seem to concern him. One thing that worries me is that his youngest son is only ten years old and is going through a bad time because of his parents' broken marriage. I decide that I cannot possibly judge the situation as I do not know his wife. I tell myself that these things happen.

In the weeks since I have met him we have talked a lot about art and music and our children. I have many grandchildren already because I had my own children when I was young. All these conversations are carried out in my daughter's living room. I have been here for nearly two months now and I begin to wonder where this is going.

I have booked my flight home and feel that it is safe now to leave my daughter. Even so, it will be a terrible wrench. Usually my daughter comes with me to the airport. I am very frightened of flying and find airports a nightmare of confusion, which is all part of the fear. But mostly she comes because it is the last time we will see each other for many months or even longer. When I go through the final barrier she cries and I know that she watches me until I vanish from sight. I never look back because then I could not bear to leave her.

A few days before I leave my son-in-law hands me the telephone. It is 7.30 a.m. and I wonder who could be ringing me so early. It is, of course, my mountain man. '*Shalom* Anna,' and then in English, ' would you like to meet and talk some more? It could be at your daughter's house if you would prefer.' He is so formal. We agree to meet the next day, the day before I fly home. I decide to see him away from the house because of the curiosity of my grandchildren who are finding it difficult to understand my friendship with him. I think though that my granddaughter is already formulating a plan for my wedding and permanent stay in Israel, which of course is what she most wants.

The time arrives, but he doesn't. He is late. I am ridiculously nervous and my son-in-law keeps grinning at me as I do my hair for the tenth time and re-apply my lipstick Finally he is at the door and looks strangely different. It's because he is wearing a tweed jacket It doesn't go with him really, but is obviously his attempt at looking smart. We set off in his car. He drives like most Israelis and we hurtle along roads that take us higher into the hills. We come to a halt in the middle of a forest and in front of a tea house cum restaurant. He takes my arm and guides me to the edge of the hillside to show me the land that he loves. The air is as cool and clear as crystal, the sky a cloudless sapphire. Dark cypresses wind through the valley below us and the horizon glows soft and pink towards the sea. All around us is the smell of cedar.

The tea house is built of wood; there are carpets and beading on the walls and the scent of patchouli oil hangs in the air. The smiling woman who ushers us to a table overlooking the valley, has long dark hair and she wears beautiful flowing clothes of rich colours.

We eat bread and olives, humus and eggplant, drink beer and black sweet coffee. We talk about our lives. He finds it difficult to live alone. I think women can cope with being on their own much more easily. In fact many women have a liberating new lease of life when they are divorced. We talked about music and love and all the time I want to touch him. He smells of fresh air and the smell that clings to clothes that are dried in the sun. He has the whitest, most even teeth that I have ever seen. He puts his hand over mine on the table and tells me that I am beautiful. I blush like a schoolgirl.

We only spent two hours together. He had to drive down to the Negev to give a lecture. So, on my daughter's doorstep, he held me in his arms, kissed me on the cheek in farewell and was gone.

By the time I got back to England his voice was on my answer phone, and so our love affair began. How is it possible to feel such strong emotions for someone that you hardly know and whom you have hardly even kissed. But I did and so did he. He rang me obsessively everyday, sometimes twice a day. When he unleashed emotional tirades at me about his children, his loneliness, his need of me, I began to wonder what I had let myself in for. Then he would phone the next day as if nothing had ever happened. These bizarre swings of mood were the rhythms that shaped his life. I should have walked away from him then, but I was too smitten.

****

The path to the *moshav* shop is strewn with pine needles. The air feels soft and a slight breeze brushes my skin. Soon the summer heat will begin to rise but at the moment it is cool enough to carry the shopping back to the caravan.

I meet no one on the way except the odd car on the main *moshav* road. I am in the Judean mountains and when you stand on the edge of the hillside you can see across the valley to vast fields of sunflowers and to the blue hills beyond, where the horizon meets in a dark line of tree and bush. Sometimes when I make this walk I just stand still under the tall pines and breathe in the sultry aromas of the forest. Birds of extraordinary colour watch me and are remarkably unafraid. The wild mixture of arid road, rock, and spiky shrub dried to the bone, gives the landscape a sculptured beauty.

Opposite my lover's caravan the edge of the hill is fringed by a verge of lush grass; palms and olive trees whisper in the breeze and wooden benches give a resting place to enjoy the view. A stone monument faces inwards to the *moshav*: on it the photograph of a smiling young man, killed long ago in the Yom Kippur war.

The *moshav* is next to Abu Gosh, a fairly prosperous Arab village. Its inhabitants live amicably enough with the *moshavniks*. We often buy our *Shabbos* bread and vegetables in the Arab shop on the main road leading to the *moshav*.

Eli, my lover, fought in the Yom Kippur war as a young man and then in the Lebanon. He has some terrible memories of those times. When he is stressed he cannot stop eating. In the *Yom Kippur* war he sat in a trench and ate everything in his pack. It was the only way he could cope with his fear. War changes people; it has to. Where do you hide away your fear and your grief? I think that many of the problems that beset our relationship were caused because he had too much inside his head that he could never confront or talk about.

A fleet of helicopters disturbs the morning stillness. The sound of them is a constant reminder of the endless war that has claimed so many lives. There have been a lot of shootings recently, day after day. Every time there is one of these incidents I phone my daughter in Bet Shemesh as I never know which road they may be travelling on, while Eli paces the caravan, his face dark and closed off to me. When a bomb went off in a pizza restaurant he wailed with despair and anxiety. He did not know where his teenage sons were. When he finally found them he raged at them for their casual neglect to phone him to say they were safe. When he is like this he frightens me, then it passes and once again he is funny and loving and wonderful to be with.

This is the first time since my daughter made *aliyah* that I have not stayed in a religious community. I am freer to wear what I please and to do all manner of things that I could not normally do. But I see a lost innocence in the faces of the youth that I meet. I miss the easy friendship of my daughter's women friends and the welcome that I get from her neighbours. Here people swim in the pool, sunbathe on the lawns, Walkmans pressed to their ears shutting out the world. Sometimes I long for the conversations I shared with my daughter and her friends on all matters, both serious and trivial.

I have met Eli's children many times now. His eldest son, who was later to come and stay with me in London, is very handsome and the image of his father when he was young. His eyes are wary and secretive. He has the habit of concealment, mainly from his father whom he loves and fears in equal measure. It worries me that this boy is so afraid of Eli. Sometimes we talk alone together. We sit on the bench facing the valley and he tells me that all his childhood was spent in the shadow of his father's moods. And so he lives his life in aimless occupation and keeps as far away from Eli as possible. Soon he will go into the army and then he will be confronted with even more dilemmas. I try to talk to Eli about how he behaves around his eldest son. I hope to make him see that you cannot own your children and force them to be what they are not. That you can go much further with acts of love and trust than you can ever go with disapproval and rage. But although he listens to me I know that he sees this defence of his frightened but defiant child as a betrayal on my part.

When things are good between us he makes me feel the most beloved of women but the dark moods seem to increase the longer I am there. It is a terrible thing to love someone who you know is a bully and a tyrant and I know that this man will eventually control me in every aspect of my life.

I think that we all have several internal voices. My daughter would say that the true voice that guides us is that of the soul, the voice of God. I choose to call it the voice of reason. When I left Eli and the *moshav* that was the voice I listened to.

Lydia Rivlin

Lydia Rivlin was born and brought up in Britain. She completed her education at Stanford University, California. She has written mostly comedy for radio and TV. She lives in London with her husband and three children.

'Though aware of their faults, I am proud of the contribution the British and Jewish cultures have made to world civilisation. As a writer, it is amazing luck that I can call upon two such great traditions. As for being a woman—no woman, no me.'

The Night Watch

When can you say a light has gone out? Is it out when it is extinguished, or when no one is there to see it? Does the light burn in my heart because I know it is there; does it burn in Elisa's heart even though she is not aware of its existence?

I left the cosy confines of a middle class Reform Jewish household in Great Neck to see Europe (or, as my sister irritatingly kept calling it, 'Yurp'). I started out in Italy and worked my way westwards towards England, taking in as many centres of European Culture as I could. I wanted to be a cultured woman. I still want to be a cultured woman—but which culture? I say that, because I became much more aware of my Jewishness on the way around Europe than I ever had before. The American Patriot might insist to you that the USA has plenty of history: she might even get quite heated up about it; but you can see more history in an afternoon in Florence than you could in a whole lifetime on Long Island, that's for sure. I tried to concentrate on the stuff you are supposed to look at when you visit 'Yurp'—the art galleries, the palaces. But sometimes I was called by the faintly heard, exotic cry of my own religion: I saw the Italian ghettos; I read the brochures describing Jewish populations destroyed here, or moved on long ago from there; I was shown around deserted synagogues with nothing left but the dusty memories of prayer. It was when I went to see one of the concentration camps that I realised what loss there had been. The guides talked about the passing of Jewish culture from their lands as a thinning of their local cultural diversity, but not as a loss to themselves. I began to realise the loss to me; how traditions and practices and thoughts which had taken generations to develop had simply blown away like dry leaves in a New Hampshire Fall. In Madrid a priest told me about the Marranos who, in the 15th century, pretended to convert to Chrisitianity, but said Hebrew prayers under their breath after each verse of the Mass; they tried, but after a few generations they ended up good Catholics anyway—the priest seemed quite proud of it. When I learned such things in comparative religion seminars back in Brandeis, they held a quirky sort of interest; but the clean, empty synagogue-museums and the melancholic sterility of wistfully remembered Jewish Quarters, gave every scrap of information a force that I had never previously felt. It was as if there were a candle in my heart, glowing so faintly it might as well have been out altogether. The remorseless wind of European history forced the candle into sputtering light. The longer I travelled around these countries of exile, the brighter the candle burned in the deepening darkness.

Things had begun to stack up on me. Isolated from my family, cast adrift and wandering from country to country, culture to culture, I wondered what I might have done to preserve my roots. To what subterfuge would I have been capable of descending in order to stay in my home and not be forcibly moved on? I could hardly look at that jolly priest—so much persecution with so little meaning. I began to feel emotions I could scarcely recognise. Okay, maybe I was brought up on re-runs of *I Love Lucy* but I have done my reading too. I have sat through the lectures from my English professors on classical allusions in Shakespeare's plays and the workings of fate in William Faulkner—I could not understand it. I should… I feel I should.

I had been to Italy, Germany, France, Spain, England and Belgium before I finally made it to Holland. I went to Belgium for the battlefields. After seeing the nurseries of European civilization, I wanted to visit its graveyards. It would have been more poetic to have done Belgium last, but the charter conditions made it cheaper to leave from Amsterdam. It is not unknown for Economics to beat Poetry.

I was pretty tired and a bit lonely and very shellshocked by the time I made Amsterdam, but I was determined to do it as much justice as the other places I had visited. That's how I ended up in the Rijksmuseum on the Friday afternoon, looking at the cleaned up *Night Watch* from near the top of a flight of stairs. I was going up, craning my neck round to look at it. Elisa was coming down the stairs with her husband, similarly absorbed in the painting and we bumped into each other. There I was, on my knees, grabbing the chilly stone banisters while she was sprawled on the stone steps, when we looked at each other, and burst out laughing. While her husband retrieved her handbag and some scattered books and leaflets, we both sat on a step, helpless with laughter. We had each been trying to take the blame and had ended up playing a sort of ping-pong game with the word 'sorry'. Finally we gave up and went to a coffee shop to recover.

Elisa had married young so she was not as old as my mother, but she and her husband had children of around my age. My new friends were as different from my parents as it was possible to be. An elegant, cultural Spanish couple, they knew all of Europe as I knew Long Island. They made me feel scruffy and illiterate. And yet, they were lonely too. Their youngest child, their only daughter, was studying Engineering at the Max Planck Institüt in Stuttgart. The previous day had been her birthday, her first away from home. Elisa and Arturo seemed only too glad to spend some time with me. I knew I was standing in for Isabella but I was so glad of the company, I didn't care.

They invited me to dinner that night and I accepted gladly. Did I mention that my money was running low? I am not mad about 'Dutch fries' with mayonnaise. I was getting a bit sick of cheap hamburgers, and a good dinner is a good dinner.

I turned up at the Sonnesta that evening in my cleanest clothes and sat back and enjoyed the quiet surroundings, the elegance and the free food. Elisa told me all about her home near Madrid and I told her all about Great Neck and Brandeis University. It didn't sound like the Max Planck Institüt at all. I started to feel really small and even a little nervous. That is probably how I came to spill coffee all over my skirt. Elisa and Arturo eyed each other and I knew they were agreeing that I was probably the most clumsy person they had ever met. I almost burst into tears. I had got round a continent with nothing worse than one missed train; now, right at the end of my trip, I looked like an oaf in front of two people I would really like to have impressed—even though I would probably never see them again. Elisa saw how upset I was and asked me if I would like to clean myself up in her room.

When Elisa opened the bedroom door, the soft glow of candles wavered in front of my eyes before it was overpowered by the electric light. As we passed the dressing table, I noticed that on a little ceramic plate there were two small candle stumps, one of them already dying in its own melt, flickering in front of the mirror. While I was sponging down my skirt in the bathroom, I thought about those candles. It was strange that they should be there, especially on a Friday night. It reminded me of home. Was it some Spanish custom of which I had never heard? Was it a memorial to a dead relative? Perhaps it was all that was left of a romantic episode between Elisa and Arturo before dinner. I could not be so indelicate as to ask.

We were on the way out of the bedroom. What did I have to lose? In any case they thought I was extremely gauche. I blurted out: 'What are those candles for?'

'It is a family custom,' replied Elisa. 'My mother always lit two candles in the bedroom on a Friday night. Her mother did it too. She told me that the women of my family must light two candles every Friday night whatever happens, but that we must not put them in a public room. I have told Isabella to do it, now she lives away from home. My mother said she was told by her mother that if she did not keep up the custom, a misfortune would befall her family. My grandmother was told the same thing by her mother and so on. I do not believe this myself but it is a tradition that links me to my family. I think it must be a very old custom… Many, many generations.'

I was unable to speak. I looked at the remains of the candles—one already out, the other hissing and spitting in its misshapen collar of molten wax. Oh Elisa! How could I tell you what you were doing? Would you stop lighting the candles if I told you that you were Jewish; that your mother and grandmother and great-grandmother and who knows how many generations of mothers were also Jewish; that this was the only thing they had left of their tattered and secret religion that they could bequeath to generations of daughters. Blinded by the long, long night the women kept a vigil measured out in Friday night candles that burned even after the unrecognised dawn had broken; until, in a hotel room in Amsterdam, far away from its origins, a traveller from even farther away had decoded the unseen message burned into the air of the hidden rooms. Generations of Jewish women trying to keep the flame lit, filled my brain with their silent cry, their blind watch. I reeled from the shock of it but I told Elisa that I was just tired. I thanked them, I excused myself, and I ran.

Later on, back in the safety of Great Neck, I wrote to Elisa and she replied. She gave me Isabella's address and suggested that I email her. Perhaps I will. Perhaps one day I will tell her what her mother has passed on. Will I be granting her a blessing or burdening her with a curse?

And I ask again, does a candle give light, even when no one can see?

Shelley Weiner

Shelley Weiner was born in South Africa and worked as a journalist for many years before turning to fiction. Her published novels include *A Sisters' Tale, The Last Honeymoon, The Joker* and *Arnost.* Her short stories have appeared in several anthologies and on BBC Radio 4. She currently lectures for Birkbeck College and is a founding director of London Open Book.

'I have never set out to project or define myself as a Jewish writer, yet the themes that obsess me (exile, loss, family ties, engagement or disengagement with the past) all seem to find shapes in narrative that is informed by the Jewish experience. My parents were Holocaust survivors, and that shadow will never cease to haunt my fiction or my life. More positively, the richness of Jewish folklore—biblical and otherwise—is for me, a wonderfully creative source.'

Naomi's Lament

It should be a triumph—a vindication of all my suffering. As I gaze on the classic configuration of mother nursing child in the stillness of a summer afternoon, I can acknowledge the beauty but feel little joy. I hear the sucking sounds made by Buddy's mouth around Ruth's overflowing nipple and involuntarily cross my hands over my own breasts, now withered and dry.

'He's beautiful,' someone says. A neighbour, one of the stream who keep calling in to pay respects. 'What a proud grandmother you must be.'

I nod, smiling, as though in agreement. But instead of celebrating the birth of a new generation, all I can think about is how much I have lost. I have come full circle, back to the sunny yet dreary gentility of suburban Port Elizabeth. Like a disintegrating comet, I've shed pieces of myself along what has seemed like a preordained orbit, until all I have now is my stony heart.

Or have I always been this way?

Let me get this straight from the start—leaving South Africa wasn't my idea. Not that I supported that awful regime, but I'm passive by nature. I was comfortable. I wanted to wait and see—which wasn't what I tried to tell Eli after he announced his decision during a particularly bad patch in the seventies. I said the country had been good to us, kind to us. We owed it to… to…

But he interrupted, the way he generally did when I hesitated. 'What the hell are you talking about, Naomi? We owe nothing,' he declared, and immediately launched into a list of his good deeds: sponsoring the education of six indigent blacks (all children of our various servants); raising copious sums for the Mayor's School Feeding Fund (he and the Mayor were members of the same Lodge); chairing the steering committee for the establishment of a Multiracial Cerebral Palsy Centre, et cetera, et cetera.

'Tell me,' he said (rhetorically of course—the last thing he ever wanted was for me to tell him anything that would deflect his stream of righteousness). 'Tell me if there's anyone in this city who could call me uncharitable or accuse me of leading a selfish life?'

'I didn't mean…' I began, but again he stopped me.

'Are you saying you're happy for your two boys to serve on the border, to get killed maybe? For what? How good would the country be to you then?'

I didn't answer, for he had raised implications far beyond civic duty or affection for a land of plenty. I loved Marcus and Hilton. In those days I loved them defiantly. Risk-takers, both, only two years apart, I could imagine them volunteering for foolhardy missions, each fired by the other's bravado. I wanted to surround them with safer challenges. I wanted them alive.

So I agreed and we sold up and made arrangements to leave for London.

Eli travelled ahead of us to establish his credentials as a man of independent means and therefore an asset to the great UK. He acquired a powder-blue Mercedes, a late Lutyens 'semi' in Hampstead Garden Suburb, and membership of various local benevolent societies. He found places for Marcus and Hilton in colleges of dubious distinction: Marcus would do business studies while Hilton, being good with his hands, would study mechanics. He also joined the most prestigious synagogue in the area and bought the most comprehensive BUPA plan. During that month of ceaseless and tireless setting-up and settling-in, Eli noticed but dismissed the odd tightness in his chest.

He certainly said nothing about it to me when I arrived with the boys bearing (as carefully instructed) as much of value as could be physically, if illegally, extracted from South Africa. All he could talk about were his purchases, his new connections and his unbelievably successful four weeks. All Marcus and Hilton could talk about was the awful fucking weather.

And I? As I handed over the smuggled gold coins and was taken to see the house, I was aware of an ache that I identified as longing. Which was strange, since I thought I'd had no particular fondness for the life we had left behind. Amidst the pushy, glamorous

Port Elizabeth wives, I'd seen myself as a drab nonentity, lacking in fashion and card sense and conversational skills. I had neither problem servants nor an adored gynaecologist and my sons, alas, provided little in the way of maternal points-scoring. Yet there I was, blinking furiously, for the ache threatened to make me cry, which, even then, I didn't do easily.

Not even when, two and a half years later, Eli was rushed to the Intensive Care Unit at the Royal Free Hospital, having suffered a major heart attack. At least a dozen tubes attached him to various drips and monitors and his ashen face was in unfamiliar repose. I sat dry-eyed at his bedside for thirty-six hours, studying each line, each fold of flesh, observing the emergence of grey stubble through each follicle; thinking how little I knew this man I had known for twenty-six years and how seldom I had watched him being still; and how little I knew myself and how seldom, since sternly dismissing the ache and the almost-tears, I had dared to be still.

In the time we had been here I had overseen an unremitting series of workmen in the house—gutting and rebuilding the kitchen and bathrooms, extending, repointing, redecorating, landscaping. Alongside home improvements, I had engaged in serious self-improvement and was now conversant in basic French, psychobabble and Weight Watchers' Points. Eli had noted and appreciated all the changes for the better and, typically, not questioned my inner state. To be fair, I'd noticed how, from time to time, he would wince and clutch at his chest, but didn't question him either. We allowed one another to have private pain.

We also allowed the boys to explore the terrain of late adolescence without much intrusion. Perhaps, having spared them the physical dangers of soldiering, we assumed that London couldn't be anything but safe. Now I had a sense of them having inflated to manhood without substance, but had long lost the will to challenge them in any way.

'Mrs Morris.' A nurse had entered the room and placed a warm firm hand on my shoulder. 'I think you should go home. You need to rest.'

I nodded, for there was truth in what she said. I was exhausted. I had lost track of time. I had thought too much and stared too hard until the thoughts and the object of my thoughts had become a meaningless muddle accompanied by the echoing intrusions of Marcus and Hilton ('Mom?'... 'Mom? ... 'How is he, Mom?'... 'Will he be all right, Mom?') and the metronomic bleeping of machines. 'I can't leave him,' I protested. Weakly. I wanted to be ordered to leave.

'You must,' she said, the pressure of her hand on my shoulder increasing. I looked down at the hand and saw that it was brown and plump, and was suddenly assailed by a recurrence of the ache so severe that tears escaped. Dabbing my eyes, I rose unsteadily to my feet, resisting the impulse to seek consolation in the cushion of her chest.

'Are you sure...?' I glanced at Eli. A flicker of... something ... passed across his face. Did he want me to stay? Was he aware that I was here?

'His condition has been stable for several hours now. We'll call you immediately, Mrs Morris, if anything changes.'

I allowed her to escort me out of the room, leaning on her arm, looking back only once to etch Eli's presence into my memory. Despite the nurse's assurances, I knew that I would never see him alive again.

The funeral was lavish. Eli had bought Full Family Burial Benefits when he joined the synagogue, thus ensuring that we would all enjoy interment plus extended gravestone maintenance in Bushey Cemetery. His dedication to good causes, and widespread sharp practice, made for a multitudinous and well-dressed crowd of mourners. Flanked by my sons, I stood numbly at the graveside, hardly hearing the prayers or the praise. I was led home and seated on a low stool where the obligatory seven-day period of mourning ensued. At night I would hear the thudding of earth against the lid of Eli's coffin and in the morning my pillows would be damp with tears.

But it passed. The void that once was Eli, dynamic and large with life, was soon filled with mundanities and displaced by minor anxieties, and finally smoothed by time. I was astonished by the speed with which the habits of wifely ministration could be undone, and how quickly I found new activities to fill the slack. Having been Eli's bedfellow for twenty-six years, I was now content to administer his

Trust.

As for my fatherless sons—after a week of desolation during which neither left my side, they suddenly saw possibilities. They had youth, good looks, few marketable skills, but a copious annual income that rendered them free of economic concerns. They were rich. They were free. They played the field with abandon.

I didn't mind. I'd long given up on either boy achieving professional success. Marcus had failed his business studies course and been loosely employed in one of Eli's companies; Hilton's career as a mechanic had never quite taken off. Apart from that single week of mutual grieving, my two sons and I weren't close.

Not that I was close to anyone at the time. I didn't even notice my isolation. Chattering crowds with couples in huddles seemed remote and irrelevant. Alone in my beautifully renovated home, I had no need for friends or emotional ties of any sort. Or so I believed, until four years to the day after Eli's death when Marcus and Hilton each came home with a girl in tow and said, 'Mom, we're both hitched.'

Thus they entered my life. Olga and Ruth. Looking back, I suppose they were gains but how could I see that when I'd hardly begun to count my losses? 'You mean… you're *married*?' I asked in bewilderment, for my sons had taken me totally by surprise. 'You just went and married?'

They stood, each son proffering his spouse, as proud as tomcats who had captured choice canaries. I wondered what drunken escapade had led to these hasty unions. I wondered what kind of treasure-grabbing pleasure-seekers these two useless young men had brought into our lives. And while I wondered, I looked the girls up and down.

'Mrs Morris,' said the blonde, breaking free of her new husband and stepping towards me with outstretched hands, 'this must be a shock to you. It's not the way it seems—we didn't *have* to do this.'

'Have to?' I echoed, for the thought hadn't occurred to silly me. Anyway, the simultaneous impregnation of two random women seemed an unlikely achievement for sons as unproductive as mine. 'Then—why?'

'I love him,' she said, gazing back at Hilton who seemed disconcerted by my response.

'And I love Marcus,' said the other, drawing closer to my younger son and nuzzling her cheek against his. She was statuesque and stylish. Her skin was pitch black.

'You're…?' I asked.

'Ruth.'

She smiled at me, and despite my reservations I almost smiled back. 'But I still don't understand,' I said, shaking my head.

'Mom,' Marcus said impatiently, 'it's not *so* difficult. We've all known each other for —oh, ages. Several months, at least. Ruth and I have been going out. I've met her sisters, other members of her family. We got on really well, didn't we, Ruth?'

She nodded, encouraging him with her dark eyes. I was becoming mesmerised by those eyes.

'Mrs Morris, it's the same with me and Hilton,' put in Olga. 'We've had a real thing going… I know it's sudden and you could easily jump to the wrong conclusions…'

'I haven't,' I lied. 'I'm surprised, that's all.'

I invited them in, for it seemed I had no choice. Eli's absence had suddenly become palpable again, a gaping hole. I longed for him to be with me, sharing the impact of this blow and bolstering my parental disapproval. Then I remembered how much he'd blamed me for not being firmer with the boys, for not insisting that they identify actively with the faith of our forefathers. Yet how could I, in all honesty, when all that primping and praying and imprisonment in dietary law meant so little to me? But now I was seeing the fruits of my non-intervention: a pair of daughters-in-law of indeterminate extraction, decidedly not Jewish. Eli, I thought, it's better for you—and for me—that you're dead.

I offered them tea, but Marcus produced champagne. We drank, and as the bubbles floated to my head I started enjoying the novelty of noise and hilarity in this house that had become a silent shell. Olga told jokes about parrots in pubs and disabled donkeys, dissolving into a throaty chortling that was quite at odds with her doll-like façade. We laughed at her and with her. I was out of breath, with streaming eyes and a strange fullness in my chest. After they left, I realised I'd been happy.

But daylight brought reality. As I lay in bed, trying to make sense of what had happened, stray remarks lingered in my mind.

Hilton, thickly: 'We knew you'd be okay… they're great girls … it was going to be just a laugh, then we got serious and thought 'Why not?'…'

Why not, indeed?

Marcus: 'You'll see, Mom—they'll do us proud…'

Olga, catching her breath between jokes: 'Gosh! Bloody hell! Never thought married life would be such *fun,* did you, Mrs M… Goodness, there are three Mrs Morris's now. Can I call you Naomi? I'm not always like this—truly. I do have my responsible side. Don't I Hilton? Hilton? Hilton—tell your mother what a good influence I am.'

I dismissed the clamour of their voices, telling myself that if my Marcus and Hilton wanted to complicate their existence and risk their inheritance in this idiotic way, then they'd have to put up with the consequences—without me. As for pretty, coarsely-spoken young Olga—she could exert her 'good influence' on another woman's son.

I sat up, determined to proceed with my morning routine, but was unable to stifle the fourth voice, with its rich velvety texture. Ruth, who had found a moment of calm in the hilarity to crouch by my side and murmur: 'I have always known I would marry a Jew—even as a child, I knew it was my destiny. When Marcus came along, there was no doubt in my mind. He was the one, yours was the family. I'll be a good daughter-in-law—you'll see.'

If not for her ebony eyes I'd have shrugged her off with a light laugh and retreated from her intensity. But she locked me in her gaze and continued: 'And you know, there's another link. Africa. My family were exiles too—they were sent as slaves to Barbados. It's different, of course: you left voluntarily, but Marcus told me how much you and his father did for black people, how much you're doing still—'

'Nonsense,' I interrupted sharply. This was going too far. Eli had given his donations and I'd offered dutiful support to various soup kitchens and other benevolent organisations favoured by the white middle-class. But those who stood up to be counted against the system tended not to have left bearing Kruger Rands. 'There are people being tortured in prisons for opposing apartheid,' I told her. 'The most I can claim is that I'm not a hypocrite. We're the lucky ones—the beneficiaries. We walked away.'

She had frowned and nodded, but I could see she wasn't convinced. The conversation hadn't ended there, I knew. I'd have to stamp on her ardour for Jews and the heroic Morris family as hard as I could.

Ruth, however, was tenacious. A fortnight later she arrived to announce that she was set on the path to Jewish conversion: she'd visited a rabbi, convinced him of her integrity and been accepted for classes. She and Olga, both.

'Olga too?' I was astonished. Hilton's flaxen-haired comedienne wanted to be a Jew?

'I persuaded her. I said it would be best for our children if we all had the same faith.'

There was no argument in that. I shrugged away the unease that had began to prickle with her words.

'I've also joined the anti-apartheid movement,' Ruth went on. 'I thought about what you said that night and decided: right—even if it's holding a placard in Sainsbury's against South African fruit, at least it's something. Something's better than nothing.'

The unease had grown to agitation. This girl—woman—was choking me. She had slid into my life like a serpent and was squeezing out and feeding off bits of me that I had long dismissed as irrelevant: the Jewish bit; the South African bit. I'd lopped them off successfully, but now, thanks to this so-called daughter-in-law, I was suddenly aware of pain. Phantom pain, I told myself as I faced her, assuming my most 'don't-care' stance. 'Ruth, darling,' I said, lacing the endearment with flippant irony, 'as I believe I've mentioned, I'm neither religiously nor politically involved. You must do what you feel is right.'

That should have been the end of it, but Ruth was impervious to my lack of interest, immune to my disdain. She persisted, charmingly: wouldn't it be wonderful if we marked the start of Sabbath together—the boys, their wives and me? Couldn't I spare a few hours to accompany her to Trafalgar Square for a peaceful demonstration?

Could I? Just the once? Wouldn't I at least try?

I did. And as I complied with her requests, I found, miraculously, that my unease dissipated. I came to tolerate and—would you believe?—to enjoy the ritual of lighting Sabbath candles. I started to look forward to the arrival of my daughters-in-law as darkness fell each Friday night. And as we ate together—usually fish, for Ruth was adhering to a *kosher* diet— our conversation would settle on God, Judaism, justice and South Africa. Neither Olga's banter nor my scorn could distract Ruth from the ardour of her quest. She had the steadfastness of an explorer bent on unearthing the fascinating secrets of a strange new land, and I was the appointed bearer of these secrets. Which became seductive—for a time. I started reading religious texts to anticipate her questions. I began to follow the news about possible changes in South Africa. Was it possible that Mandela would be released from prison? Could a new era of liberty and equality be possible, after all? Perhaps I should be more engaged with the country of my birth? Maybe I could…?

Meanwhile Marcus and Hilton were increasingly absent from these gatherings. I hardly noticed—to my shame, even welcomed—the fact that on most Friday evenings Ruth and Olga came alone. I made perfunctory enquiries and readily accepted their pat replies: meetings, business trips, headaches, colds. Why didn't I probe deeper? Why did I choose to ignore the unhappy glances they exchanged, the awkward silences, when I alluded to future grandchildren? Could I not have pursued my sons and given them some of the compassion and warmth I was lavishing on their wives? No—I was too busy being bewitched and amused. Until the crunch came, on a Friday night ten years after that hasty double wedding.

The candles had long burnt themselves out and we were in the kitchen, the three of us, deciding whether or not to prolong the evening with more coffee. I had observed (but not mentioned) that Olga's eyes were puffy and her face strained; that Ruth was more reticent than normal; that both of them seemed, several times, on the brink of saying something, then held themselves back. Would it have made any difference if I'd coaxed whatever it was out of them, or asked them directly what was wrong?

I didn't. I didn't want to know.

But when the doorbell shrilled, there was no way I could repress the certainty that something terrible had happened. We stared at one another, all frozen by dread, until at last I forced myself back to mobility.

'Mrs Morris?'

The chilling banality of it. A policeman standing at the door, helmet in hand, eyes lowered respectfully.

Bad tidings.

They had both been drunk but Hilton, at the wheel, had been responsible for the collision that caused their death. At least it was quick. At least no other vehicle had been involved. At least there were no children to grieve their fathers' passing.

How hollow the crumbs of comfort that are tossed to the bereaved. Olga and Ruth were dry-eyed, shocked to the core, unable to absorb what had happened. This was what they had been afraid of—Hilton's drinking, Marcus's bouts of depression, their sudden dangerous mood swings veering from mania to despair—all coming to a sudden, violent end. They had wanted to talk to me about it—to share with me their concern. But I hadn't wanted to hear.

And now, now when it was too late, I was inconsolable. Never before, certainly not after Eli's death, had I felt such devastating sorrow. I was filled, bursting, overflowing with an unstoppable fount of bitterness and remorse. It choked and nauseated me. If I'd been able to, I would have ended my life too.

But that, I knew, would have been a final evasion in a life that was nothing but evasion. I regretted everything, all the choices I had never made. I deplored my passivity and the emptiness of my existence. And mainly because they had witnessed my shame and disgust, I began to hate my daughters-in-law. This was unfair, I know, but it was a response I was unable to suppress. I resented Olga, with her tear-rinsed blue eyes and valiant attempts to be jolly despite all. Most of my anger, though, was reserved for cloying, cleaving Ruth.

I hid it, of course. They gave me time to wail and moan, medication to sleep and food to refuse. They stayed in the house with me. I was never left alone. 'Please,' I begged, 'please go. Let me be.' But they refused. They would stand by me. They would help me through this. We would all endure it together.

They didn't have a clue.

They also seemed unaware of our dire financial circumstances. I had always relied on Eli's business acumen and, in his lifetime, it had proven more than sound. He made me a rich widow, but also left far too much cash and monetary control to his feckless sons, who blew the lot and then some—liquidating or borrowing against everything we owned. All but the Full Family Burial Fund, which had turned out to be his shrewdest investment, long term.

Despite my misery, however, I decided not to take advantage of that particular resource. Not now, not ever, since the small print restricted burial to Bushey Cemetery. I had made up my mind that, taking everything into account, my only way forward was to sell the house and convert what change remained into more lucrative rands.

I would head back to Port Elizabeth, South Africa, where I would re-make my home.

They were appalled. 'What? You can't mean it! What will you do there? You're in no fit state to travel… to pick up the threads… to manage alone…'

I had told them about our near-destitution, and they'd listened, nodded, accepted it calmly, for in spite of my early suspicions about their motives for marrying, they were not materialistic at heart. They were far from calm, though, about my intention to leave the country. Olga sat, hugging herself, sobbing forlornly. Ruth flung her arms around me, pleading for me to stay. Couldn't they see the sense in my decision? Was there no way I could convey to them that I wanted to be free of their oppressive omnipresence?

Then, current events gave me an argument that they couldn't possibly oppose. South Africa announced its first democratic general election and I, latching onto the news with glee, proclaimed my intention to be part of it. I wanted to contribute to the momentous changes that were sweeping the country. I was determined, at last, to be counted in the land of my birth.

They changed their tune. They couldn't stop me but now resolved to come with me. There was nothing left for them in England.

They would share my commitment to the new rainbow nation. There was no way they were letting me do this alone.

No, no, no, I wanted to scream. Let me go. The harder they insisted, the more I was determined that I had to leave them behind. I was bursting to tell them the brutal truth, but refrained. As calmly as I could, I cited reasons why their future lay in England: they were young, eligible, had families who would love and support them.

'I'm not being a martyr,' I said, at the end of my tether, for my protestations were falling on completely deaf ears. 'I'll manage on my own.'

This was on the morning of my departure. The debate had been raging for two months and, even now, with the taxi waiting to take me to the airport, they were imploring me to change my mind.

'Good*bye*, my darlings,' I said in desperation.

They begged me to postpone the parting: couldn't they come with me to Heathrow Airport, at the very least? It would have been churlish to refuse them that.

I've always hated scenes. If there's any theme that runs consistently through my life (apart from chronic bereavement) it's the avoidance of public scenes. And here we were, at the South African Airways check-in desk, being ogled by a thousand milling passengers and their mates, engaged in a loud and extremely public scene.

'Contain yourselves, girls,' I pleaded, extricating myself from Ruth and placing a calming hand on Olga's arm. 'You can come and visit, I promise. It's for the best that you remain here—I've explained why at least a hundred times. Please. People are staring at us. Let's take a grip on ourselves and say goodbye?'

Olga's sobs subsided with my words. She wiped her eyes, blew her nose, kissed me on the cheek and said she would always love me. I believed her. As she turned away, tucking a stray golden hair behind her ear and straightening her back resolutely, I was aware of the onset of that long dormant ache and for a moment wanted to call after her—to ask her to laugh with me one last time.

I didn't. Instead I turned to Ruth, expecting her to follow behind Olga for she, too, had gone quiet. She was rummaging in her handbag.

'Here,' I said, offering her a tissue in a bid to hasten her exit. It was almost time to board.

Then she produced the object of her fumbling: an air ticket to South Africa and a valid UK passport.

'What?' I managed. 'You can't!'

But she could. She did. 'I go where you go,' she declared, in a show of defiant loyalty that was almost biblical. What could I possibly say to that? I was saddled. Willy-nilly she was coming along. I decided to grit my teeth, made for the departure gate and hoped for the best.

But inside I was fuming. I had taken charge of my life, determined on a course of action—only for Ruth to undermine my autonomy. *I go where you go*. Couldn't she have got it into her stubborn head that she wasn't wanted?

'It's not going to be easy,' I muttered, after the plane had reached cruising altitude.

'Of course not,' she said. 'That's exactly why…'

'I mean for *you*. South Africa has *officially* changed, as we know. I'm not sure about attitudes, though. Port Elizabeth is a small provincial city. You might find that some people are… well, less than friendly.'

There was silence while she made inroads into her tray of food. It further infuriated me that she'd been so sure of her place alongside me that she had pre-ordered kosher. 'Because I'm black?' she asked at last. 'Or because I wasn't born Jewish?'

I glanced sideways to see if she was teasing and, if possible, grew even angrier. 'I assume,' I said icily, 'you're aware that we're not arriving with much in the way of assets.'

'Money, you mean?'

'That's exactly what I mean.'

'Don't worry, Naomi—we'll get by.'

Would we? I knew that had I been returning alone, Eli's cousins would have taken care of me. Having Ruth with me changed things; her presence raised complications that, resentful as I was, I was reluctant to explore. As we flew ever southward over Africa, my foreboding increased. I had no illusions about the reception that would greet us.

It was cool, to say the least. Two rather juicy items of gossip had failed to reach the Port Elizabeth branch of the Morris clan until now. The first, which I couldn't hide, was about our son's grossly unsuitable match. The second, about which I swore Ruth to secrecy, was the wild profligacy of Marcus and Hilton and our resultant destitution. 'You're not to breathe a word about it to anyone—ever,' I warned her melodramatically, for the whispers and sniggers round the table at our family 'welcome' meal had made me mad with acrimony and regret. I blamed Ruth entirely, swore to myself that somehow she would pay for ruining my homecoming.

For instead of being feted and indulged by adoring relatives, here I was in a narrow bed in a seedy seaside hotel. The noise of pounding surf and roaring traffic kept me awake. I tossed and groaned and muttered complaint while in the bed alongside mine, Ruth snored gently, sound asleep. Surely there was a way out of this mess? Someone upon whom I could dump this clinging daughter-in-law of mine? Someone who could alleviate our destitution? I tried counting relatives and began to nod off.

Then I remembered Eli's cousin Barney, now a fifty-something bachelor, who owned a thriving men's clothing factory. Barney had been the subject of scandal about liaisons with nubile Xhosa servants in the heady old days of the Immorality Act. There was a fair chance that he'd find the sultry beauty of my daughter-in-law irresistible. There was an excellent chance that he would bail us out.

Next morning over breakfast, in a casual sort of way, I mentioned his name and the size of his company. Naturally, I said nothing about his notoriety.

'Fine,' Ruth said immediately. 'I'll see if he can give me a job.' Which she did, in her imperturbable way. Within days she was on the temporary catering staff, and within a week had somehow found her way into Barney's office and made her presence known. Predictably in this small-town environment, Barney had heard all about us and was full of praise for the nobility of Ruth's sacrifice of homeland and family in order to be with me. That was the way he saw it. More to the point, he offered her a permanent position with statutory sick-pay, a pension and four weeks annual leave.

Each evening, she would return from work laden with delicacies. Smoked salmon, caviar blinis, champagne. 'It's what rich businessmen have for lunch,' she giggled. 'Leftovers. Cousin Barney said I should help myself.'

'You get along well then, you and cousin Barney,' I observed.

'Oh, yes. We certainly do.'

So it continued. Each day Ruth left at eight-thirty sharp for the factory, and at least twice a week she arrived home bearing gifts. On bad days, chopped liver and pickled herring; on good days, pike and exotic fruit.

Meanwhile I was hard at work trying to find a way to promote this promising relationship. Careful probing of key family members had confirmed Barney's healthy bank balance, his cloudy sexual history and (probably to compensate) his obsessive sense of duty. Most importantly, I had also discovered, via key Jewish texts, that when a man dies childless his nearest kin are responsible for ensuring that his widow doesn't do likewise. To translate: since Marcus hadn't done it, then Barney—as the closest, wealthiest unmarried cousin I could lay my hands on—should.

As I pointed out to Ruth, jokingly. She laughed, but her eye remained serious. She understood.

'D'you know something…' she said casually, 'Barney usually stays really late at work on a Thursday night.'

'Is that so?' I answered with matching nonchalance. 'Perhaps you might put in some overtime then as well?'

She nodded.

The following Thursday morning I encouraged her to take particular care with her appearance. She left for work in a cloud of Chanel No 5, with firm instructions from me that she shouldn't appear before Barney until after he'd finished his supper and fallen asleep on the leather sofa in his office. At that point she should kneel beside him and gently uncover his feet. Knowing Barney, he would take it from there.

I waved her off and waited. The day passed in delightful solitary anticipation, and the last thing I expected was for her to return to the hotel that night. But at 9.15 I heard the sound of the key in the door.

'I'm back, ' she called.

'What happened?' I couldn't keep the anxiety out of my voice. 'Why are you so early?'

Then I saw her. Far from sporting a two-carat diamond, my daughter-in-law was wearing a wry smile and a grey flannel suit. 'The factory,' she announced, handing me half a dozen cotton blouses, 'is diversifying into ladies' wear.'

'Excellent,' I said drily. 'What wonderful news.'

We sat down and stared at one another. I wondered what had gone wrong. I'd been convinced that a nubile, fragrant young women plus a leather sofa had been an infallible combination for the entrapment of a randy old goat. Apparently not. Duty had proven more powerful than lust. Honourable Barney had refrained from sex and balked at marriage. Why? It seemed that he had decided the age gap between the two of them was too great. He had no qualms about a mixed-race relationship but was reluctant to be seen as a 'cradle-snatcher'.

'A cradle-snatcher?' I repeated in disbelief. 'Ruth, dear, you're thirty.'

'Exactly. Barney's a kind man, Ruth—I think he cares for me, but he believes I should be with someone closer in age. There's an unmarried cousin who lives in Despatch. David Morris. Nice looking, clever, but hasn't quite found himself. Barney thinks David and I would be good for each other.'

'And you?' I asked. 'What do you think?'

She shrugged, sat down next to me, put her hand on my arm but didn't answer. I knew that whatever she thought, she would do as I wanted—and I certainly didn't want to foster an alliance with the penniless Despatch branch of the Morris clan.

'Let's go to sleep,' I suggested. 'You must be tired. We can discuss this further tomorrow morning.'

I had no intention of discussing anything with her the next morning. Leaving her fast asleep, I headed for Cousin Barney's office to see what I could do about his sudden and perverse attack of rectitude.

'Do you want Ruth?' I asked boldly. There was no time to be lost on niceties. Next thing she'd be meeting poor handsome David and falling in love. That wouldn't do at all.

He nodded. It was soon clear that in spite of Barney's unease about the disparity in their ages, he was desperate for reassurance that the match would not be frowned upon—not by me, at any rate.

'Are you sure?' he asked.

'Positive.' I was about to add that it was heaven-sent, but thought that might be overdoing it. 'I left her fast asleep in the hotel room. Why don't you take your chances? No time like the present.'

It worked out beautifully. Urged by me, Barney hastened to Ruth's side and, with courtly charm, knelt down and formally offered to marry her. She,having just awoken and too sleep-befuddled to question the disappearance of his misgivings, looked across the room to me as I stood at the door witnessing the scene. For a moment— and it was the last time this happened—we made eye-contact. Then she quickly turned away.

'Yes,' she said to Cousin Barney. 'I will.'

So here we are, a year later, and I suppose I should be happy. Buddy is the closest I'll ever have to a grandson. I now have money in the bank and my status in Port Elizabeth has been fully restored. I should be happy, but I'm not. Ruth doesn't look at me and Olga, pretty giggly Olga, has stopped writing to me. Of all the things I've lost—husband, sons, adopted home— it pains me now that I couldn't see what I had in such abundance. Their loyalty.

Michelene Wandor

Michelene Wandor is an award-winning playwright, broadcaster and critic. Her dramatisation of *The Wandering Jew* was produced at the Royal National Theatre, and her radio work includes *The Clock of Heaven, Orlando and Friends* (plays), and dramatisations of novels by Dostoyevsky, Austen, Drabble and Wilson. Her selected poems appear in *Gardens of Eden Revisited* (Five Leaves).

'My writing draws in different ways on my main cultural sources of Britishness, Jewishness and being a woman (not necessarily in that order). While constantly reshaping the combination of those influences (along with feminism, socialism and an interest in combining artistic conventions), I hope I am more than the sum of these parts, as well as the sum of these parts.'

Yom Tov

She can hear the music from her hotel room. It clashes with the early morning TV, where an edition of *Whose Line is it Anyway?* is garnished with Hebrew subtitles. She switches the television off, and the music from outside fills the room. She checks her watch. Half an hour before the taxi is due.

The hotel receptionist tells her that there will be a *hamsin* today. Along the sea front the sun already burns beyond the shade. The air is still. She crosses the road and walks between two towering hotels, down a wide sweep of stone steps onto the beach.

At the back of a large square of concrete at the edge of the sand, are two enormous loudspeakers, belting out a medley of numbers: Israeli folk songs, Arab pop songs, the occasional Beatles track. On the square of concrete itself, people are dancing, freely, sinuously, some in couples, some alone, sometimes all in lines which join and break. This is not the Israeli folk dancing she remembers, this is something soft and sexy and deeply rhythmic. People join the dancers for a while, and then wander off. She watches, her body responding to the rhythms, her feet shifting in rhythm. She longs to join the dancers, but she doesn't know the steps, so she buys an ice cream. As the kiosk vendor gives her the change, he wishes her a *Yom tov*. Have a good day.

On the way back to the hotel, she passes a restaurant that lists a ham omelette on its menu.

The taxi arrives and carries her away smoothly. The music fades away behind them, an Arabic song, with an obbligato piping line, singing and sliding its notes alongside the voice.

****

The kibbutz now has a Macdonalds outside it, in the road's elbow, where you turn right into a wide drive. The taxi stops by a tree and a low, sprawling cactus bush, just before the houses begin. She pays the driver, and arranges for him to call back for her in an hour.

She has no idea where to go, no memory of the layout of the place. Just beyond the first two small houses is a larger building. She recognises the *heder ha'ochel*, the dining room, still there, but the simple, oblong block has had extensions built out to the east and the west, rather like a simple cross-shaped Christian church. Outside the main door of the building is a notice-board, listing the week's events: a birthday party, a *bar-* and *bat-mitzvah* celebration for twins, a meeting of the Kibbutz Council. She walks round the side of the building and peers through the windows. What was the kitchen is now an office, with computers and desks. The dining room looks as though it is no longer used for meals, no longer the hub of the kibbutz.

Further along the path down the left-hand side of the former dining room is the *beit yeladim*, the children's house. This now seems to be an outlying building for a series of large classrooms, a school which perhaps takes in children from the surrounding area. A bus timetable pinned onto a tree seems to confirm this.

She realises she has been looking upwards quite a lot: the trees —of course, the trees are taller. After forty years, she thinks, what do you expect? The grass is certainly much greener now, the irrigation pipes concealed beneath the ground, no longer trailing between flower beds or along the edges of the paths.

She wanders in and out of the houses, never straying far from the old dining room, in case she loses her way. Vaguely, she is trying to find the house she lived in with her family, but her memory fails her and none of the houses looks or feels right.

The air is close, heavy and silent, except for an occasional child cycling along the quiet paths, a woman carrying a shopping bag, a small tractor breaking the silence, and distant traffic on the main road. She makes her way back to the dining room, and, listless in the weighty heat, sits down on a bench under the tree, by the taxi's tyre marks.

Beyond, Tel Aviv, Europe and America are hidden in the swirl of the *hamsin*. Sand blows invisibly across the buildings, landing on car tops, the sky a thick, yellow-grey colour, reminiscent of London in the days before smokeless fuel cleared the air.

To one side of the bench on which she sits, is a cactus, gnarled, but still standing warningly green, the prickly pear, the *sabra,* the word for a native born Israeli.

We used to knock the pears off the cactus with a stick, then roll them in the sand, with our shoes or the stick, then pick them up with thick canvas gloves. Cut the resilient flesh sideways with a knife, and then, and only then, allow the bare, clean hand to grasp the edges of the dark pink, moist and slithery pear, peel back the skin, take the whole pear in your mouth, protected from the outer layer and sweetly eat it.

Casually, she sweeps one foot backwards and forwards across the sandy soil, scraping a shallow bowl at the side of the cactus. Her foot knocks gently against something unyielding. She bends down, scrapes away a light layer of sand and finds a *hallilit* buried in the sand. A recorder. Black wood for the head joint, a light wood for the body joint. An old soprano recorder. Carelessly and urgently, she plunges her hands into the sand to extricate it.

One day, foraging for sugar cane, avoiding the cactuses, a snake slid between the rising tiras, *the corn on the cob, shiny slim green leaves arching backwards from the central stem, the cobs proudly standing in the crook of the leafy branches, upright, cocooned from light and heat, silky brown fronds protecting the top.*

She holds the instrument finally, her hands now the colour of the ground, her fingers tingling with invisible transparent tiny spines which have mingled with the sand. It is exactly like the first recorder she was given. Ten years old, an English child, not a word of Hebrew, just a musical instrument with which to invent sounds.

She hid, trembling in the high, soft jungle of corn plants. The snake disappeared, and as she plucked up her courage to move out of the green shelter, onto the path beside the fields, shots rang out. Before she had time to react, cry out, arms picked her up, and she was held close to a man's chest, his footsteps pounding on the dry path, along the furrows of the freshly ploughed field, his feet slipping, never losing his grasp on her, his feet sliding on the clods of the dark, fertile, watered earth.

She remembers a prickly pear, eagerly bought in a London greengrocer's, tasting dry and dull. She remembers the recorder, unthinkingly left behind, replaced with a wooden equivalent, made in Germany, never with quite the same wayward sweet sound she remembered.

There were more shots, but as the man ran, they seemed to recede. As he reached the edge of the field, he tripped and fell, his body still shielding her from the hard ground. Momentarily, his heart skipped a beat; his close warm, sweaty heartbeat had caught its breath. Then her mother was running to meet them, her father lifted her and they ran back to the house with her, white with relief.

She brushes the sand from the surface of the wood, takes a tissue out of her bag, spits on it, precious spit in this dry and dusty heat, and wipes the outside clean. Her fingers rest comfortably on the holes, and dance to tunes she remembers.

The man was never mentioned, but a few days later, playing on the hilltop, in renewed relative calm, she heard other children talking about a man who had been arrested for trying to steal a Jewish child.

Her terror had smudged her memory; she thought she was the child, but she wasn't sure. But she was sure that he had saved her, this man. When she asked her parents, they hugged her and told her not to worry. She was safe. She must not go into the fields on her own again. Dangerous snakes, that kind of thing. The shots were not mentioned.

She hears the sound of a rough diesel engine, putt-putt, its regular whining rhythm occasionally missing a beat. A dusty black taxi turns into the drive, and then slows. She gets up from the bench and walks towards the taxi, the *hallilit* still in her hand. The driver opens the door for her, and she notices that there is a green prickly pear painted under the door handle. She chooses to sit in the front, beside him.

She makes conversation in her halting Hebrew. About the heat, the dust, how long will the *hamsin* last. She realises that as she gestures, she is waving the *hallilit,* still in her hand. The driver asks her what she is holding. She shows him. A dusty descant recorder, the instrument she taught herself to play, which she lost when the family packed up to leave the kibbutz. Later, in England, she replaced it with a dark brown plastic recorder. When she told people with pride that she played the recorder, they laughed, so she called it a flute, and everyone nodded, impressed. The *hallilit* became the *hallil*. The recorder became the flute. The girl became the woman.

She doesn't tell him all these things. She becomes aware that the car is slowing down, and for a moment she is scared. The road is deserted. Then he begins to speak to her in English. Do you mind if we stop? I want to look at the *hallilit*, he says.

When the car has pulled over onto the hard shoulder, he takes the instrument, rubs the sand off on his T-shirt, takes off the upper joint, places his right forefinger over the vent, and blows into the head joint. A cloud of earth sprays out. He takes a bottle of water from the glove compartment, and, opening the car door, pours the water through the head joint onto the dusty road. Then he replaces the head joint and plays a C major scale. It is a dusty and slightly muffled sound, but nevertheless almost in tune. He hands it back to her, and she plays, haltingly at first, then, as her fingers remember, the tune from a movement from one of Bach's French suites. He joins in, singing the bass line, a grounding harmony.

She stops before the repeat of the second half. This is ridiculous, she says. Why, he asks. We know the same piece of music. Do you live round here, she asks? Of course, he says. I was born here. A *sabra*, she comments. Not exactly, he says. I am an Israeli Arab. A contradiction in terms, she suggests. He shrugs. Do you live here, in—near the kibbutz, she asks? Yes, he says I lived on the kibbutz until a few years ago. Now I live in Tel Aviv. I run a small cafe, and my taxi service.

Some time later there was an Arab labourer with a bad limp who worked in the fields and did odd jobs around the kibbutz. Nothing was ever said. One day he brought a handful of recorders for some of the children, showed them how to find some notes, and gave them some tunes written on a piece of paper.

He gets out of the open car door to stretch, then returns to his seat and closes the door. It is my leg, he says. I was injured many years ago and it has never healed completely. Without knowing why, she hears herself ask, were you shot? Yes, he replies. Who shot you? she asks. I don't know, he says. I saved a child one night in the kibbutz, and I collapsed when we got back to the kibbutz. When I recovered in prison, I realised that I had been shot. It could have been anyone. It could have been a fellow Arab, thinking I was an Israeli; it could have been the Israeli police. After all, he added, I am one of those despised by both sides. An Arab who has lived all his life in Israel. An Israeli Arab. A contradiction in terms.

What happened afterwards, she asks. I came out of prison after six months. I was never charged because they couldn't remember why they had arrested me in the first place. Just as well. No one would ever have believed that an Arab would save a Jewish child from the guns. I got a job sorting fruit.

Why did you stay here, she asks. After all that had happened? This is my home, he says, looking straight at her. This is where I was born. This is where I live. He turns back to the steering wheel. Shall I take you back to your hotel now? Yes, please, she says. He starts the engine and they begin to drive again, in silence. I am sorry if I upset you just now, she says.

No, he says, you did not upset me. I married an Israeli woman, he says. We didn't marry in Israel. Here Arabs and Jews are not allowed to marry each other. We flew to Cyprus to marry. Here, of course, we are living in sin. But then, in a country full of sins, one more little sin doesn't make much difference. Both our families accept us, he says. Our children speak Hebrew and Arabic. You are the ideal family of the future, I say, trying to joke. He smiles.

When we arrive outside my hotel, he waves my money away. It was a pleasure to drive you, he says. A pleasure to hear you play. It reminded me of a child I knew once. And it reminded me of a dream I have often. In it I am chased by a Palestinian Arab sniper because he knows that I saved the life of an Israeli child.The man wants to explain why I was wrong. Because he can no longer live in his father's house. Because a snake bit him. Because he was forced to leave his home. I understand what he is saying, and yet I cannot speak to him. And when I am about to wake up, the man leaves me, playing a tune I have not heard for years—until today.

If any of the fine, invisible spines stayed in your fingers, the only way was with fine tweezers. You had to hold your fingers up to the light, to catch the shine on the spines which otherwise would embed themselves deeper into the skin when the hand brushed against anything. Absorption. Concentration.

The hotel lobby is cool, the fan circulating air round the dim space. I order tea and iced water. I sit by the window, looking out over the deserted swimming pool. The *hallilit* is in my bag. My tea and iced water arrive. The waiter asks me if I have had a *Yom tov.*

Bobbie Dahdi

Bobbie Dahdi is a mother, journalist and businesswoman who, after a life-threatening illness, decided to fulfil her lifelong dream to write fiction. Her play *Question Time*, about breast cancer, won the Bromley Arts Festival Award, 2000. She is writing a novel set in Ireland, which inspires her with its sense of peace and dramatic scenery.

'What I like about being a Jewish woman in the UK is that, whether you are Liberal, Reform or Orthodox, there is room for women's spirituality, participation and learning, whether at synagogue, local *Rosh Hodesh* or national women's groups.

Recipe for Moussaka

As the men before your coffin bowed rhythmically to punctuate the Hebrew prayers, I stood, dry-eyed, with our non-Jewish friends, watching for clues as to what was expected of us.

I imagined myself dead, buried in some C of E cemetery (as in 'Can't think of anything Else'), or my ashes scattered about my nameplate, stuck like a plant label in a municipal rose bed. Either way, I was alone. They wouldn't have me here. I wasn't in the exclusive club.

Your mother and sister planned to lie with you one day, and I could just go to hell. They urged Josh from my clasp so he could join them by your casket, with its bronze plaque, as the rabbi they'd retained, a black-locked Rasputin, gave an incomprehensible address in thickly-accented English.

My eyes followed a breeze that moved like a Mexican wave down the maples that lined the rows of Hebrew-inscribed stones with their Stars of David. Did I see or imagine you, Michael, my sweet, barefoot in a white suit, looking back at us all with a puzzled expression, before continuing weightlessly on your way?

After the funeral, Anne told me I could take as long as I needed to pay what I owed your mother.

Since then, I've thought about getting you exhumed, a sort of elopement plan, the details of which remain unclear. These last fourteen months, I've been too miserable to organise anything much, going through the motions at work, and even with Josh. But the idea has germinated. I'll get there.

On a fine September day like today, our last free Sunday, our little family should have been kicking up leaves in the park or exploring a medieval castle, not hanging around a cemetery with long faces, staring at two pebbles lying on your grave. They told me that Anne and your mother have visited. Your sister might have suggested that Josh and I join them in her car, and saved us two hours travelling on trains and buses across London.

I let Josh run off to dodge between the auburn maples, leading a sortie of his imaginary troops, and took a peach-coloured, blood-shot rose from the bunch I was carrying, to place before your gleaming headstone, wondering what lay beneath. It was hard to believe that you, my husband—the man I loved and made love to—were now no more than skull and bones.

In the faith of my childhood, your spirit could expect a place in heaven, life without end, *amen*. From what I've picked up, the Jewish after-life is hazy. But then, you didn't 'believe' anyway.

Josh and I approached the School of Religion classroom of Mr Fry—tall, dark and with features a little too like Barbra Streisand to call handsome. He was hugging a pair of dark-haired girls, his daughters presumably, not twins but close in age, maybe about thirteen.

'Be kind to your teacher,' he counselled, releasing them and laughing.

'In your dreams!' threw back the taller of the two, as they sauntered away.

He turned to us with a smile. 'Hello. This is…?'

'Josh Mousstaki,' I replied.

'Moussaka's back!' cried a child from under a table somewhere inside.

'Welcome, Josh,' said Mr Fry. 'Go in and sit down with the others.'

Josh glanced up at me and I nodded, giving him my most reassuring look. Dragging his feet a little, he entered the class. Mr Fry smiled, expecting me to leave. I hovered, tempted to retrieve Josh and take him home. Eventually, I blurted out, 'I don't know if they told you, Mr Fry…'

'Adam.'

'… But Josh missed the whole of last year. I'm not sure he should be here at all.'

He raised a kindly eyebrow.

'I'm not Jewish.' There was a lump in my throat and a cry in my voice. (Oh dear.)

He poked his head into the classroom and told a girl with dark features like his own, that he'd be a few minutes and that she was in charge. Then he led me by the elbow to a musty, book-lined room, where we sat by a desk strewn with papers.

He put his hands in his lap and leant towards me a little. His sympathetic expression made the tears well up in me again.

When I could control my voice, I said: 'Michael, my husband—my ex-husband—my late husband, wanted Josh to attend Religion School. I don't really know why. He was brought up an atheist. He took Josh to the Orthodox Synagogue, where my sister-in-law goes, but they expelled him when they found out I wasn't Jewish—even though her kids go there and her husband's not Jewish. So he brought Josh here, and you took him…'

'Liberals accept that Judaism can be passed on by either parent,' he said.

'I don't understand these rules. Why should it have to be passed on at all?'

He opened his mouth, but I'd already opened mine.

'Michael died in July last year.' I paused. I could see the jet-ski bearing down on him all over again. I took a deep breath and continued. 'I was in a state and didn't get it together enough to bring Josh.' That was only part of it.

'Actually, I was reluctant to bring him,' I admitted. 'I couldn't see what Judaism ever did for me. I'm sorry, Mr Fry. You really don't need to hear all this, I'm sure.'

'But you've registered him for this year?'

'Your rabbi said it would be all right. I offered to become a member but I'm not allowed.'

He frowned. 'That's not my question. I'm wondering why you wanted to bring him at all?'

The answer was pretty obvious to me. 'Because it was what Michael wanted.'

'And how do you feel about his growing up Jewish?'

'Ignorant.' I laughed mirthlessly.

He touched my arm. 'We'll see how he gets on, shall we?'

I managed a smile. 'Thank you, Mr Fry.'

'Adam.'

'Adam.'

'And you?'

'Vicky.'

'How was it?' I asked Josh later that morning, as we walked home hand in hand.

'Good,' he replied. I waited, but he volunteered no more. His mouth made machine gun noises at a cat on a fence. The cat hissed after us.

'What did you learn?' I tried.

'About *Rosh Hashanah*, Jewish New Year and *Yom Kippur*, the Day of Atonement.'

'The day you say sorry?'

He nodded. 'You won't be forgiven unless you apologise to the person as well as to God.'

'Right.' An image popped into my head of Anne, in a beautiful hat, as she was for her sons' *bar mitzvahs*, standing primly behind the screen to which they relegate women in her synagogue, chatting to her friends.The idea that she might ever seek forgiveness for her sins seemed laughable.

In our little kitchen, where the light is always on, I emptied Josh's Spiderman rucksack. He sat at the table, picking the tomatoes from his cheese and tomato sandwich. I knew, of course, that he didn't like them, but I kept trying.

I pulled out a little booklet the cover of which read *Affirmations*.

'What's this?'

'It's from Mr Fry.'

I flicked through the book. It contained the tenets of the Liberal Jewish faith. Clearly, I was the target of a conversion crusade.

My mother-in-law likes to see Josh, so I brought him on Saturday afternoon to the hat shop she keeps with Anne. Marie is five-foot-nothing, wide, with tidy grey hair and has in common with her stout, taller daughter a taste for dark-coloured serge dresses of impeccable cut.

They didn't think much of my ragged jeans and hippy tops. This was not a guess. They told me.

As we arrived, Marie, beaming, hauled herself out of the chair where she sat, sipping Greek coffee and guarding the till, to cup Josh's face in her pudgy hands and plant noisy kisses on it. He loved it.

'My poor boy, my poor boy,' she murmured, holding him away from her. Her mouth contorted and I knew she was thinking how like his father he looked.

He certainly didn't take after me, petite, with blond hair, blue eyes and pale complexion. Sometimes, as now, I'd catch Anne's speculative gaze, wondering what Michael saw in me. She grabbed Josh dramatically from her mother and hugged him, smothering him in her bosom.

'Look at him, only nine, and grown so tall!' cried Marie. 'You don't come and see me enough, *ineh*, young man, that I should notice.' She looked balefully in my direction, then waddled out the back, tempting Josh with a promise of *loukoums*. I gave a little wave. 'See you.' But they'd gone.

I forgive my mother-in-law a great deal because Michael told me about her terrible childhood in Greece during World War Two. Marie, then ten years old, returned from buying bread one day to see a dark lorry outside their apartment block, and her whole family being herded into it. Her mother waved her away, urgently. Marie returned later to find their home ransacked and deserted. Her mother, father, brothers and sisters all perished in the camps.

After Michael's accident, Marie berated me for enticing her son to holiday in the cursed country of her birth. Anne also gave me a tongue-lashing for flying home with Josh and abandoning Michael's coffin.

A clock ticked the passing seconds. I looked around the shop with its richly coloured felt and wool hats for winter, all tilted at just the right angle on chrome stands of varying heights. Tall, gilt-edged mirrors sat on white dressing tables and swathes of gold net decorated the window.

'I'll bring Josh back after we close,' said Anne, going behind an elegant display of gloves on the glass-topped counter.

'Okay,' I replied, feeling dismissed.

'I hear you've registered him for *cheder*.' Her words caught me as I turned to go. 'Religion School,' she added, in response to my quizzical expression.

I felt prickles on the back of my neck. Her spies were everywhere. 'Yes.'

'Would he like to come to our *shul* for *Kol Nidrei* with his cousins?'

'What?'

'*Erev Yom Kippur*, the evening of the fast.'

I noted that I was not invited.

Apparently taking my hesitancy for a logistics problem, she added, 'I could pick him up.'

'Well, fine then, if Josh would like to,' I said, as lightly as I could, though I felt she was trying to steal my son away. I headed for the door.

'So you're planning to bring him up Jewish?'

I took the plunge and strode towards her. 'What is Jewish?'

'What do you mean?' She fingered the rim of her winged glasses.

'I can't work out whether it's a race, a nationality or a creed. If you want to join, you should believe, but you can be Jewish your whole life without believing, like Marie. So for outsiders it's a faith, but for insiders it's like a birthright. But, then, your mother couldn't relinquish it, even though she hates religion, which hints at it being a race.'

Anne's mouth gaped. 'Shit, I don't know.'

For the first time in my life, I felt warmth towards her.

The evenings, after a long day at work are precious, especially if I'm not wallowing in my usual self-pity. This evening, Josh was already tucked up in bed and I was getting cosy, curled up in the armchair with a cup of cocoa, thinking about reading my book or maybe watching a sentimental movie. The doorbell rang. I sighed as I went to open the door and was surprised to find Adam Fry on my doorstep.

'Have you come to give me the Jewish version of *Watchtower*?' I asked crossly, remembering the unsolicited *Affirmations*. The smile was wiped from his face.

'Well?'

'Can I come in, Vicky?' he asked, sounding like a little boy, despite his stature.

'I don't think so,' I responded, popping briefly out from behind the door to flash my pink candlewick dressing gown and bootie slippers. At this point, I remembered the night cream I'd slapped on. I probably looked like an iced bun.

'I should have phoned,' he muttered.

Yes, you should have, I thought.

He took a deep breath. 'I wanted to ask you and Josh to break the fast with us on *Yom Kippur* evening.'

'We can't!' I cried and immediately felt guilty at his crestfallen expression. 'I mean, we shan't be fasting.'

'That doesn't matter.' He looked down, shuffling the toe of his trainer back and forth.

'Why are you asking?'

He frowned. 'What an embarrassing question.'

I didn't understand. 'I mean is it for Josh's or my edification?'

There was a pause. He said, 'I hoped we might become friends.'

Oh, right, the 'softly softly' approach. 'Look,' I said, finding myself wagging a finger, 'If Judaism had been a nationality, I'd have taken it on long ago, because it would certainly have made life a lot easier. But it's not. For converts, it's about belief. So I wouldn't do it for Michael or for Josh. It'd have to be for me.'

He looked flummoxed, then exasperated. 'We're talking about supper on *Yom Kippur*! Just supper!'

'Oh.'

He sighed. 'Shall I take that as a 'yes' then?'

'Yes!' called a little voice from upstairs. We both laughed.

On *Yom Kippur* morning, the prayers were moving, and the ranks of men and women, standing to admit to their shortcomings, made me feel that today there was space to think about new beginnings.

Contrary to expectations, I was enjoying my day, despite being as conspicuous as a bride, in white smock and slacks. I thought this was the colour to wear for *Yom Kippur*, even though it was now grey-skied autumn, but no one else, except the rabbi, was in white.

At lunchtime, I found myself watching Josh eat. 'Why are you fasting, Mum?' he asked.

'Perhaps I'm feeling solidarity with the others,' I replied. 'They're not eating.'

'Should I be fasting?'

'You did a half day. That's pretty good.'

I asked him about the previous evening with his aunt and cousins.

'It was wicked, Mum! The singing in *shul* was great! It made me feel all tingly inside.'

'Really?' He'd never said anything like that before.

'It was cool—like midnight mass at Christmas, when we all held candles and it was spooky around the edges of the church! Only we didn't get mince pies and a drink after, of course.'

Poor, mixed-up kid.

As we left the synagogue in the evening and my eyes readjusted to the gloom outside, it was the traffic and the bustle of the rush hour that seemed unreal, not the calm world within that we were leaving behind.

We joined Adam Fry, his class assistant and the girls we had seen him hugging on the first Sunday of term. I learnt that they were his sisters, Rachel, Esther and Naomi.

'I thought they were your daughters,' I said as we walked to his car, munching biscuits.

'Please!' he exclaimed. 'The fact is, Esther and Naomi were after-thoughts.'

At this, the two younger girls set upon him playfully. When they released him, he ushered me towards the front seat.

'I suppose if I had another child, Josh might be taken for his or her Dad, eventually,' I mused. For some reason, my words made me blush. Hopefully, he hadn't noticed.

'Where's Mrs Fry?'

'Getting supper ready,' he replied, taking the wheel. 'She was here this morning.'

I was looking, but I didn't see her.

As we made the short journey to Adam's house, my good spirits began to evaporate and I found myself dreading the evening. What if Adam and his wife quoted the bible at us late into the night? I saw Josh and me, seated at a bare table, a naked bulb shining into our eyes until, browbeaten, I submitted to their demands to convert and they smugly toasted themselves—with *schnapps*—for fulfilling the commandment to help the widow and the orphan.

'Penny for them?' asked Adam, as we drew up at a Victorian

semi.

I jumped.

'Sorry. Are you all right?'

'Fine!' I retorted.

As we got out of the car, a man and woman in their fifties came out to greet us. Adam introduced them as Mum and Dad.

'*Lashanah Tovah,*' said Mum, shaking my hand. 'Please call us Sam and Margaret.'

She had a waxy complexion, big brown eyes, silver hair and spoke with a trace of a foreign accent, French perhaps. He was tall and plump, his features clearly the source of Adam's Streisand looks.

They seemed nice. Encouraged, but still on my guard, I followed them inside.

'No standing on ceremony, everyone,' cried Margaret. 'We're all hungry. Let's tuck in.'

In the high-ceilinged dining room, a white tablecloth was decked with old-fashioned lemonade, fried fish, potato salad, coleslaw and, what I was told was Adam's speciality—*moussaka*.

'In honour of your nickname,' said Adam to Josh, who grinned. 'Hope you don't mind,' he added, turning to me shyly. 'It's what the other kids at Religion School call him.'

'Not at all,' I replied, taking my place at the table. 'My in-laws are Greek.'

'We guessed that from your surname,' said Sam. 'Margaret's family is Greek too, though she was born in Egypt. They all left for France in 1956, which is where I found her. Isn't it, dear?'

She smiled. 'Bowled me off my feet, even if you were *Vouz-Vouz.*'

'Dad's *Ashkenazi* and Mum's *Sephardi,*' Adam explained. 'Different branches of Judaism.'

'What a hotchpotch we are,' laughed Margaret. 'And we all have our own ideas. There are probably as many forms of Judaism as there are Jews.'

'Perhaps this'll start a new tradition, eh Moussaka?' said Adam's sister, Naomi, planting herself next to Josh, who nodded and lifted his knife and fork, ready for action.

When we were all seated, Adam proffered a basket of bread.

'So where's your wife?' I asked, noting that every place at the table was filled.

Surprised looks were followed by raucous laughter all around.

'I'm not married,' said Adam.

My face burned. 'You said she was preparing supper!'

'You asked about Mrs Fry. I thought you meant Mum!'

I kept pretty quiet for a while after that, listening to the conversation, which was lively and increasingly noisy as empty bellies were filled. I told Adam that his moussaka was delicious.

'My own recipe,' he said.

'Everyone has their own recipe for moussaka,' Margaret declared, waving her fork. 'They're all good in their own way. But Adam's in the business. He's a chef.'

'Really?' I said.

'He's just returned from nearly eight years with the Voluntary Overseas Service,' she enthused, 'working with nutrition projects in the Third World. But he's back now to stay, we hope!'

'Proud Jewish mother,' laughed Adam, gesturing like a compère introducing a star guest. 'Stereotype.' Margaret looked delighted. To me, he added, 'I'm working in a corporate restaurant right now, but my plan is to open my own place.'

'Greek?' I asked and they laughed.

'Maybe,' he replied.

The conversation then passed me by for a while, because I was looking at Josh, who was the centre of the girls' attention and basking in it. I began to feel a warm glow. Eventually, he noticed me and poked his tongue out.

I turned away, smiling, to absorb my surroundings—white-painted wallpaper, tapestry of Moses with the Tablets of the Law, ornate mouldings, red velvet curtains, blue and red patterned carpet, glass-fronted mahogany cabinet with a silver chalice, candlesticks and a brass nine-branched candlestick.

'You have a lovely home, Mrs Fry,' I said later, as we adults cleared the table, the kids having stampeded upstairs like elephants to play on a computer.

'Margaret,' she corrected. 'And thank you. We have a lot of Judaica. I suppose that's because Judaism's first and foremost a religion of the home.'

'Is it?' I asked cagily. Here we go, I thought.

'We only really need to attend synagogue on *Yom Kippur*, though I'm sure the rabbi wouldn't agree.' Adam laughed.

'Anyone'll tell you that the rest of Judaism's about eating!' chipped in Sam, patting his belly.

'Especially you!' exclaimed Margaret.

I thought about Anne's home, where Michael, Josh and I have attended so many barely-understood festival meals, and it clicked with me that, by feeding us, she was doing all she needed to be a good Jew. As Adam, over tea in the lounge, brought alive for us stints he had spent in Nigeria and Brazil, I realised how much I'd been starved of adult chat, by widowhood and a demanding job directing plays for women prisoners.

There was a gleam in Adam's mother's eye as he spoke. He touched her hand unconsciously. I hoped that Josh and I would remain as close in years to come.

It seemed no time at all before we were climbing into Adam's Peugeot for the drive home. The evening had turned out to be a perfect end to a special day.

As we reached our house, I thanked him, yet again, for his family's hospitality.

'I'll just see you in.' He followed us to the porch.

Josh tramped blearily upstairs and I turned to Adam on the step. 'It's been great. Thanks for not spending the time in trying to convert me.'

He was dumbfounded.

'The *Affirmations*,' I explained. 'Not very subtle.'

'The *Affirmations*?' He scratched his head. 'Oh!' he exclaimed with sudden realisation. 'All the kids took copies home!'

'They weren't just for me?'

'We don't do that,' he confirmed anxiously. 'Proselytise. We never do that.'

'Ah.' My cheeks turned crimson again. This was becoming a habit. 'Look, Adam…'

'Yes.'

'Nothing. Goodnight.' I made to close the door.

He cleared his throat. 'Um, I won't turn up unannounced again, but would it be okay to call you?'

'Yeah.'

'Goodnight then,' he said, with a wave.

'I'm sorry, Adam, that I prejudged you,' I gushed.

There, I did it! Now it was his turn to look embarrassed. 'Goodnight,' I whispered and closed the front door.

A lemon sun tried to peep out from behind rain clouds as I stood at Michael's grave, telling him about the Rememberance Service on *Yom Kippur*. Fallen maple leaves, some soggy and some curling crisply, lay around his gleaming headstone.

'Your name was one of a long, long list,' I whispered. I thought they'd never stop. The silence had been electric, as if we were all holding our breath together, waiting.

The old man who was standing beside me dabbed his eyes.

Then I recognised the rhythm of the *kaddish* prayer: *Yidtgadal ve yit kadash shema rabo*... and I was back once more at your funeral, watching you walk away from me. Only this time, you stopped and turned. Smiling, you came right up to me, your eyes gazing steadily into mine. I sighed, kissed you.

A gust of wind lifted a flurry of leaves. They swirled about my ankles like a tiny twister, returning me to the present.

My body aches for you, Michael.

I'll always be here, said the breeze. Your gentle palm touched my forehead. I couldn't believe I'd found you again. The tension, which had become so much a part of me that I hardly noticed it any longer, left me. It was as if every muscle in my body was released to start anew. The experience was a shock. Tears welled up and streamed uncontrollably down my cheeks. Tears of joy.

A car purred to a halt beneath the maples. I was hardly aware of it until a door slid open. 'Mum!' cried Josh and ran into my arms. He was followed by Anne, Brian (her husband), their boys and Marie. Hurriedly, I wiped my eyes and greeted them.

'You should have told us you were coming,' said Anne. 'We'd have given you a lift.'

To my surprise, after a moment, she took out a prayer book

and began to read the *kaddish* prayer. Her boys joined in and Josh seemed to know some of it too. I put my hand on his shoulder. He melted into me, and didn't pull away, as he does when he's being big and tough.

The biggest surprise of all was Marie. She was reciting the prayer too!

Afterwards, I said to Anne, 'I didn't know you knew Hebrew.'

'I'm a woman of many talents,' she replied glibly, and smirked. Brian, put an arm around my shoulder. 'You okay?'

I nodded.

'Come home with us,' he said.

We left a heap of pebbles on Michael's grave.

Sally Cline

Sally Cline's most recent biography *Zelda Fitzgerald: Her Voice in Paradise* (2002) was entered for the Whitbread Prize. She is also an award-winning author of non-fiction and short stories. She is the Royal Literary Fund Project Fellow at Anglia Polytechnic University, Cambridge, and teaches Social and Political Science for Cambridge University.

'Born into a white middle-class orthodox Jewish family in North West London, I see my identity as a writer, mother, feminist and lesbian. These six significant elements of which I am proud, are crucial to both my writing and to my spiritual self.
Writing is my guiding star; my daughter is a magical gift; my lesbianism has given me courage and my closest friendships; Cambridge has offered me my community; and being born British and Jewish, despite the challenges of each, has rooted me.'

A Small Number

There were just twenty people in the London gallery—a small number. Not many paintings either, by Charlotte Salomon, a young German artist. Well, she had been young when she painted them. They were wild, strange, bright: lots of blue, a great deal of red, some startling cadmium yellow, a small number of pigments that shone and battled.

The catalogue described her work as 'a tri-coloured play with music'. The painter, it stated, used only three pigments. 'A small number' the catalogue said: just red, yellow and blue. Black had not been found.

Charlotte Salomon, it seems, was unusual in not using a greater number of colours. Why she used only three, confessed the catalogue writer, will remain her professional secret.

It probably will.

Charlotte Salomon died aged twenty-two in 1939—not a great number of years for a woman to help herself to a variety of colours. There were not a great number of women either, in Charlotte's family, and no one else was a painter. All the women in Charlotte's family had killed themselves: her mother had killed herself; her grandmother had killed herself. Two isn't that many, you could say: but two was all she had. Charlotte, the gallery guide told me, was always afraid she might do the same: kill herself.

She need not have worried. In the event she did not have to face that fear. The matter was taken out of her hands.

In 1939, when a great number of other women (and children and men) were facing their own fears, Charlotte was deported to the Auschwitz Women's Camp. She had just married one of a number of men she had been courting—a man called Alexander Nagler. On the day she left home she was five months pregnant. A small number of months, but enough to see a baby develop and live, had Charlotte stayed home and not taken any chances.

Charlotte was just one amongst a great number of women deported to Auschwitz that year. A large number were pregnant.

Charlotte was amongst the number (we don't know the number)

who did not survive, did not come back, did not get to use black in her paintings, or purple or green or heliotrope.

A poet who was standing next to me in the gallery scribbled a poem about Charlotte Salomon's paintings. One verse ran:

Red yellow and blue
These caught every relative
And you.

I'm not a poet but I wanted to write a story about Charlotte's life. There were not many months in her life—two hundred and sixty-four. A mere two hundred and sixty-four months lived in red, yellow and blue.

There was no further information about Charlotte Salomon, the painter: only that she had painted in three vivid tones—a woman, a young woman, who had used a small number of pigments.

I wondered what Charlotte's own number had been in the camp. I asked the poet. She had no idea. 'Phone Auschwitz', she said. 'They'll tell you her number.'

Phone Auschwitz? I could not believe that anyone could pick up a public phone and dial Auschwitz—not on BT. I shall do it, I thought. I'll get Charlotte's number.

I did it.

I went to a phone, in a red box, outside the gallery—just red, not yellow, not blue. I got through to someone in Auschwitz. 'I'd like Charlotte Salomon's number in the camp. 1939,' I said. They put me on hold, then on to Archives. I repeated my request. 'Please send a fax with your request', said a metal voice in the Auschwitz archives.

I faxed Auschwitz. Auschwitz faxed back. 'Dear Client, After research in our archives we wish to inform you that Alexander Nagler's registration number in the camp was 157166.' (Alexander Nagler, you may remember, was Charlotte's new husband, one of a large number of men who had courted her.)

'It is not possible', continued the fax,'to establish Charlotte Salomon's number. It is very probable that she, being pregnant at that time, was selected to the gas chamber on her arrival, which happened in most such cases.'

There the fax ended. 157166 was the only number available.

But it wasn't *her* number.

Charlotte, who I assume was selected (their word, their selection) out of a great number for the gas chamber, went into that chamber numberless: no number of her own.

I keep wondering about the red, yellow and blue. I discovered that cadmium yellow, Charlotte's particular shade, was named for a furnace used for smelting zinc. You could say the colour was relevant.

But what about black? No black has ever been found.

This story was written in appreciation of a poem and an account by Jane Liddell King. It was revised and performed at Hawthornden Castle during Sally Cline's 2003 Hawthornden Fellowship.

Marion Baraitser

Marion Baraitser's published plays (Oberon Books) have received Arts Council awards: *The Story of an African Farm* (The Young Vic and BBC Radio 4), *The Crystal Den* (The New End), *Louis/lui* and *Winnie* (Soho). In 1996 she founded her own press specialising in new work in translation (finalist in the Women in Publishing Pandora Award 2002). As editor of *Plays by Mediterranean Women*, she attended the *Women Writers Talk Peace* conference in Israel on a British Council award. She lectured in English Literature for Birkbeck, London University, for many years, and taught Creative Writing at City Lit and Scriptwriting at London Metropolitan University. Her short stories and journalism have been published in various magazines. She lives in London with her family.

'As a writer, a woman, a Jew and a Londoner with a South African upbringing, it is not surprising that I am concerned with knowing who I am. Perhaps this is because my identity was partly 'lost in translation'. In my plays and stories, I like to write about the personalities of others with whom I can identify, which is a way of getting to know myself. I am disturbed and excited by the writings of the modern Jewish philosopher Emmanuel Levinas, and his ideas on striving to know and to take responsibility for the *other.*'

Something Chronic

So, let those druggies in Hackney shove in at me at the lights. I'm a small guy, but I'll move, boy. Drive this car straight through them and get to Malka's house. I'll leave those boys standing. No flies on me. Listen, she's alone there and I'm going to reach her, even if it kills me. Then I'm going to take her where she wants to go. Now is the moment that I can do something true for her. If only I hadn't sat on my *tokhas* all those years, like a *nebekh*. I stood by and watched her marry the wrong man.

One thing bothers me, though. Will she recognise me? Since she has been in hospital, something's not quite right with her eyes. At the reading circle, Malka's mother Gittle, says to me: 'She can't see things straight now. You get the picture?' She stresses the *you*, so I feel stupid.

'You know I love my daughter Malka, and I think she's fond of you. But after an operation like that, she can't drive anymore. Not in her condition. Not in her state. She's *in drerd.* Not even a wheelchair can she drive, never mind getting on and off public transport. And her husband has the business to run. So, we must drive her, *got tsu danken,* you and me. This is the position—I must drive my own daughter, when she should be driving me! And look at me!'

Everyone in the reading circle looks and nods, except myself.

She's a tough old rooster is Malka's mother. Seventy going on forty, and still crowing, even after a handful of kids, two husbands, two hip replacements, facelifts, a cyst the size of a football lodged in her stomach, and a bad appendix.

She says to me: 'I should have had them done years ago. My boobs. Instead of *shleping* them round all my life. All those years and me not getting into a bathing suit on account of these articles. I didn't have the guts.'

Not that she's yellow, Gittle. When they finally got Malka to hospital, Gittle left her own sick bed, with her appendix stitches still in place. Yes, doubled up with pain, she drove herself to her daughter's bedside. But then, unlike me, she likes driving. It's her favourite pastime, and she prides herself on her skill. What else is there for her to do? When Gittle's behind the driving wheel, she thinks she's Jesus Christ. She tells me: 'If I had another life, I'd be a taxi driver. Anticipation, that's what it takes. Anticipation. And that's what I've got.'

Personally, I drive like nothing on earth. The last thing I ever want to be is a taxi driver. So, as far as this woman is concerned, I don't even qualify as human.

She says: 'If you don't use your *kop* when you drive, you're nothing. Not worth the time of day.'

Anticipate? Who the hell can know what's coming?

If Gittle saw me driving now she'd call me a maniac, but I just want to get to Malka, without those East End thugs stopping me at the next lights and taking the car, or spilling my brains on the floor.

I should have seen more of Malka, but you know how it is? We used to meet at the reading circle, but I don't go much lately. To tell the truth, I don't see the point of books. I went to the book club only to lay eyes on Malka. All those years meeting her at the reading circle, she grew on me, until on her wedding day, it came to me that I loved her. But what would she want with a salesman of second-hand fancy-goods in the Hackney Road. Now Malka respects books. Works for nothing in the school library so she can take out the books she wants. Her husband, Colin, does not understand this, but then Colin makes money and he holds the purse strings so tight, I swear one day his fingers will drop off. He flies to Hong Kong to pick up orders for kiddies' underwear and sells it on commission to stores for a small cut. It's a good business and he's a rich man and accordingly, his wife stays home. It's infradig for his wife to work, you see. He considers himself a good cut above the *shtetl*.

Between Colin and Malka, it goes like this:

'What's the point in your coming with me, *Mamele*?'

He dusts off his suit. 'Makes a change.'

She strokes the cat.

'You'd leave our house with just the maid in charge?' He shoves away the cat with a sharp kick.

'We can make a plan... Max could come.'

‘So who will organise things? You know what your mother says? Anticipate…’

‘I do my best.’

‘Who anticipates? Me. Who thinks it all out: how to boil a chicken, how to put flowers in a vase?’ His temper rises. ‘How to stop the cleaner pinching?’ He clenches his fists. ‘Me! Haven’t I got enough to do?’

Once, at the book club, Gittle says to me: ‘It’s true. Malka is no organiser. Now I am what you call an *organiser.* Every little thing, her husband has to think of. In case someone should come in and he should feel ashamed. Is it her fault she can’t anticipate? Is it her fault she’s not like me? Is it her fault she has got no confidence? Is it her fault he gets so angry he wants to throttle her? You see, as far as Colin’s concerned, his wife doesn’t have s*eykhl.* You either have it, or you don’t. Now Colin wants a wife he can show off, be proud of.’

While the mother is talking, I’m thinking to myself: Okay, Malka is a little on the big side. So what? Who cares about a waist—if it’s there, or not there? You just need to look into Malka’s velvet eyes and her soul is coming up in them like great sad moons. It just so happens Gittle never looks into her daughter’s eyes, and neither does Colin. He didn’t marry Malka for her eyes; he married her for her father, a *ganser* big *makher* in the medical profession. Never mind his money, that’s how Colin went up in the world. And don’t think Gittle didn’t know all about that. But to have a daughter on the shelf, you are not doing yourself a favour. So Colin took Malka over from her Daddy the Doctor, dressed her according to the standards she was used to. His wife must be seen wearing a pearl choker with a gold heart as big as a plum, never mind what his own heart was doing. And who can blame him? It happens.

So here I am, safe and sound, having arrived at Malka’s house. I’m finally looking at Malka standing in the doorway, eyes like brown velvet, leaning on her walker in her purple vinyl blouse, colourful as a parrot in a cage. She’s not alone because, as usual, wound round her gentle neck is—Cat.

Listen, I am not fond of cats, but I restrain myself out of respect when I'm with Malka. Cats are important to her. Malka uses cats like I use the fax machine, to get through to people. Sometimes it's the only way she can talk to Colin.

Malka says: 'Now I've turned fifty, now that I am old, Cat says you should give a person some respect.' This is how she talks to her father the doctor, too: 'Give Pussy a stroke.'

I'm not surprised Malka has such an attachment to this animal, because her son Max is away most of the time at the university, and Colin doesn't have much to do with her except when they go to synagogue together, where he's the model husband, calling her '*Mamele*' and 'Sweetie'. Butter wouldn't melt in his mouth.

But I haven't forgotten what he did, already. You're not going to believe me, but who did Colin invite to accompany him on his trip to Hong Kong just now? His mother-in-law. Yes. Gittle. And did she refuse? No. She jumped at the chance. Colin thinks Gittle's fun, that she has plenty of spunk. And Gittle's not going to be caught mooning.

Gittle says to her daughter: 'Stop being a *nebekh,* can't you? Get a life.'

See how it is in this world, if a girl can't even trust her own mother, even if she is seventy going on forty already, and tough as an old rooster?

Anyway, you won't be surprised to hear that Cat can't stand the sight of Colin or Gittle. In fact, Cat runs a mile when he sees Colin coming in at the door.

So this is how it happens that I am helping Malka into my car, locking the doors, checking the windows are rolled up tight so I can drive at a heck of a rate, in case some criminal decides to wave his thingamy in my face or smash the windscreen with a crowbar and take the car, never mind shoot us dead. And Malka is talking, in her high childish voice, as fast as I am driving. And when you butt in to say something, she finishes your sentences along with you, like she always does—like someone singing in tune, which drives Colin crazy. What is more, every now and then, she laces her flow with her favourite sayings: 'She's losing her marbles' and 'Watch out, this is a test.' I find this sweet and something to do with her very special and delicate sense of humour, but to Colin, it's like someone flinging handfuls of gravel at his *yarmelke*. So now I'm asking her what happened to her and how she landed in hospital. As I listen, her talk becomes faster, higher in her throat until I'm straining to catch her meaning. This is what she is saying to me:

'How did it happen? I don't know. It was sudden. We're having people round one evening, clients of Colin, and I know I must be on my best behaviour and come up with the right pudding. A Japanese buyer and his wife, who is... well, naturally Colin thinks she's perfect. You know the sort? A bone china doll with long red nails? I think to myself: This is a test Malka. Are you going to lose your marbles or are you going to lose your marbles? So I pick up Cat, and I open the door and there stands Colin holding a bonsai tree in a pot in one hand and the smiling Japanese couple in the other.

Okay, so Colin has had a bad day. The fax had broken and Max had just called saying he can't stick this dump a day longer and he's going back to Canada where we sent him in the first place. And Colin's brother has been *haking* him a *tsaynik* about money Colin owes him. What do I know? They have secret meetings about *gelt* all the time. Anyway, I come to the door holding Cat because this little dinner party is a test, and you know, not even Cat is keen on my cooking. So I'm trying very hard. My face is gorgeous already, flushed with Clinique Beige. Nothing but the best for Colin. My hair spray would stop a hurricane. The chicken is in the pot since yesterday and not too mushy to eat, and the *tsimes* is shining, sweet as honey on one side, and I'm keeping *stum* about the other side which is a teeny bit too browned for eating. The only thing missing from the table is the pot plant (which Colin is holding), because I usually make such a mess of arranging flowers.

As I say, I'm holding Cat on account of my nerves and I open the door.

Oy vey!

Cat sees only Colin, and before I can blink, she is out of my arms like a shot, and on her way out, knocking the bonsai clean out of Colin's hands, so it goes flying and it smashes on the floor. And suddenly I hear Colin screaming and I see him kicking out and swinging his arms all over the place, and a noise is coming from his throat like he's choking and then he's coming at me like a lorry and he's on top of me and I'm on the floor and my head goes bang on the tiles. I'm sure he doesn't mean any harm, but my head is paining. And in the corner of my eye are the Japanese buyer and his wife, frozen, with their mouths open. And I'm thinking: Poor Colin, when he comes round, the humiliation will kill him. Then someone switches off the light, and when I come to, I'm in the hospital and Colin is kneeling next to the bed and I can hardly see because my head is going like a gong, and I'm seeing double, but it looks to me like Colin is crying… As God is my witness, I am not telling you a lie, the tears are dripping through his fingers and on to the sheets and this I only saw happen once before, at his mother's funeral. And I'm not losing my marbles. This isn't a test. And through the terrible pain in my head... where they took out this clot of blood pressing on the nerves in my brain making me see double... I'm watching the tears run over my husband's hands and wetting the sheet. And something happens to me. Something very strange, more strange than the gong or the bandages, or the seeing double. And I'm trying to find the word for it. It's like, well…something I haven't felt in donkey's years. I'm feeling so… yes, that's it! A real surprise. You see, for the first time in ages, I am feeling … happy! Why? Because he's crying for me!'

This is what Malka is telling me, as I am driving like a maniac, as her mother Gittle would say, through our mad city streets, hardly stopping at the lights, hoping those thugs won't get us this time. And who can blame them?

Yes, I am driving my friend Malka where she wants to go because Colin and Gittle aren't there to drive her anywhere. They're in Hong Kong. Together.

And do you know where we're going? We're going to her synagogue, so she can pull herself up the stairs, on her walker, to the woman's section at the top, so she can drag herself to the front row and thank God for giving her a husband who cries because of her.

****

Note: Generally, where acceptable spelling exists in English, this is used. Otherwise, modern Hebrew transliteration rules are used, and Yiddish words are written according to the Yivo system.

The editors wish to thank Barry Davis for his invaluable help in compiling the glossary.

Glossary

abba	father
aliyah	journey from any other country to Israel
Ashkenazi	Jew from central or Eastern Europe
bar mitzvah	celebrated by Jewish males on reaching the age of 13 years; *bat mitzvah*: the same, for a Jewish girl
bechas	beaker
bimah	platform in the centre of the synagogue; desk for reading the *Torah*
bubba	grandma
charoset	paste of sweetened, cooked fruit and nuts, symbolising the morter used by the Jews to build the pyramids, when enslaved to the Egyptians
cheder	Jewish religious elementary school
cholla	milk loaf served at a Jewish Friday night supper; *challot* or *chollot* (pl)
chutzpah	supreme self-confidence, gall
datiyim	observant Jews
doven (daven)	to pray
feygele	little bird, in this context
frum	religious or observant in Jewish practice
ganser makher	important man
gefilte fish	poached fish balls made from fish forcemeat

gelt	money
genizah	storeroom for sacred books
got tsu danken	thank the Lord
Hag Sameyah	Happy Festival
hak a tsaynik	to irritate
hamsin	a hot, dry, desert wind
haredim	Orthodox Jews
Hasid	a member of a Jewish ecstatic, charismatic religious revival movement amongst East European Jews, dating from the mid-eighteenth century; *Hasidim* (pl)
Intifada	Arab uprising
kazatska	a popular, vigorous, Russian folk dance
imma/ ineh	mother
in drerd	in trouble
Ivrit	Hebrew
kaddish	a Jewish prayer recited in the daily ritual of the synagogue and by mourners at public services after the death of a close relative
kasher	the process of making *kosher*
khazeray	bits and pieces, junk
kibbutz	a Jewish communal agricultural settlement in Israel
kiddush	ceremonial blessing pronounced over bread or wine, recited on the Sabbath and holy days
kindertransport	the rescue of Jewish children from Germany, Austria and Czecoslovakia between 1938 and 1939
kodesh	holy
Kol Nidrei	prayer on Yom Kippur to cancel all vows rashly made to God
kop	head
kosher	sanctioned by Jewish law, particularly

	ritually
kotel	the surviving Western wall of the Temple in Jerusalem (the Wailing Wall)
kneidlekh	*matzo* dumplings
kristallnacht	'the Night of Broken glass', the pogrom launched by Goebbels against German Jews
kurve	whore
Lashanah Torah	May there be a good year
l*oukoums*	Turkish Delight
Lubavitch	a Hasidic sect founded in the late eighteenth century
Mamele	Mother
Mashiah	the anointed one (the Messiah)
moshav	Jewish settlement
matzo	unleavened bread used at Passover to symbolise the Jew's hasty flight from their enslavers; *matzot* (pl)
mazzel	Modern Hebrew for 'luck' (from the Yiddish *mazel*)
mazzel tov	good luck
mensh	man
misvoth	plural of *mitzvah*— a commandment of the Jewish law, or a meritorious or charitable act
mezuzah	small parchment on which are inscribed the first two paragraphs of the *Shema*, placed in a case fixed to the doorpost by some Jewish families as a sign or reminder of their faith
meshuggener	a foolish or crazy person; *meshuge* (adj)
nebekh	a man who counts for nothing
Oy(oi) vey!	Goodness me!
pareve	a dish made without milk, meat, or their derivatives
Haggadah	the Passover book containing the *seder* ritual
rav	rabbi

Rosh Hashanah	the Jewish New Year
Rosh Hodesh	New Moom: the beginning of the Hebrew month
sabre	a native-born Israeli
seder	Jewish service at home on the first or second night of Passover, in commemoration of the exodus from Egypt
Sephardi	Jew of Spanish origin: now predominantly from the Middle East and North Africa
seykhl	intelligence
Shabbat	the Sabbath day (modern Hebrew). *Shabbos* (Ashkenazi pronounciation)
Shalom	Hello
'*Shema*'	'Hear', the first word of *Deuteronomy* 6.4, 'Hear, O Israel, the Lord is our God, the Lord is one'
shiksah	a non-Jewish woman
shivah	seven days of mourning in a Jewish home following the death of a close relative
shlep	carry
shmattes	clothes, especially in a ragged condition
shtetl	a small Jewish town or village formerly found in Eastern Europe
shul	synagogue
stum	quiet
Talmud	the vast body of rabbinic, civil and criminal law, regulations, traditions, and the disputa tions of the rabbinic sages
tokhas	bum (behind)
Torah	the corpus of Jewish sacred literature
treif	forbidden food according to the Jewish dietary laws
tsimes	a dish of cooked sweetened carrots

yarmelke	a skull cap worn by the religious
yeshiva	institute devoted to the study of the *Talmud*
yiddishkeit	the essence of Jewishness in the East European tradition
Yiddishe	Yiddish-speaking; can mean Jewish
'Yitgadal ve yit kadash shema rabo'	'Magnified and sanctified be God's great name'— from the beginning of *kaddish*
Yom Kippur	Jewish holy day observed with fasting and prayer (Day of Atonement)
Yom tov	a Jewish festival; a good day

OTHER TITLES BY LOKI BOOKS

LOKI INTERNATIONAL FICTION SERIES

- ***DOLLY CITY*** by ***Orly Castel-Bloom***

Paperback ISBN 0 9529426 0 7 £7.99

An irreverent and witty satire, an original and timely tour de force about the Yiddish-mamma complex, and Israel today, by a triple prize-winning new young voice.

'A novel of Joycean insolence—A beautiful book whose non-conformism is a delight.' (*La Marsellaise*)

'Castel-Bloom writes with such freshness, such dash and panache that I was willing to follow her anywhere.' (Eva Figes)

- ***APPLES FROM THE DESERT: SELECTED STORIES*** by ***Savyon Liebrecht***

Paperback 1SBN: 0 9529426 1 5 £9.99

Foreword by ***Grace Paley***

Introduction by **Lilly Ratok, Tel Aviv University.**

Savyon Liebrecht's short stories are **classics in new Hebrew literature.** A broad panorama of contemporary Israeli society in '**bitter-sweet tales of fury, passion and disenchantment.'** ***(Ha'aretz).***

'...beautifully, affectingly plumbs profound and painful themes...Be sure to read them.' (*Washington Post*, 1998)

• *CHERRIES IN THE ICEBOX*
CONTEMPORARY HEBREW SHORT STORIES

Editors: ***Marion Baraitser*** **and** ***Haya Hoffman***
Introduction by Haya Hoffman
With The European Jewish Publication Society

Papaerback ISBN: 0 9529426 5 8 £11.50

A unique collection of twelve of the best, daring, young multicultural voices, writing in Hebrew today, these stories encapsulate the diverse mosaic of a society that is uncomfortable with itself, as it comes to terms with violence and dislocation, with wry wit and hope that counters despair.

'Excellent and stimulating anthology' — *Jewish Chronicle*

'The easiest way to find out who will be the next Amos Oz' — *Jewish Renaissance*

LOKI INTERNATIONAL PLAY SERIES

• ***ECHOES OF ISRAEL: Contemporary Drama***
ed. ***Marion Baraitser***

Paperback ISBN: 0 9529426 3 1 £9.99

From the Royal National Theatre.

'Bold dramas...revealing the rifts and taboos in Israeli society at this crucial time in the nation's history.' *New Statesman*

A FAMILY STORY by **Edna Mazya**
Winner of the Israeli Theatre Award 1997/8

MURDER by **Hanoch Levin**
Play of the year and Playwright of the Year, 1997
SHEINDALE by **Rami Danon** and **Amnon Levy**
'A vital subject .. an intriguing merciless play' *Al Ha'Mish Mar*
MR MANI, a monodrama by **A.B. Yehoshua** . ***'A fascinating insight into the British presence in Palestine by the Israel Prize winner.'*** *Ha'aretz*

- ***BOTTLED NOTES FROM UNDERGROUND: CONTEMPORARY PLAYS BY JEWISH WRITERS***
ed. **Linden S, Baraitser M.**
Paperback ISBN: 0 9529426 2 3 £9.99

From Sobol to Schneider—a barn-breaking collection of five popular award-winning new plays of excellence from London, New York and Israel. Features Israel's greatest living playwright **JOSHUA SOBOL's** ***The Palestinian Girl***
with **Carole Braverman, Marion Baraitser, Sonja Linden, and David Schneider.**

- **T*HE DEFIANT MUSE: HEBREW FEMINIST POEMS FROM ANTIQUITY TO THE PRESENT: A BILINGUAL ANTHOLOGY***

Editors: ***Shirley Kaufman, Galit Hasan-Rokem,*** **and** ***Tamar Hess***
Paperback ISBN: 0 9529426 4 X £12.99

Poetry Book Society Recommended Translation, 2000

Unprecedented in its scope, many of these poems are unknown to an English speaking audience. A unique volume of 100 poems by 50 writers from antiquity to the present, which transforms the perception of Jewish women's poetry in Hebrew.

- Unique bilingual anthology transforming the conception of Jewish women's poetry.
- New material, new translations.
- Introduction placing the poems in historical, cultural, and literary perspectives, and full bibliographic and biographical notes.
- Arts Council of England and European Jewish Publication Society support. Published in association with The Feminist Press at CUNY

Shirley Kaufman: prize-winning American Israeli poet and translator who has published seven volumes of poems, as well as translations from Hebrew and Dutch.
Galit Hasan-Rokem: professor of folklore at the Hebrew University of Jerusalem, translator, scholar, and poet:**Tamar Hess**: teacher at the Hebrew University.

All books available from good book shops or from amazon.co.uk, or LokiBooks, 38 Chalcot Crescent, London NW1 8YD:all@lokibooks.vianw.co.uk http://www.lokibooks.u-net.com. Trade: Central Books.99 Wallis Rd, London E9 5LN: tel: +44 (0)845 4589911 : fax:+44 (0)845 4589912: orders@centralbooks.com